Till the Mountains
Turn to Dust

Also by J. S. Volpe

The Chronicles of Eridia

Anomaly Hunters

Rare Finds

*ebook only

Till the Mountains Turn to Dust

J. S. Volpe

Peridor Press

CE-12013

For Tiffany

CONTENTS

1

New Portland
5 A.C.

Reynard ran.

Behind him a sound like thunder filled the world. Closer to its source—probably around the city center by now—the sound would resolve itself into a thousand separate elements: screams, explosions, the roar of collapsing buildings, the whir and rattle of machines, the crunch of skulls under all-terrain tank treads. But distance mercifully fuzzed them into that single incessant rumble.

He was racing down a cobblestone street, a narrow channel between row houses, all of which still sported damage from the Cataclysm five years earlier. The cracked brick facades on either side resounded with the clattering footfalls of himself and the ten or twelve people behind him. He didn't know any of these people and had no idea whether they were following him on purpose or just fleeing in the same direction he was. Too bad for them if they thought he was heading somewhere specific—a safe house, say, or a rescue transport. He had been in town only two days and didn't even know what neighborhood he was in right now. All he knew, all that mattered, was that he was heading south, away from the implacably advancing army of the self-proclaimed robot-god 1000001, the army that had already obliterated countless other towns amid the southern foothills of the Salt Stairs.

A harsh mechanical buzz suddenly drowned out the rumble as a swarm of link drones shot onto the street from an alley half a block back. Reynard forced himself to run faster, a feat he would have thought impossible a second earlier. Behind him the buzz swelled rapidly. Then came screams. Then came a series of electrical crackles and snaps, and some of the screams abruptly stopped.

And then from a building to his left a young woman's voice called, "In here!"

Without even looking, relying only on the survival instincts that had helped keep him alive for over seven centuries, he veered toward the voice, barreled through an open doorway, caught a fleeting eye's-edge glimpse of a whitely clad figure, then stumbled to a halt the moment the door slammed shut, cutting off the buzz.

He had covered the three miles here from the city center in one continuous run, and now that he had stopped, now that survival was assured at least for the moment, his legs lost all strength and he dropped to his knees. As he hunched there, gulping down breaths, sweat dripping from his nose and chin, he stared absently at the frayed maroon carpet beneath him. After a moment a pair of feet in white lace-up ankle-high leather boots stepped into view. The hem of a starchy white skirt floated above the boots.

Nostrils flaring, he sucked in another breath and with it came an interesting admixture of odors: fresh linen, oiled leather, and above all else an unfamiliar scent that reminded him of exotic spices. It was the unique scent of the person who stood in front of him.

"Are you hurt?" the woman asked. Her voice was gentle and strangely accented. Not that the latter fact meant anything; strange accents, strange languages, strange entities, strangeness of every sort abounded since the Cataclysm.

Normal didn't exist anymore.

He raised his head, eyes quickly and thoroughly exploring the figure before him: up the stiff cotton skirt; over an old white leather belt, cracked and worn in places, especially around the hole the silver tongue was thrust through; up the column of carved ivory buttons that divided the high-collared tunic; over the tunic's slightly puffed shoulders; down the form-fitting sleeves that dead-ended in neat, even lines at the wrists; briefly beyond the sleeves to the slender hands, open and empty, nails clipped short; then back up this outfit whose uniform-like primness and whiteness led him to surmise its wearer was a nurse of some kind, up to the head and face that crowned it all.

She was a lovely specimen, eminently fuckable, with light-brown skin and long, straight black hair, both of which contrasted strikingly with her white outfit. She looked young, perhaps only twenty or twenty-one, but her expression was calm and assured as she peered into his face.

"Are you hurt?" she repeated.

"No, just run ragged."

She let him catch his breath a few more seconds, then extended a hand. He took it, reveling in the feel of her soft, smooth palm as she helped him up. Yes, he would definitely have to bed this one.

"Thanks," he said, wobbling a little on still-shaky legs. "I owe you one."

"No no," the girl said. "We—"

A loud flat bang smacked the house as something exploded nearby. The windowpanes rattled in their frames. A faint haze of plaster dust drifted down from the ceiling. In the depths of the house something small and fragile shattered.

The girl grabbed an oil lamp that sat burning on a table

beside the front door. "We need to go."

"Good idea."

She brushed past him and strode down a hallway that led into the depths of the building. He followed.

Halfway down the hall she led him through a door on the left and across a kitchen/dining room. They passed an old iron stove that still radiated residual heat, a white ceramic sink heaped with unwashed cookware, a wooden counter littered with crumbs and flour. A table opposite the stove was laid out with a meal for four, the plates and platters covered with cooling roast beef, potatoes, carrots, biscuits. China teacups contained a brownish fluid—tea or coffee probably—that sloshed about like storm-tossed waters as something else exploded outside, closer this time. A crystal decanter in the center of the table thunked to its side and purplish liquid glugged out across the white tablecloth.

The girl strode past all this without a glance. On the far side of the room, she threw open a door and led Reynard down a dim musty corridor, then through a door on the right and down a flight of wooden stairs. The smells of dirt, clay, mildew grew strong as they descended.

At the bottom was a cellar with a hard dirt floor, bare wood walls, unmarked sacks and crates stacked here and there. The light from the girl's lamp threw ever-shifting, sharp-edged shadows across everything.

She led him straight toward a shadowy corner on the far side of the room. As they neared the corner, the lamp-light thinned then banished the shadows, revealing a rough, moldingless doorway cut into the wall.

"Where're we going?" Reynard asked.

"Safety," she said simply, passing through the doorway. "The others have already gone ahead."

"Others?"

She didn't answer. He passed through after her.

They headed single-file down a narrow corridor rough-hewn through striated limestone. The walls were stacks of colored ribbons, each ribbon representing centuries of lives and weather and occurrences compressed to mere centimeters. The corridor ended at what Reynard at first thought was a huge room, but soon discerned was a thirty-foot-wide arched brick tunnel that ran perpendicular to the limestone passageway. A gutter ten feet across and six deep extended down the tunnel's center, its bottom caked with a hard, greenish substance.

Turning right, they headed along the wide, flat stone expanse that ran between the gutter and the wall. At intervals rusty lamps of a design Reynard didn't recognize were affixed to the wall about eight feet up. None of them were lit. Several hung askew, their glass covers missing or broken. On the floor were signs that people had recently passed this way: prints in the dirt, hairs, a piece of yellow thread.

"What is this place?" Reynard asked. "A sewer or something?"

"We don't know exactly. My friend Grace thinks it might be an old underground roadway of some kind."

While technically answering his question, she had done so in a way that flung up a host of new ones. Who constituted the "we"? Were they the ones who cut the limestone passageway? And had whoever cut the passageway known this tunnel was here, or had it been discovered by accident?

Before he could ask anything, the girl glanced at him and said, "My name's Solace, by the way."

"I'm Reynard."

"I haven't seen you around town before. Are you a newcomer?"

"Yeah. I was really only just passing through. As usual, I

was in the wrong place at the wrong time. Story of my life. What about you? You a resident?"

She hesitated a moment, then gave a small, self-conscious laugh. "Yeah, I guess I must be by now. Like you, I was just passing through on my way to…somewhere else. I only meant to stay a few days, but I found I liked it here, so I decided to stick around an extra week or two. Then I met some people and got a job at the House"—the way she said it made it a proper noun—"and the extra week or two became six months."

"The House? Was that the building we passed through? You work there?"

"Yeah." She raised the lamp higher and peered down the tunnel at a small light approaching. "I think that's Grace. She works at the House, too." Her shoulders slumped a little, and she let out a small sigh. "Well, *worked*, I guess."

As the two lights converged, Reynard discovered that the bearer of the new one was a short stocky young woman with curly red hair, a pug nose, acne scars mingling with her freckles, and an outfit similar to Solace's. The woman waited for them to reach her, then fell into step alongside them, heading back the way she had come.

"For a second there I was afraid you might be a robot," the woman said with a nervous laugh.

"Thankfully not," Solace said.

The woman shifted her gaze to Reynard and scrutinized him with cool, guarded eyes, as though unsure if she should trust him.

"Hey," she said.

"This is Reynard," Solace said. "Reynard, Grace."

"Nice to meet you," he said.

Grace eyed him a moment longer, then gave a small nod, her scrutiny having apparently ended in his favor. She returned her attention to Solace.

"The others are waiting at the gate," she said. "I didn't want to go ahead until you were there. If we got separated…" She shrugged, various unpleasant outcomes hanging unspoken in the air. "I don't understand why you stayed so long anyway."

"I just wanted to check for any last survivors," Solace said. She gestured at Reynard. "It's a good thing I did, too."

"Yeah," he said. "Thanks for that." He grinned. "Though I know plenty of folks who'd tell you you shouldn't have bothered."

Solace laughed, revealing teeth that were enviably white and even. Reynard didn't think he had ever seen teeth so perfect.

"I'm sure you're worth it," she said. "Everyone's worth it."

They walked in silence a while, their shadows on the curving brick walls lurching in synch with the erratic movements of the lanterns' flames. Occasional faint rumbles testified to New Portland's still-ongoing fall.

"So, uh, you never explained what this House place is," Reynard said.

"Oh!" Solace said. "It's the House of Good Karma. It's basically just a bunch of us doing whatever we can to make life better for everyone in these difficult times."

"Very admirable."

"It's good work," Grace said with a vigorous nod, eyes bright with the ardor of a True Believer. "We like to think of ourselves as a sort of army of love, a force of light and hope and order nonviolently combating the chaos that's overrun the world. We feed the hungry, we house the homeless, we build, we educate, we salvage useful goods and distribute them to the needy. That's what I mainly do: salvage. The landscape's full of stuff just sitting around. About six months ago we stumbled across the ruins of a huge warehouse that contained nothing but shoes. There were thousands of pairs, all different sizes, all of them in beautiful condition. We gathered them up and handed them out to anyone who needed them. We've found tons of clothes, non-perishable food, oil, tools, pretty much everything you can think of. You'd be amazed what kinds of things are just sitting around out there."

"Wow," Reynard said, not even remotely amazed. He knew exactly what was out there. Indeed, he himself spent a great deal of time hunting around for worthwhile items. But his idea of worthwhile differed vastly from Grace's. He was looking for things he could sell or use to his advantage, things far more remarkable than clothes and food, things like the fist-sized ruby he had snatched from a coffin in a sprawling necropolis and later traded to a powerful regional warlord in exchange for a suit of black-dragon armor (now sadly lost); or the laser torch he had discovered in the wreckage of a high-tech factory and subsequently used to break into the treasure hall of the Phantom Palace and rob it of seven sacks of gold (now sadly spent).

No one was sure what the Cataclysm had really been—the most logical theory he had heard so far was one advanced by an otherwise dotty scholar, who insisted the event had been the merging of many alternate worlds, sort of like a thousand different decks of cards all violently riffled together—but whatever the truth, it had thrown together more people and creatures and places and things than Reynard had ever imagined existed. There was no telling what you might come across next in this strange new world. Opportunities and possibilities abounded. Everything was sheer chaos, and it was wonderful.

Which was an attitude that would no doubt horrify his current company. It was certainly disappointing to discover that the scrumptious Solace was a silly do-gooder, a Pollyanna, and quite likely religious to boot. It would no doubt make it that much trickier to get her into bed. Not impossible, though. Manipulating people was his stock-in-trade. It was all a matter of figuring out which buttons to press to get a person's psychological machinery working the way you wanted it to. In some cases, with some people, it was all so simple it bored him. Solace, he sensed, would be more of a challenge. And that was fine. The harder the challenge, the sweeter the victory.

"So what about you?" Solace asked him. "What do you do?"

"Well, for the most part I'm a merchant," he said. This was arguably true: He did indeed buy things and sell them; except sometimes he stole them and sold them; and sometimes the things he sold didn't actually exist. "Lately I've also been doing some charitable work that isn't really too different from yours."

He went on to explain that when 1000001's forces attacked, he had been in Kingston Square soliciting donations for the Orphans of the Storm Relief Fund, a humanitarian effort to aid children orphaned by the Cataclysm. As incentive, donors received crude but cute hand-painted ornamental orbs that had been made by the children themselves.

In truth, there were no orphans. The only beneficiary of the fund was Reynard. His scavenging hadn't been turning up very much lately—that happened from time to time—so he concocted the orphan scheme to generate some quick revenue. New Portland was only the third town he had tried it in, and he had already amassed nearly two hundred of the crude copper pieces currently used as currency in these parts. As for the orbs, he painted them himself. Underneath the paint were dragon eggs he had discovered in a cleft in the mountains last month. He cackled whenever he imagined the mayhem that would ensue when they hatched.

He was in the middle of extemporaneously waxing poetic about how aiding children and showing them the virtues of goodness and cooperation would instill valuable lessons integral in furthering the return of order and sanity to the world, when he spotted a dot of light in the darkness ahead. Unlike Grace's lamp, this light didn't seem to be moving.

"What's that?" he whispered.

"The gate," Solace said. "We're almost at the end of the tunnel."

As the trio walked on, the light grew larger, brighter, took on a circular shape, parsed into colors: sky blue, leaf green, stone gray. A cluster of shadowy figures moved about along the bottom half of the light. Soon, dim lines became discernible, gridding the view.

The tunnel ended at a rusty metal grate twelve feet across. Beyond it, a rock-strewn slope gently descended to a stream. On the far side of the stream was a grassy field dotted with small yellow flowers. Beyond that, a forest. Of the robots, the city, the battle, there was no sign. Nearly a dozen people stood on the other side of the grate, all of them staying safely within the shade of the overhanging cliff above. In silence they watched Reynard and the two women approach.

"We were getting worried," a man told Solace as he opened a door in the grate, its ancient hinges squalling. He was twentyish, gangly, with long brown hair and a wispy goatee. He gave Reynard a chilly, appraisive glance. Reynard realized the man either was or wished to be Solace's lover.

Probably the latter, given how the man made no move to make physical contact with Solace once she had stepped through the gate. Competition, then. But not of a serious sort. The man was barely more than a child, easily swayed or spooked.

The moment everyone was out of the tunnel, the group headed east along the stream's bank. It was a little past noon, the sun high overhead, the sky cloudless, the air warm and still. A perfect summer day. At least meteorologically: Very faintly over the stream's steady burble, Reynard caught the sounds of distant explosions and the indecipherable droning of a deep mechanical voice. He looked north, but the high, tree-crowned cliff obscured New Portland from view.

"How far are we from the city?" he asked Solace.

"Half a mile. Not far enough."

A short walk brought them to a wooden footbridge over the stream. On the far shore, they headed across the field toward the woods, heedlessly tramping the yellow flowers as they went.

They were twenty feet from the tree line when the buzz of link drones grew audible over the sound of the stream. The buzz was coming from the north, the direction of New Portland, and it was approaching fast.

"Split up and run!" cried a balding man with cracked spectacles. "Meet at Grazinwyr!"

Everyone sprinted for the woods. As he ran, Reynard glanced over his shoulder. At first all he saw was the field and the stream and the cliff with its fringe of trees and the hazy white peaks of the Salt Stairs just visible above the treetops and, rising above them all, pillars of smoke from the still-hidden city; and for a moment he wondered if it had been a false alarm, if perhaps a drone patrol was merely passing by in ignorance of the refugees not far away. But then several dozen of the football-sized drones shot from the trees atop the cliff in a flurry of leaves. They streaked down and across the stream, converging on the crowd of fleeing humans, their shining silver link-cords trailing behind them.

Reynard tried to keep close to Solace as they ran, but in the jostle of panicked bodies they got separated, and once they hit the woods he lost track of her completely. He lost track of everyone. All he had were quick glimpses of figures hurtling through foliage and a confused jumble of sounds—thudding footfalls, branches snapping, brush rustling—all of which slowly faded as the group spread out, giving the drones a host of targets to track, hopefully so many targets that there would be no drones left to follow Reynard.

He headed due south, away from the robots and toward Grazinwyr, a bucolic little town ten miles distant. He had passed it in his travels a few times but never thought it looked rich enough to be worth visiting.

Before he had gone very far he heard footsteps pounding toward him from the right. From the same direction came the swelling buzz of drones.

Reynard dove behind a bush, then peered out through a gap in the branches in time to see a pudgy brunette from the group—not anyone he had had any real contact with—race into view, her face warped with terror, her cheeks streaked with tears.

She dashed toward the very bush Reynard hunched behind. He silently cursed and wished her away, wished her to trip on a stone or a root and succumb to the drones before she could unwittingly reveal his position to them.

To his relief, twenty drones shot out of the brush and streaked toward the woman while she was still a dozen paces away. There was no way she could make it in time.

She knew it too, and emitted a single wordless wail.

As the drones flew forward, their link-cords stiffened and swiveled about until the cords' tips touched those of neighboring drones.

Today was the first time Reynard had seen link drones, but he had heard a lot about them as he conned his way through town after town in the region over the last few months. Individually each drone was no smarter than an insect, basically just a machine responding in simple ways to the environment. But when the link-cords connected one drone to another, they shared their memory and processing power, and the individuals became components of a larger, colonial organism. The more drones that linked up, the smarter the colony became. Also, the more powerful. The drones generated electricity, which they used to further their prime directive of exterminating all higher biological life-forms. Each drone by itself could unleash only a meager amount, perhaps enough to kill a rat. A larger group of, say, twenty, as now…

"No, please!" the woman screamed. "God! Why? This isn't fair!" She knew pleading was as useless as running, but she couldn't stop herself from doing either, her innate organic will to survive unquashable even now, even as the linked drones floated above her like a net about to fall.

But it didn't fall. Instead lightning arced down from a small metal nodule on the underside of each drone. The woman stiffened as twenty bolts snapped through her. Her mouth stretched wide in a silent scream, and a curl of gray smoke emerged. Reynard shut his eyes and turned away, but nothing blocked the stench of burning hair and meat.

A few seconds later the crackling stopped. There was a thud of something heavy landing on the grass.

He peeked out through the bush again in time to see the

link-cords separate and the drones drift apart. Slowly they turned about as if scanning for something, each one rotating individually while maintaining its position relative to the others. Then as one they shot away through the trees and out of sight.

Reynard waited until the drones' buzz was lost amid the rustle of leaves in the breeze, and then waited some more. When ten minutes had passed with no further sign of the drones, he stood up and resumed his trek south, this time at a fast walk.

It was early evening when he got to Grazinwyr. After stealing a string of sausages and a potato pie from a vendor's stall and devouring them in a few greedy bites, he made a circuit of the town, carefully scanning the crowds, finding only the usual assortment of farmers, laborers, watchmen, merchants, whores, and mercenaries. He saw no one from the group that had fled New Portland. It occurred to him as he roamed the manure-caked streets that perhaps the others in the group had agreed on a rendezvous point before he joined up with them. Or perhaps to them the place was obvious. He systematically checked everywhere that struck him as a logical location to meet: the run-down manor house that served as the seat of what passed for the town's government; the small square around Grazinwyr's only monument—an eroded granite statue of a buckskin-clad woman in a canoe; the market with its stalls of floppy lettuce, dirt-flecked carrots, and scrawny chickens in rickety wooden cages; the two inns; the five taverns.

It was in the last of these taverns that he overheard drunken talk of a man in the town of Slake who possessed a cache of working automatic weapons that he guarded with bloodthirsty zeal. This bore investigation. Reynard immediately set to work finding a horse that could cover the eight miles to Slake that very night. He was eager to find out if these weapons really existed, and if they did, how well guarded they really were. Not well enough to protect them from someone with Reynard's skills and experience, he felt sure.

As he sped out of town on a horse stolen from the inn's stable, he spared one last passing thought for Solace. He felt a twinge of regret that he hadn't gotten to fuck her, but it didn't matter that much. The world was full of fuckable girls.

Besides, who knew? Perhaps their paths would cross again someday.

2

Drell
926 A.C.

Reynard was grinning as he skirted the ragged edge of the midday market crowd. Everything was going exactly as planned.

Using blueprints stolen from a dead inventor's lab, he had spent the morning convincing a hastily convened assembly of merchants and minor members of Drell's government that he was a brilliant if absent-minded engineer interested in making his designs reality and thereby providing the city-state with a massive mobile flame-thrower that would help protect them from the countless threats abroad in this wild world. To construct a prototype, he told them, he required not only funding—to the tune of several thousand gold pieces—but also access to the extremely rare, extremely valuable, and extremely flammable Phlogiston-22 stored in sealed subterranean vaults on the outskirts of the city.

His performance as the scatterbrained genius had been so good he nearly fooled himself. He had mixed up everyone's names, stammered out faux pas both endearing and embarrassing, and unleashed strings of incoherent techspeak that glazed all eyes. And in the end he had won them over. They hadn't said so, of course; bureaucracy dictated a series of further discussions and negotiations, the next one to be held tomorrow morning at the Merchant's Guild. But their delighted smiles as they rose and thanked him for his time told him all he needed to know.

If everything went as planned, he would soon wind up with not only enough gold to snap a mule's back, but several canisters of Phlogiston-22, which he could then auction off to the highest bidder.

Life was good.

An explosion of laughter drew his attention to a large crowd off to his left. They were watching what was now called a Punching Judy show, a common marketplace entertainment in which a pair of leering puppets, a he and a she, shrieked and squawked and battered each other with blunt instruments.

He watched the silly puppets for a second, then swept a bored glance over the audience. Then he froze in his tracks.

At the far edge of the crowd stood a woman whose face was maddeningly familiar. She had light-brown skin, black hair that had been cropped to a fine down—a style currently popular among both men and women—and a red-and-green linen kirtle. Slung over her shoulder was a gray hemp bag weighed down with something heavy and angular.

Reynard stood there staring at her for well over a minute, trying to recall where he had seen her before, while market-goers streamed past him and the early spring breeze, which retained just the faintest trace of winter's chill, gently tousled his hair and tugged at his clothes. He was fairly sure she wasn't one of his sexual conquests, though admittedly the list was so long not even he with his near-photographic memory could remember every single one. If indeed she wasn't, it was a major oversight he ought to rectify. But he didn't want to approach her until he had identified her, for she might be a former mark, and right now he couldn't risk stirring up any unnecessary trouble, what with his Phlogiston scheme nearing fruition.

Then she smiled at the puppets' violent antics, and the sight of her perfectly white, even teeth—a sight rarer than comely whores in these diseased and brutal days—unlocked the right memory.

It was the girl from New Portland, the one who had saved his life.

Nine hundred years ago.

"Son of a bitch," he muttered.

As he crossed the crowd toward her, his eyes never once wavering from her face, barely aware of the toes he tromped and the shoulders he bumped and the murmured imprecations he received, he tried to remember her name. It was something odd. A regular noun with pleasant and comforting connotations. Beginning with an S.

Serenity? Solidarity? No, not quite, but something *like* that. Her redheaded friend had had a similar name...

Grace! That was the friend's name. Grace. Grace and...

Security? Stillness?

Crap.

Oh, well. No big deal. He knew all kinds of ways to get people to reveal their names to him without their realizing he didn't already know.

He was still a good fifteen feet from her when the audience burst into applause. Glancing stageward, he saw that the show was over, and the puppeteer had stepped out of his booth to take a bow. The puppets were still on his hands like a pair of grotesque mittens, and as he bowed he held up his arms and made the puppets bow, too.

When he turned back to the girl, she was striding away toward Spear Street, shrugging her bag into a more comfortable position as she went.

If he could just remember her name he could shout it out and make her stop. But the name (Sympathy? Satisfaction?) wouldn't come, so he hurried after her, hoping to catch up.

It wasn't going to be easy, he soon saw. She walked fast and maneuvered through the ever-shifting mass of people with practiced ease, an ease he simply couldn't rival, not with him having to split his attention between navigating the crowd and keeping track of her at the same time. It took all his effort just to match her pace.

She exited the market and headed down Spear Street, a major thoroughfare lined with inns and taverns and shops and stables. Horses clopped along on every side. Wagons creaked and rattled. Blacksmiths' anvils rang. A thousand conversations merged into a single ceaseless drone. The air stank of shit and straw and wood smoke.

Six blocks down, with the neighborhood slowly growing seedier, she (Sweetness? Safety?) slowed to a near stop at the intersection of Spear Street and Cobbler's Lane. Grinning, he hurried to close the remaining fifty feet between them. But then he saw the reason for her slowing down, saw what her attention was riveted on: one of Drell's armored guards, standing tall and stiff with self-importance as he questioned an old man outside a stonemason's a few doors past the intersection. Reynard also noted how her arm clamped the hemp bag against her side as if to hide it. Reynard himself slowed, intrigued by this unexpected development, and waited to see what the girl would do next.

Keeping her wary eyes on the guard, she veered left onto Cobbler's Lane, a quiet, sparsely traveled side street lined with artisans' shops that sold specialty items—dolls, scrolls, baskets, and the like. The traffic here was very light, and he had no problem keeping track of her. He would have had no problem catching up to her, either, but the incident with the guard had piqued his curiosity, and he wanted to find out what she was up to before he revealed himself. Knowledge, after all, was power.

As they made their way down Cobbler's Lane he stayed a good thirty feet behind her and made sure to keep his eyes off her at all times, fixing them instead on the trio of children who happened to be racing past her, or on the window of a fletcher's in which her reflection just happened to be visible. This, he quickly found, had been a wise decision, for a few times she half turned as if to examine the goods in a window she was passing, while no doubt in reality stealing a quick glimpse behind her to ensure the guard wasn't on her tail.

After a block and a half she turned down a narrow alley that connected Cobbler's Lane with Twittenbrake Road. Reynard paused just short of the alley's mouth and waited a few seconds, listening for any sound from the alley. He heard nothing. After a count of five, he strolled casually into the alley just in time to see her reach the opposite end and turn left.

He trotted down the alley, splashing through puddles of unidentifiable muck and sending rats and roaches scuttling for cover. When he reached the far end, he stopped and peered around the corner in the direction she had gone.

Twittenbrake was much busier than Cobbler's Lane, with constant traffic into and out of and between the numerous taverns the street was infamous for, and for a few worrying moments he couldn't find her amid the steady flux of bodies that moved about with varying degrees of co-ordination.

But then he caught a quick glimpse of a figure with a black-fuzzed head and a red-and-green dress darting into another alley a hundred feet down on the opposite side of the street. He raced across Twittenbrake, swerving around startled drunks and bounding over a mangy yellow dog that was lapping up a puddle of vomit.

When he reached the alley mouth and peered down it, he again caught only a fleeting glimpse of the girl (Succor? Support?) as she turned down a side alley. Not good. This was one of those areas where the alleys branched and twisted to form networks so mazy you could get lost even with a map. If he didn't catch her now, he might lose her completely.

He rushed down the alley. The instant he rounded the corner into the side alley, a pair of huge meaty fists grasped the front of his shirt and slammed him against the side alley's brick wall. The back of his head thwocked against the wall hard enough to make him see stars.

"The hell you think you're doin'?" growled a sneering, blond-stubbled face only inches from his. A thick scar as white and shiny as candle wax ran down the man's right cheek. His breath stank of sardines and tooth decay.

Reynard opened his mouth to respond, then paused, having spotted the girl over the man's massive right shoulder. She stood ten feet away, watching blankly, her hemp bag and its mysterious contents held tightly to her chest. He met her eyes, hoping she would recognize him and call out for the blond man to stop, but her face remained blank.

The man shook Reynard hard enough for Reynard's head to smack the wall a second time.

"Well?" the man snarled. "Answer me!"

"I...I..." He inclined his head toward the girl. "I know her."

The man's blond unibrow descended in a dubious frown.

"Zat true?" he called back over his shoulder.

The girl studied Reynard's face. She shook her head.

"I've never seen him before."

"'S what I thought." The man grinned at Reynard, revealing teeth in worse shape than his face. It was the grin of a man who knows he'll soon be doing what he loves best. "Now you tell me what the hell you's really up to."

Reynard looked at the girl again, desperately trying to remember her name. It was his only hope. What the hell was her damn name? Sanity? Solace?

"Solace!"

The man's grin collapsed, and he emitted a surprised grunt. Solace blinked at Reynard in startlement. Then she frowned and shook her head slightly.

"Have we met?" she said.

Now that the immediate threat of violence was gone (or at least forestalled), he thought of more things he could say to try to jog her memory, things he probably would have thought of already if his head hadn't been getting smacked against a wall.

"Fall of New Portland," he said to Solace.

She looked blank again, and for a second he was afraid that she had forgotten the whole event, or that this wasn't really her after all, only someone coincidentally similar, or, perhaps more likely, a descendant, recipient of similar genes and a name handed down through generations like a family heirloom.

Then her eyes went wide.

"Oh!"

She regarded him with fascination for a moment, then said, "Yeah, now I remember you. But your name...I don't quite..."

"Reynard," he said.

"Of course! That's right. Reynard." She looked him up

and down while a marveling smile spread across her face. "Wow. This is certainly a surprise." To the blond man she said, "You can let him go, George."

George squinted balefully at Reynard, silently telling him not to try anything funny or something bad and painful and quite possibly fatal would happen. The hands released Reynard's shirt. Reynard slumped against the wall, gently rubbing the growing bump on the back of his head.

George stepped away as Solace stepped forward.

"Are you hurt bad?" she asked Reynard.

"Nah. Worst damage is to my pride. Well, unless I'm too concussed to realize it."

She smiled, relieved by his good humor. Then she looked at him more seriously. "Why were you following me like that?"

"Honestly? I couldn't recall your name until just a second ago. And you walk so fast, I couldn't catch up. I didn't want to just shout, 'Hey, you girl there!'"

Solace laughed. "I guess I do walk kind of fast."

"And, you know, people like us, we don't really want to attract too much attention to ourselves, you know?" This was something of an understatement. The centuries since the Cataclysm had been an age of chaos, full of wars and invasions and betrayals. For safety's sake, people stuck close to those most like themselves and shunned or killed anyone too different. Under such circumstances, you quickly learned to keep your differences to yourself.

"After all," Reynard concluded, flicking his eyes toward George, who stood scowling a few feet away, his arms folded across his chest, "you never know who might be listening."

She understood. "He knows. It's okay."

"Ah."

"I know what?" growled George.

"That I'm an Elder," she said in a low voice. She gestured at Reynard. "He's one, too."

At this, George's whole demeanor changed. His face went slack with shock, his mouth dropping open so far you could have parked a cart inside. His arms fell from his chest and hung limply at his sides.

"Uh…whuh…heck, I didn't realize…" George flashed Reynard an obsequious smile and ducked his head in a little bow. "Sorry if I hurt you or anything, but, you know, you was followin' Ms. Solace, and—"

"Oh, I understand," Reynard said. "It's fine. Any decent man would've done the same."

"Thank you, Mr., um…"

"Reynard's fine."

"Reynard. Right."

"Um, if you don't mind my asking, what's an Elder?" Reynard asked Solace. "I think I understand from the context, but…"

"It means someone who was alive before the Cataclysm and is still around today," she explained.

"Never heard the term before."

"It's kind of newish. I heard it for the first time about fifty years ago in Cennomac, but it seems to be spreading fast."

George shifted uncomfortably and cleared his throat. "Uh, if guys're gonna talk about stuff like that, maybe you oughta get off the street. Plus, there's, uh…you know. The thing." He glanced meaningfully at Solace's bag.

"What thing?" Reynard asked.

"Um…" Solace looked at George, then back at Reynard, then out the side alley's mouth to the main alley beyond. "Let's get inside first."

They headed a short distance down the side alley to a door Reynard hadn't noticed before, mainly because it was painted the same color as the bricks around it. There were no signs on or around it, no windows, no indications of what was inside.

George took out a heavy iron key ring, picked out a key, and unlocked the door. Pushing the door open, he motioned for them to enter. Reynard and Solace stepped into a narrow room that contained a bare, rough-hewn trestle table but no other furniture. A pair of lanterns sat on a shelf next to the door. The walls and ceiling were made of crudely cut planks of wood, clearly a recent replacement for whatever the original materials had been. The floor was old, cracked concrete. Opposite the entrance was a steel door painted green. This looked like part of one of the city's original pre-Cataclysm buildings.

Solace took one of the lanterns from the shelf and lit it. She turned and nodded at George, who had remained outside. He nodded in reply and shut the door.

"He's not coming in?" Reynard asked.

"He's the guard. That's why he was a little...rough with you."

"Just a little," he said, rubbing the back of his head with a grimace.

She winced apologetically. "Sorry about that, but I'm kind of twitchy about strangers following me. Or old acquaintances I don't remember right away. Sorry about that, too. There's a lot up here." She tapped the side of her head. "It takes some time to sort through it all."

"I know the feeling. Luckily, though, it's usually not much of an issue. I don't often run into people I haven't seen in nine hundred years."

"Same here. I've met only a few others like us, though

25

I've heard about maybe two dozen more."

"Yeah, that about tallies with my own experiences. So just how long-lived are you?"

She laughed. "Thanks for not saying 'old.' No woman wants to hear that, even if she *is* functionally immortal. Anyway, if you must know, I celebrated my thousandth birthday about two decades back. You?"

"Nearly seventeen hundred."

"Wow. I think that might be the oldest I've heard of. Well, at least as far as humans go. I talked to a robot once that claimed to be over sixteen-thousand years old. And I've heard that fairies and dragons—"

There was a click, and the steel door opened just enough to allow a woman's worried face to peer out.

"Hey, Dwan," Solace said. "It's okay. You can come out. It's safe."

The door swung wide, revealing a tall, gray-haired woman in a brown wool tunic dress. Despite the hair, she looked to be only around thirty-five. In her hand was a burning lantern similar to Solace's. Behind her, a door-lined corridor stretched away.

"I wasn't sure," Dwan said, stepping into the room with a smile that was half relief, half embarrassment. "I heard the outer door open, and then some voices, but no one came in." She eyed Reynard, then glanced questioningly at Solace.

"This is Reynard," Solace said. "He's an Elder."

Like George's, Dwan's face collapsed in amazement.

"Well now!" she exclaimed, giving Reynard a big, starstuck smile. "It's a great pleasure to meet you."

"It's an even greater pleasure to meet *you*," Reynard said. "When most people find out what I am, they want to set me on fire."

Dwan gave a derisive snort. "Most people are superstitious primitives, ready to kill anything they don't understand. Some of us know better."

"They're just afraid," Solace told her a little wearily, as if this were an old, recurring argument. "With all the chaos and strife in the world, who can blame them?"

"They're adults. They have eyes and ears and brains. They should know better."

"So, what are you guys?" Reynard asked. "Some kind of pro-diversity group?"

Dwan flashed Solace a shocked look. "He doesn't know?"

"We just met up," Solace said. "I haven't had a chance to tell him."

"Well, you better show him around the place!" She grinned at Reynard. "Trust me: You'll love it."

"You're welcome to join us," Solace said.

"Can't. Gotta finish the inventory before the meeting." She heaved a sigh. "My slave labor is never done."

She began to turn back toward the hallway, but then started a little, suddenly remembering something, and turned to Solace.

"I almost forgot. I take it everything went okay?" She gestured at Solace's bag.

"It was all completely hitchless," Solace said.

"Good."

Dwan headed down the hallway. Reynard and Solace followed, Solace shutting the metal door behind them. Halfway down the corridor Dwan stopped before a door on the right.

"Well, I will be in my usual prison cell here," she said. "If you need anything, just holler." She paused a moment, eyes and smile fixed on Reynard. "I hope I get to see you again later."

"Likewise," Reynard said.

Dwan's smile split into a grin. With a nod she opened the door and slipped into the room beyond. Reynard caught a quick glimpse of a wooden desk heaped high with papers, and then the door clicked shut.

"She's nice," Reynard said.

"Oh, she is. Very nice. But be careful: She's also a scholar. Give her a chance and she'll interrogate you about every minute detail of your life until you want to throw her out a window."

He laughed. "Sounds like you speak from hard experience."

"Alas."

She led Reynard to a blank metal door at the end of the corridor. Taking a key from a hidden pocket in her kirtle, she unlocked the door.

"Welcome," she said with a playfully melodramatic intonation as she pushed open the door, "to the Database."

On the other side of the door was a long concrete room full of wooden shelving units that were packed with books, parchments, boxes, statuettes, clothing, crystals, and a bewildering variety of other items. Luminous silver spheres the size of pumpkins had been strategically placed on pedestals throughout the room to provide light.

"What is this?" Reynard asked as he followed Solace inside. He studied a row of scrolls on a shelf next to the door. They were written in a language he had never seen before. "Is it like a library or something?"

"In a manner of speaking," Solace said. She dimmed her lantern and set it aside, the weird glowing globes having rendered it unnecessary. "The Database started out as a way of preserving knowledge from pre-Cataclysm civilizations. It was actually begun by the government of Drell shortly after the Cataclysm to gather information about monsters they were facing and technology they came across and things like that. Over time it became a bit less utilitarian and began to include pre-Cataclysm artifacts of any kind. More recently, it's evolved once again to include items from all the different cultures and species of Eridia." She glanced at him. "You've heard 'Eridia' before, right?"

He nodded. Eridia was a term that had been swiftly gaining ground among humans as the name of the known world, which at this point extended from the Akai Desert in the west to the Ocean in the east, and from the Northern Wastes to the South Sea. No one was sure what, if anything, "Eridia" meant or where the word had come from, but most folks were relieved to finally have a halfway decent-sounding name for the landmass they lived on other than "The Land" or "The World" or something equally banal.

"Now I understand your concerns about security," he said as he examined a fist-sized cube made of bone, every side of which was carved with stars, skulls, trees, and other simple, iconic images. "Lots of people would love to raze this place to the ground. I take it the local government isn't involved anymore?"

"No. A few hundred years ago, they decided to shut the Database down and throw everything away to make room for an expansion to the city's armory. Fortunately, the person in charge of the Database at that time—a fellow named Lummy Hood—managed to convince the government to let him cart it all off and store it at his own expense on the condition they be allowed to look at it whenever they wanted. As far as I know, they never wanted to, and at this point I doubt a single individual in Drell's government even knows the Database ever existed, let alone that it still does."

"And you want to keep it that way, eh?"

"Exactly. The militaristic xenophobes currently in charge would probably label the Database a 'harmful outside influence' and torch it on the spot."

They made their way through the room, pausing often while Reynard inspected some of the items: a pamphlet titled "Waste Disposal Procedures for BioDome 8 (NorthAm)"; two dozen color slides showing a black-walled room equipped with manacles, metal tables, floor drains, and scads of sinister implements bristling with blades and hooks; a bundle of letters addressed to someone named Appolei f'fff Kei AGA who resided in a place called Upper Quayr; a bright yellow oboe-like instrument that branched into two separate mouthpieces; a fold-out street guide to a city named Doomstadt; a red, white, and purple pin-back button that read "Re-elect Pandufin in '06!"; and a textbook titled *An Introduction to Therianthropic Cellular Biology (Second Edition)*.

"This is incredible," Reynard muttered. And he meant it, though not in the way Solace probably thought. A lot of this stuff would be worth a fortune to certain collectors. He glanced around, trying to estimate the potential value of the room's contents. He gave up around a hundred thousand gold pieces. Maybe if his Phlogiston scheme allowed him the time, he could orchestrate a little heist…

Solace interpreted his looking around as an attempt to grasp the room's layout.

"The section we're in is all pre-Cataclysm stuff," she said. "There are artifacts from thousands of civilizations here. As far as we can tell, most of those civilizations are just gone, with no known members surviving the Cataclysm. We've got old books no one can translate, images of creatures and things no one recognizes, machines no one can figure out how to use. Sometimes it gets to me a little. Sometimes I feel like I'm working in a graveyard."

"What's the story with those?" Reynard asked, pointing at one of the glowing globes that lit the room.

"Aren't those amazing? They never stop glowing. They're some kind of special crystalline thingies that were used as a natural light source by a pre-Cataclysm elf society. A Database scouting party found them amid some ruins in a ravine in the Peletite Mountains. We're not entirely sure how they work, but they sure work well. I wish someone would figure out their secret so we could make them for everybody."

Reynard put his hand over the globe. He felt no heat, no sensations of any kind. "You sure it's safe? These things could be radioactive."

"They seem to be safe. They've been in use here for over two centuries now without a problem. Besides, if they were radioactive, they would've affected the elves, too. After all, we're not *that* biologically dissimilar. Which reminds me…"

She opened her bag and carefully withdrew a large rectangular object wrapped in a cloth. "Our latest acquisition. Something really unusual."

"What is it?"

She set the object on an empty patch of shelf and unwrapped it, revealing a box made of bright green coral. She flipped a latch and lifted the lid. Inside were twenty compartments, each containing a small ovate stone in a nest of intricately woven strips of seaweed. The stones bore tiny images of sea life and ocean-bottom geography, the images having been made by delicately chipping away at the stones' outermost layers to reveal bits of other layers beneath, each layer being a different color due to some peculiar process of lithification.

"This was donated to us by the sister of a woman who recently died," Solace explained. "The story goes, the dead woman fell in love with a merman when she was a teenager, and he gave her this as a gift. Shortly afterward, he returned to the sea and never returned."

"Typical male."

Solace tutted, but couldn't suppress a smile. "Cynic."

"Realist."

Still smiling, she shook her head, then picked up the coral box. "Come on. I need to put this with the other new acquisitions."

She led him through the stacks toward the far end of the room.

"I'd hate to be the guy responsible for dusting all this stuff," Reynard said.

She laughed. "You think this is bad? This place is nothing compared with the Peridor Archives."

"The what?"

"Peridor Archives. It's a much, much bigger version of this. So far, it fills about five rooms the size of this one. And I hate to say it, but it's much better organized. Then again, the woman who runs it is an Elder like us, and boy, is she a stickler for proper categorization. And I've heard there are a few other, similar data-preservation projects here and there, but none as big as the one in Peridor, or even this one."

"I had no idea this was such a booming business." Maybe once he had heisted the Drell Database, he would move on to Peridor.

She snorted. "A handful of rooms in all of Eridia versus enough armies and arsenals and irrational hatred to sink a continent? I'd hardly call that booming."

"It's better than nothing."

"Very true. Here we are." They had come to the room's far wall, against which stood a trestle table that matched the one in the anteroom. Solace set the coral box on the table, where it joined a Palu-Batatan slave collar, a cameo of an old woman with a pair of stubby horns sprouting from her forehead, and a stack of moldy paperbacks written by an author named J.T.P. Bromanski.

There were four chairs at the table, and Solace pulled one out, turned it to face the room, and slumped into it with a weary sigh.

"I hope you don't mind," she said. "I've been on my feet for hours."

"Same here, actually," Reynard said. "I could use a sit-down."

He settled into the chair next to hers, likewise with his back to the table. They sat in silence for a moment, staring out at the assorted products of this world and a thousand vanished others.

"I keep hoping one day I'll find something from Interon," Solace said. She glanced at Reynard and answered the question forming on his lips before he could ask it: "That's where I'm from."

"Ah."

"So far, though, nothing's turned up."

"What was Interon like?"

"Very technologically advanced. Nothing like this world. Everything was regulated and sanitary and safe. There wasn't any war or poverty or disease. It was nice, if sometimes a bit dull. My crazy family more than made up for any dullness, though."

"Crazy how?"

"Oh, all kinds of ways. For one thing, I had four siblings, two sisters and two brothers, which was highly unusual. In Interon it was frowned upon for any family to have more than two children. But my parents were iconoclasts, freethinkers who followed their own hearts. To be honest, I think they kind of regretted it a little in this case; my siblings and I were quite a handful. My parents had to develop a different parenting strategy for each one of us, because we all had such wildly different personalities."

"Really?"

"Oh, yeah. My oldest brother, Jonquial? He was the nicest guy you could ever hope to meet. He ended up becoming a peace liaison."

"A what?"

"Um…kind of like a city guard, only…different."

"That's helpful," he said dryly.

"It's hard to explain. Let's just say he served the peace."

"Got it."

"And then on the opposite side of the scale there was Ashema, my youngest sister. She was, shall we say, a bad seed. A *very* bad seed. We tried to help her as best we could, tried to get her to change, but nothing ever stuck. We finally had to let my brother arrest her. I mean, we loved her, of course. We never stopped loving her. It's just…we didn't know what to do with her."

"What was she up to that was so bad?"

"Drugs, mostly."

"Ah. What was she taking?"

"Oh, she wasn't taking anything. She was *making*. And *selling*. It was this highly addictive stuff called Eclipse. I am *so* glad that stuff didn't survive the Cataclysm. But anyway, it was the same way with all my siblings: No two of us had the same interests or temperaments or anything. My mom always hypothesized that our differences were due to the effects of her erratic diet during pregnancy on our sensitive fetal brains. But then, she *was* a biochemist."

"What about your dad? What did he do?"

"He taught philology. University level."

"And you? What did you do for a living?"

"Well, at the time the Cataclysm struck, I wasn't actually working at all. I was back in school studying for my tenth degree, this one in Sociology. But as I'm guessing you'll understand, I'd held a wide variety of jobs, everything from a political campaign aide to a nutritionist." She flapped a hand dismissively. "I think that's more than enough about me for the moment. What about you? What was your homeworld like? What did your parents do?"

"My homeworld was a lot more primitive than yours, so there were fewer options as far as careers. My father was a farmer. My mom was a seamstress." This was a complete fabrication. He never knew his father, and his mother was a whore. "Honestly, there isn't really much to tell about my early years. Most of my childhood was spent on a farm." This, at least, was partly true. He had spent three years working on one as a child; it was punitive labor, consequence of a pyromaniacal phase he had gone through at the age of seven. "It was all very...simple. Low-tech."

"You must feel kind of at home in this world, then," she said. She tried to sound chipper, pleased for him, but behind her gladness, something troubled lurked. Based on what she had told him about her own origins, it wasn't hard to conclude that she herself didn't feel even remotely at home in this world, that she felt alien, lonely. These were feelings he could use to his advantage.

Before he could employ any of the stratagems that were rapidly unfolding in his mind, she said, "So how did you get to be immortal, if you don't mind my asking?"

"Magic," he said, lying. It was a lie he had told before. The truth was, he had no idea why he stopped aging in his late twenties. The truth was dull, though, so he invented something more interesting. "I took part in this battle against a gigantic magical monster that was trying to conquer my homeland, Greater Teutonia. After a long, vicious battle, we finally managed to kill it, but as it died, all the powerful magic it contained exploded outward, altering reality in the immediate vicinity in strange, chaotic ways. Nearly everyone present was killed, and the handful who weren't were changed in various ways. One guy had been turned into metal. Another had been literally turned inside-out. And me? I stopped aging."

"Wow. You got lucky."

"I know. There isn't a day that goes by that I don't tell myself that." He turned sideways in his chair, facing her, and rested his elbow on the tabletop. "So what about you? I told you my secret origin; you tell me yours."

"Believe it or not, I volunteered for an experiment. I chose to be like this. See, this scientist in Interon had developed something he thought would halt the aging process. He'd tested it on a few lower mammals—mice, monkeys, stuff like that—but he needed to test it on some humans, so he asked for volunteers. I was one of six. The experiment was a rousing success for all six of us."

"So, what, you drank some potion, or—"

She shook her head. "It wasn't a potion. The chemical was delivered as a gas. For sixty days we had to live in a sealed underground complex where this stuff was mixed with the air, and during that time I guess it sort of saturated our bodies, our cells, and altered them in some way. I think." She laughed, a bit self-consciously. "I was never quite a stickler for the details, especially where science is involved. But anyway, yeah, I stopped aging, and I never get sick, and I heal about five times faster than the average person. At least from normal injuries. I don't know what would happen if I got a really severe injury, like if I got a limb cut off or something. I'd really rather not find out, actually."

"What happened to the other volunteers?" he asked. "Did they survive the Cataclysm, too?"

"No idea. I kept in touch with them until the Cataclysm, but after that..." She shrugged. "Honestly, as far as I can tell, I'm the only thing from all of Interon to survive." She shook her head slowly. Her eyes were distant, unfocused, lost in memories. She gave a small sigh that hitched a little at the top. "I keep hoping the scavenging parties will turn up something." She looked down at her lap. "I know it's fool-ish—"

"Not at all," he said in a soft voice. He reached out with the arm on the table and cupped her shoulder. "I understand perfectly. I'm in the same boat myself. I mean, yeah, this world is similar to the one I came from in a lot of ways...but it's not the same. It's not mine. It'll never be mine."

She flashed him a sad, grateful smile. "It's good to know someone understands."

He let go of her shoulder but kept the arm extended so his hand lay right beside her, close enough to feel the warmth radiating from her body. She didn't object to the continued closeness. On the contrary, she turned in her seat to face him, just as he had turned to face her earlier. It was then, with that movement, that he knew he had her.

"Yeah," he said. "There aren't many like us out there. It can feel pretty lonely sometimes." His eyes flicked to her lips, then back to her eyes. "You know?"

She gave a small nod. Her own eyes likewise briefly dropped to his lips, then rose to meet his gaze again. "I do."

And here we go, he thought. He slowly leaned forward, his eyes still fixed on hers. She leaned forward to meet him...

The door opened.

"You guys still in here?" Dwan called.

Solace breathed out a small, annoyed groan and stood up. Reynard did likewise, disappointed at the interruption but sure that the moment had simply been deferred rather than killed entirely.

"We're back here," Solace said, striding across the room. Reynard followed close behind.

"There you are," Dwan said, meeting them in the middle of the pre-Cataclysm section. The trio moved doorward. "I finished the inventory, but there are a few irregularities I'd like to go over with you before the meeting. Um, that is, if you don't mind my tearing you away from our esteemed guest."

"Sure." Solace looked at Reynard. "I hate to do this, but we've got this really big meeting tonight—a Database workers–only kind of thing—and—"

"Hey, it's okay," Reynard said. "I understand."

"But I have some free time tomorrow afternoon. Perhaps if you're not busy, we could meet then. I could show you around the Database some more. Maybe you'll even find something from Greater Teutonia."

"That would be fantastic."

They reached the door. Solace picked up her lantern, and the trio stepped out into the hall. Solace shut and locked the Database's door, then turned to Reynard.

"So how about we meet here tomorrow afternoon at three?"

He grinned. "Sounds perfect."

She grinned.

Dwan loudly cleared her throat.

"Inventory," Dwan said to Solace's half-querying, half-irritated glance. "Not a lot of time, you know." She gave Reynard a wincing smile. "Sorry. I'm the bad guy. Hate me."

"Not possible," Reynard said. "Besides, I really need to

get going anyway. It was nice meeting you."

"Likewise."

He looked at Solace. "And I'll see you tomorrow."

She nodded. "Tomorrow."

Reynard headed outside. After briefly savoring the spate of servile smiling and head-ducking his sudden appearance precipitated from George, Reynard strolled away down the alley, all the while wondering what delicious pleasures tomorrow would hold.

None, as it turned out. When he arrived for the meeting at the Merchant's Guild in the morning, he found a squad of city guards awaiting him, tasked with his arrest. The fortunate placement of a window nearby allowed him to flee, and through a combination of luck and wit he managed to evade the ensuing manhunt and escape the city hidden inside a barrel of pickled herring in the hold of a ship bound for Vatch, five hundred miles south...

The next time he found himself in Drell—in 1112—he decided to swing by the Database building, just to see, just in case. Not only was the building gone, but so was the whole neighborhood. In its place stood an array of warehouses. Inquiries revealed that over fifty years earlier half of Drell, including the area in question, had been leveled in a massive conflagration after the city's stockpiles of Phlogiston-22 mysteriously combusted.

3

Den Demestrion
2135 A.C.

In the belly of his black carriage, Reynard slouched bored on a red velvet seat as Saffron, his fuck-of-the-moment, blathered on about some unseeable stain on her taffeta dress.

Outside, the Amara Theater, their destination, rolled into view. Like a lot of postwar architecture here in Den Demestrion, Röthimar's capitol, the theater's ornamentation was extravagant enough to make Reynard's eyes ache: The façade was one gigantic floral frieze dominated by roses and tulips the size of boulders; the doorframes, windowframes, railings, and cresting were choked with intricately curling viny designs; and crowning the whole mess was a series of slender decorative towers that Reynard thought resembled giant rococo birthday candles. After the privations and horrors of the War of Unification, life was re-expressing itself in a burst of fecundity both literal and figurative, from the record birthrate to outpourings of song and poetry to architectural abominations like this.

Reynard heaved a silent sigh. Though this wearisome coach ride was nearly over, the evening's tediousness had only just begun. Saffron would no doubt keep babbling all throughout the concert, and in any case, he didn't give a squirt of jizz about this ridiculous symphony anyway. He would rather be out carousing or gambling or finding this bitch's replacement, but his social standing demanded his attendance.

Fortunately his social standing—a synonym for obscene wealth, really—granted him a private box in the top tier, which meant he could sleep through the damn symphony if he wished. Other possibilities suggested themselves as well: He entertained the notion of banging Saffron the whole show through, commemorating the long-anticipated first performance of the already sacrosanct Unity Symphony with a little unity of a different sort. Alas, even that wouldn't shut the cunt up, as he well knew. Nothing could.

As the carriage rattled past the front of the theater, he smirked at the teeming mass of less well-connected and less wealthy attendees bottlenecked at the main entrance. At least he could be glad he wasn't trapped amid that crush of bodies. He had risen high in the world, higher than ever before, thanks in large part to his shrewd dealings during the war (some of which, admittedly, would get him hanged should they become public knowledge, especially his little wartime arrangement with the orcs).

At the north end of the building, the carriage turned left down a wide alley that led to the theater's side door, an entrance reserved for box owners. An instant before the crowd vanished from sight around the corner, Reynard caught a glimpse of a light-brown face topped with black hair that shone bluish in the glow from the solarite street lamps lining Grand Avenue.

"Stop!"

Before Metaturk, the coachman, could slow the horses to any appreciable degree, before Saffron could do more than screech, "The fuck?" Reynard threw open the door and leaped out. He raced toward the front of the theater, heed-less of the water splashing his silk leggings as his black troll-hide boots pounded through puddles left over from the rain earlier in the evening.

He rounded the corner and scanned the crowd as he slowed to a trot. There was no sign of her. Could he have imagined it?

And then several people moved at once, opening an avenue in the throng, and at the end of that avenue stood Solace.

She was clad in a simple black dress that hugged her body from clavicles to calves. Her hair, long once again, was pinned back from her face with silver clips shaped like open hands, a popular motif since the war. She wore high-heeled black leather boots, a small emerald pendant on a silver chain, and a pair of elbow-length black gloves. A white leather purse hung from her shoulder.

Clasped in one of her black-gloved hands was the hand of a girl about eight years old with black hair, skin a slightly lighter brown than Solace's, and a dress the bright green of budding leaves.

The girl saw Reynard before Solace did, saw him slow then stop at the edge of the crowd with his mouth hanging open in a way that must have been especially comical, for the girl giggled and tugged the woman's hand.

"Look!" she said.

Solace looked, but by then, by the time it had taken her to swivel her eyes from the back of the head of the man in front of her to the girl at her side, then up to what the girl was smiling at, Reynard had composed himself and was walking calmly toward them.

Solace watched his approach with both a faint frown and a faint smile, the expression of someone trying hard to puzzle out the identity of someone maddeningly familiar. Then the smile faded while the frown briefly deepened as a memory stirred. She stiffened with recognition.

"Well, hello," she said as he stopped in front of her. "This is a surprise."

"It sure is," he said. "It's good to see you again."

"Likewise."

He looked down at the girl. "And who is this?" he asked, squatting before her, already knowing the answer.

"This is my daughter," Solace said. "Cara."

He smiled at the girl, masking his annoyance. The presence of children always hindered seduction.

"Hello, Cara."

"Hello," the girl said, eyes probing his face with sober care.

"She's beautiful," Reynard said. He meant it, too. She was a very beautiful girl indeed. She would be quite a tasty treat in about ten years' time.

"She is," Solace said.

"And that's a very beautiful dress, too." As he said this, he shifted his gaze from Cara to Solace, covering both ladies with the compliment.

Solace gave him a small, bland smile. Above it, her eyes were reserved and a little chilly.

He stood up, stealing a look at Solace's fingers as he did so in search of a wedding ring. Her black gloves made it impossible to tell.

"So how have you been?" she asked. She surveyed his finery, eyes lingering longest on the grape-colored vest woven from Lampardian giant-spider silk and embroidered with mithril thread. It was worth lingering over; it cost more than his carriage. "Pretty good from the look of it."

"Yeah. I certainly can't complain. What about you?"

"I'm doing just fine, thanks."

"Good. You here with anyone else?"

"Um, no. It's just Cara and me."

He nodded, hiding his glee. Still, he couldn't help but wonder where the girl's dad was. Did he die in the war? Had they separated? Did he simply hate music?

Reynard gestured at the theater. "What do you have? General admission seats?"

"Yeah."

"Why don't you share my box with me? The two of you."

"Oh, thanks, but we—"

"A box?" Cara exclaimed, eyes huge with excitement. She pumped her mother's arm. "Can we? Please?"

Solace's gaze bounced between her daughter and Reynard. For a moment Reynard was sure she would refuse, but then she sighed and said to Cara, "All right. As long as you behave yourself." To Reynard she said, "Are you sure you don't mind?"

"Not at all. I'm here by myself, so there're plenty of extra seats in the box. Just...hold on a minute. Wait here. I have to check on something first."

He walked quickly back to the alley. His carriage sat next to the side entrance. Through the rear window, Saffron's blonde hair bobbed and shook as she bitched him out in absentia. He thanked every star in the sky she had been her usual lazy self and stayed put.

"Take her home," he called to Metaturk, who was twisting around on his perch to look at Reynard over the carriage's roof. "Then come back."

"Yes, sir." Metaturk bowed his bald head and turned back around to pick up the reins.

Saffron stuck her head out the side window.

There you are! Where the fuck did you get to? I mean, I've been waiting for, like, ever. The performance probably—"

"Drive!" Reynard shouted.

Metaturk snapped the reins. The carriage shot away.

"What the fucking fuck!" Saffron cried. She whisked her head back inside so it wouldn't get lopped off by one of the other carriages in the alley. A moment later her face appeared in the rear window, eyes aflame with outrage, mouth huge and black, an ugly hole. The carriage clattered out of the alley, turned right on Woomar Lane, and was gone.

Reynard returned to the front of the building. Solace and Cara had stepped out of the crowd and stood off to one side, examining the coming attractions posters in the theater's display windows. Solace was pointing at the foot-high name of Mendheina, who the poster revealed was slated to give a speech in the theater in a month's time.

"Your daddy met her during the War, you know," Solace was telling Cara as Reynard neared. "In fact, it's because of her we got the tickets. She—" Then she spotted Reynard approaching and fell silent.

"Everything's good to go," he said. "Follow me."

He led them to the side entrance, where a doorman opened the door for them with a brisk salute.

"They're with me," Reynard told him as they strode inside, even though the doorman had given no sign he found the woman and the girl's presence in any way untoward.

After the dim, cloudy evening outside, the theater's large, crowded east lobby was so bright they had to squint until their eyes adjusted. Rows of crystal chandeliers blazed overhead, and gilt-framed mirrors had been strategically placed around the room to reflect and amplify the light. The wallpaper was periwinkle with repeating lily motifs. The white marble floor gleamed like milk. A ribbon of carpet the color of goldenrod ran the length of the room from the entrance to a white marble staircase that curved away to the theater's upper levels.

Some of the wealthiest and most powerful people in this part of Eridia strolled about or stood in quietly chatting clusters. As the trio crossed the room, Reynard nodded in greeting to all whose eyes he could catch, regardless of how well he knew them, a performance calculated to impress Solace and Cara. It seemed to work.

"Was that Jamet Carchlarret I saw?" Solace whispered once they had reached the stairs and were well away from overhearing ears.

"Yep," Reynard said, voice as nonchalant as he could contrive.

"Wow. You're traveling in some pretty rarefied circles these days, aren't you?"

"Eh," he shrugged with faux modesty. "Success equals a lot of stress, actually. The more successful you are, the more responsibilities there are to deal with. I mean, I've got my shipping company, warehouses in six different Realms, various estates to maintain. It doesn't help that my mansion here in Röthimar is right next to the royal palace, and those damn animals in the King's private zoo sometimes make enough noise to deafen a goom. Keeps me awake half the night."

"Sounds rough."

The congenial sarcasm in her voice compelled him to smile. "Yeah, I know: I shouldn't complain. It could be a lot worse. I always try to remember how fortunate I am to have all this."

"That's a very healthy attitude to have."

At the third landing, he led them down a long, curving corridor that sported rich purple carpeting and elaborate pastoral murals. At regular intervals along the right-hand wall were the curtained entrances to the boxes, many of whose occupants milled and mingled in the hallway.

Cara's head swiveled this way and that as she took in every detail—the silver-handled scimitar on the jeweled belt of a bodyguard, the brown bumbler stole worn by a tall middle-aged woman with a nose like a parrot's beak and hair dyed lemon yellow, the herd of cattle crossing a field of lilacs in the mural on the wall. Solace, for her part, examined things more casually, with a small placid smile. Reynard noticed she never looked at him once.

Halfway down the corridor they passed Thayla, the wife of Obsissimant, the king's chancellor. She stood chatting with a tall cadaverous man Reynard didn't know. Though they had never done more than nod at each other in passing a few times at social events, Reynard smiled warmly at her and said, "Hello, Thayla," as if they had known each other all their lives.

Thayla gave him a thin, barely polite smile.

Once they were out of earshot, Reynard told Solace: "She's still a little sore about an argument we had over foreign policy with Grimbar."

"Ah," Solace said.

Reynard's box was the fourth from the end. At their approach, Reynard's box-man, an old, white-haired halfling named Predegar Fellowes, stepped forward and held open the red Cennomacan hemp curtain that separated the box from the corridor. As they passed through, Reynard smiled and thanked Predegar, hiding, as always, the unease he felt around the twerpy bastard. Though one would never guess it from Predegar's serene, cherubic countenance, he was a survivor of the Genocide, and Reynard always had the irrational and unnerving feeling that the halfling's survival of such horrors had somehow granted him a wisdom so deep it could see right through Reynard's every prevarication. Alas Predegar came with the box and was not Reynard's to dismiss.

The semicircular balcony beyond the curtain contained three ebony tables inlaid with white gold, and eight ebony chairs upholstered in green silk damask.

Ignoring all this, Solace and Cara headed straight to the black titanwood railing. Reynard followed, amused to watch mother and daughter thrill to the view that familiarity had made quite dull to him.

Fifty feet below was the theater's floor, over half its seats already full. Far to the right, the double doors from the main lobby disgorged a steady stream of new arrivals whom yellow-robed ushers led down the aisles and directed along the curving rows to their seats. The chatting of the waiting crowd filled the vast room with a steady, excited murmur.

As Reynard surveyed the room, he realized the view wasn't what he was used to after all, for the crowd below consisted of far more than the usual jaded Röthimaran aristocrats. Not only were there representatives from several dozen realms, including one man whose blue-and-yellow uniform identified him as a general from Uquar, Röthimar's ancient enemy, but there were representatives of other species, as well. Three whole rows were filled with figures about Cara's size whose wildly differing hair colors—from simple black to shocking orange—demarked them as gnomes. Not far from them was a section of slightly shorter, stockier individuals with long braided beards. These beings called themselves *djoren* in their own tongue, but since the sound represented by the "dj" was unpronounceable to most other sentient species, they were more widely known as dwarves. In the back row sat a dozen nyow-ha, tall bipedal cat people, who stared with stereotypical feline patience at the dark green curtain veiling the stage. And here and there were others: a pair of black-cloaked umalai, a small cluster of wochobüshkans, a few of the smaller Opalorians, even a robot that Reynard thought resembled a giant bucket on legs. The variety of entities on display didn't even come close to matching the spectacle of the Grand Assembly which had convened during the War, but it was still quite breathtaking.

When Cara began to complain of achy legs, Reynard arranged three chairs in a row facing the stage, and the trio sat down. Despite Reynard's intentions, Cara wound up in the middle, separating him from Solace. He suspected Solace had orchestrated it that way, but if so, she had done it so deftly that even he with his millennia of tricksiness wasn't sure how.

"When's the music start?" Cara asked.

"I don't know," Solace said. "Not long."

Cara slumped in her chair as if she were sure "not long" meant "three hours."

"Can I play my game?" she asked.

"Okay, but you have to put it away the moment the concert starts." Solace picked her purse up off the floor, set it in her lap, and began to rummage through it.

While she was thus distracted, Reynard studied her profile. She hadn't changed at all. She looked just as trim and sexy as she had the last two times they met. He suddenly felt keenly aware of the way his waistband bit into his distended gut. Why had he let himself go so much? It was stupid, sloppy. It made him soft and slow, and a man like him needed to be ready to spring into action at a moment's notice.

Solace pulled a small wooden box from her purse and handed it to Cara. The box's lid flipped up to reveal a wooden game board covered with alternating white and black squares, each with a small hole in the center. In some of those holes were pegs, half of them black, the others white. Cara studied the layout, then moved a white peg to a square across the board. After a moment's more scrutiny, she moved a black peg three squares forward. Then she opened a compartment to the right of the board, took out a black peg, and stuck it in the hole in which the white peg had initially sat. Reynard watched a few more moves, but couldn't grasp the logic guiding them. The fact that Cara always added pieces to the board but never removed them particularly perplexed him; it was the opposite of how most games were played.

When he finally tore his gaze from the game, he found Solace smiling at him over her daughter's head.

"Thank you," she said. He must have looked puzzled because she quickly clarified: "For the seats."

He shrugged. "It was my pleasure."

A sudden loudening of the susurrus of voices below compelled Reynard, Solace, and a somewhat reluctant Cara to peer over the railing. Striding down the main aisle were two dozen robed figures, twelve males and twelve females, all of whom had pointed ears, calm smiles, and slim, petit physiques, the tallest male being only five-foot-two. Elves. Most likely from the Kolmakendi tribe, who occupied the Kol Forest to the north.

"Isn't this exciting?" Solace said as the elves took their seats directly below Reynard's box. "I mean, who'd have ever thought we'd see the day when all the sentient species were working together? All those years of conflict and suffering, all the hate and war and distrust, and now…" She gestured vaguely, at the world apparently. "Here we are."

"Yeah. Though when you think about what it took to get us here…"

Her ebullience dimmed a little. "True. But at least we're here. And at least all the bad stuff that happened wasn't in vain."

They returned to their seats. Reynard watched Cara resume her game, then looked up at Solace over the girl's head.

"Things've changed quite a bit indeed," he said. He let his eyes drop meaningfully to the top of Cara's head.

Solace laughed softly. "Indeed."

"Married?" he asked.

"Yes." Her voice was flat and even. There was no inflection to the word, no hint of any emotion or valuation. It was a simple statement of fact.

"I take it he's not a music fan?"

Solace hesitated. Her eyes remained fixed on his. "He's...busy."

"Huh."

"You?" she asked.

"Me?"

"Married."

"Oh. No."

"Mm." A faint nod, as if it were the answer she expected. "Have you *ever* been married?"

"Nope."

"Oh, I don't believe that."

"It's true."

"Never? Not in..." She glanced at Cara. "Not in...all this time? Never? Ever?"

Interesting. Her reaction suggested Cara didn't know about her mother's extended lifespan. He wondered if hubby did. Reynard was starting to suspect that all was not well in her marriage. Which meant opportunity for him.

"Really," he said. "Never."

"Wow. And you've never had any kids?"

"Well, not that I'm aware of."

"Uh!" She rolled her eyes.

"So, your husband…" Reynard said. "Is he…" A quick glance at Cara showed she was still absorbed in her game. "You know, like us?"

Solace likewise glanced at Cara, her expression carefully neutral.

"No," she said in a soft voice. After a pause she shook her head as if to underscore the negative for some reason.

She looked away, down at the crowd, then immediately turned back to Reynard and said, "We met during the war."

"Oh, yeah?"

"I was in Carladea, a bit northwest of Nioedo, helping out in a field hospital—doing chores, helping prep food, transporting supplies, stuff like that. He was one of the injured they were treating there. At first I thought he was a soldier." She smiled, eyes distant, not seeing Reynard, seeing only her past, perhaps some jokey moment she had shared with her husband. "But it turned out to be a miscommunication. He was really a teacher who'd been helping refugees flee the war zones. We…" She paused, and then her eyes refocused and fixed on Reynard's. "We fell in love. It happened so fast." She frowned slightly, as if still baffled by the turn of events. "We got married later that month. I never imagined that anything like that would ever happen to me, that I'd ever find my soulmate."

"That's nice," he said, swallowing back his groan at the word "soulmate." Ridiculous. Teenage fantasyland pap. As evidenced, he suspected, by the fact that her husband wasn't here. "I'm happy for you."

"Thanks," she said with a small, pleased smile. She looked down at the audience below.

Reynard followed her gaze. The theater was nearly full

now. The stream coming through the double doors had dwindled to sporadic drops. The show should start soon.

When he raised his eyes again, he noticed a fat lady in the box directly across from his giving him a wide, enchanted smile, the sort of smile women give babies and puppies and other darling things, the smile of a heart that's been warmed and won. What the fuck?

Seeing that he had seen her, she gave him a nod, then fell to chatting with her fat husband and her four fat children.

And that was when it dawned on Reynard that the fat lady assumed Solace was his wife or partner, Cara their child, the three of them forming one adorable family. Probably everyone was assuming that.

Surprised by the idea for some reason, he regarded Solace—still watching the audience—and then Cara—still playing her strange little game. Just as he was about to turn away, Cara looked up. She blinked at him a moment, then smiled.

Chimes sounded, three high glassy notes, each one higher than the last, the signal that the curtain was about to rise.

Glad to break gaze with the girl, Reynard turned his attention to the stage, while beside him there were clacks and whispers and a put-upon sigh as Solace took the game from Cara and put it away.

With a rattle of pulleys, the curtain rose. The murmuring below was replaced by applause.

Onstage were three wooden chairs with cushioned seats. Behind them was a plain green backdrop. That was all. The stage's barrenness was a startling contrast to the baroque decor of most modern concerts.

After a pause for the applause to abate a bit, Muden do Korka do Djoteth, the famed dwarven drummer, walked out from stage right. He had left his long white beard unbraided, and its shaggy mass stood out starkly against his dressy black tunic. He carried a double-headed *kumbo* drum, its convex wooden sides carved with ridges and swirls that purportedly affected the drum's acoustics and helped produce its amazing range of tones.

After Muden had bowed and taken his seat, the next performer took the stage. This was Hathendomonia, a pale, long-faced Kolmakendi, regarded as the finest living player of the *deisan,* a type of end-blown flute fashioned from oak. He wore a *tavilda,* a white robe the Kolmakendi reserved for formal interactions with other sentient species. His black hair was tied back in a ponytail that extended to his waist.

He bowed. He sat. And then the third and final performer in the concert appeared. This was Cali Mwa, a human, her hefty body draped in a dress patterned with typically colorful Zumaran designs. She carried nothing, for her instrument was her voice, said to be beautiful enough to thaw the iciest heart and moisten the driest eye. Smiling and waving at the audience, she sat down between the other two.

The Unity Symphony began with Muden on the drum. For a while there was more silence than sound, the deep resounding beats coming at long intervals like the pulse of a god. Gradually the beats sped up and developed a rhythm that grew increasingly complex, especially once Muden brought the drum's treble end into play. Before long, his hands were a blur as they slapped, tapped, and skimmed the drum's variable-thickness skins, producing such a wide selection of sounds that no other instrument seemed necessary.

After several minutes, Hathendomonia proved this untrue. Rather than start off slowly as Muden had done, he unleashed a stream of notes on his *deisan* that flawlessly matched the drum's rapid and complicated beat before spinning away to craft its own complementary melody.

The two instruments played together for a time, then the drum's output deepened and slowed, while the *deisan*'s higher, faster tune whirled around it like a mammal gamboling about the feet of a trudging dinosaur. Finally the drum returned to its original sporadic beats before dying off completely.

Solo now, Hathendomonia wove an elaborate melody that swooped and spiraled in dizzyingly intricate patterns. At times the music's complexity thinned just enough to reveal that the backbone of the melody was a lighter, cheerier version of the tune played by Muden's drum.

After a while, however, the music slowed and lost its buoyancy. The notes wavered, sank, assumed lower and more somber tones. When it had grown quite mournful and torpid, Cali Mwa stood up and belted out a string of high, clear sounds that pierced the *deisan*'s gloom like a shaft of light. The sounds weren't words or even nonsense syllables. They were cries and howls and other abstract vocalisms, artfully and melodically arranged. She had transformed her voice into an instrument and was using it to convey emotions in ways no mere words ever could.

For a while, voice and *deisan* competed, each playing variations of the same melody, but tugging in opposite directions: the instrument trending lower and sadder, the voice striving to rise. Eventually Cali Mwa's voice won, drawing the *deisan* a little higher, then higher still, onward, upward, bit by bit.

When the *deisan* had regained its initial cheer, it ceased its tune, and Cali Mwa's voice continued on alone. She began to sing an actual song now, its words a paean to unity that drew heavily upon the works of gnomish poet Mogo Lobilozo, particularly the now-famous phrase "All one flesh, all one blood" that referred to the commonality of all beings. The song began in Eridian—a human language that seemed well on its way to becoming the common tongue—then shifted into a different language with each verse. Reynard identified a few other human languages, plus Kolmakendi, Olokendi, Dwarvish, both Eastern and Western Gnomish, Wochobüshkan, Alantri, Nyow-Ha, Gargoyle, and several languages he didn't recognize. As good as the drum and *deisan* had been, Cali Mwa's voice carried emotional resonance no instrument could hope to match. At times she sang with such passion, such intensity, she looked as if she were coming or giving birth, her face sheened with sweat, her body stiff and trembling, her fisted hands quivering.

After the final verse, this one again in Eridian, she resumed her wordless vocalizations, and Muden's *kumbo* drum rejoined the Symphony, providing a sturdy rhythmic framework along which Cali's trills unfurled and blossomed.

And then the *deisan* joined the mix, and together the trio ascended to the climax, an irrepressible outpouring of harmony and joy that even Reynard found somewhat moving.

As the final strains of the Symphony resounded through the theater, Reynard glanced over and saw tears spilling down Solace's cheeks. Cara's eyes were huge, her mouth parted, as if she were stunned by some divine revelation.

The moment the last echo died, the audience sprang to its feet, roaring, applauding. The performers bowed, then bowed again as the shouts and claps continued. And continued. And continued.

When Reynard felt his palms growing numb, he leaned toward Solace and said, "We should probably think about getting going, before the rush."

She hesitated, glancing from him to the stage and back

again, obviously unwilling to leave just yet. The box was his, though, so in the end she felt obliged to comply.

As it turned out, they weren't the only ones leaving early, and they joined a thin stream of people heading down the corridor while the applause thundered on and on in the theater proper.

"Thank you so much," Solace told Reynard as they descended the stairs. "It wouldn't have been half as good with floor seats."

He nodded. "It was my pleasure."

"That was an incredible concert. And I don't just mean the social significance, although that's certainly important. The music alone was worth it. I'd never heard a *kutukten dyaba* before."

"A what?"

"That's what the piece was structured on, musically. It's a dwarven form, where they play through every possible combination of instruments. If there're more than five or six instruments, it can take all day."

"Huh. I've never heard of it. But then, I never spent a lot of time among the dwarves." Which was true; he had always found that the rational and materialistic dwarves were a lot harder to con than most species and were thus best avoided.

"Oh, I haven't either. I just did a little reading on the background of the Symphony before we came. I hadn't realized this was the first time different species worked together on a major musical composition for a mass audience." She shook her head. "This was historic. They'll probably be talking about this for millennia."

"Well," he said with a smile, his voice just a touch too low for Cara to hear, "I guess we'll find out, eh?"

She breathed out a soft laugh.

They exited via the side door they had entered through.

It had rained again during the concert, and the bricks that paved the alley were dark and gleaming. Here and there puddles quivered in the warm breeze.

Reynard's carriage sat waiting amid a dozen others. The trio—man and woman and girl—stopped beside it.

"Well…thanks once more," Solace said. She sounded nervous, like someone who's about to say or do something they're afraid will make them disliked. Was she planning to bolt on him?

"So," Reynard said, hiding his suspicions behind a mask of good cheer. "Think we can manage to keep in touch this time around?"

Her mouth opened. Nothing came out. Her gaze flicked back and forth between his eyes as if unable to fix on one spot for long.

"Look," he said, "if you're upset about…before, then I'm sorry about that. I really didn't mean to disappear on you like that in Drell. I just—"

"It's not that, Reynard…"

"Then what is it?"

Another hesitation, followed by a quick glance down at Cara. Fortunately the girl was too absorbed in examining the carriage horses to pay any heed to the adults' boring blather.

"Reynard, it's just…I don't think it would be a good idea."

"Can I at least know why?"

She stared at him in silence for a moment, then her eyes slid away from his as if in embarrassment. "It's just not a good idea, okay?"

"All I'm asking is that we keep in touch. Is that wrong?"

She opened her mouth, shut it, sighed. "It wouldn't be…appropriate."

He had to restrain himself from rolling his eyes. "Look,

if it's your husband—"

"Reynard, it's—it's complicated, okay? Let's just drop it. I'm sorry, but I don't think keeping in touch is a good idea. Not…right now."

The implication of these final three words seemed pretty clear: One day not very long from now in the grand scheme of things, her mortal husband would cease to be, and maybe at that time, things once inappropriate would become appropriate.

He was sure this was just a sop, a way to shut him up. After all, if they didn't stay in touch, how would he know when that time had come? Clearly, he wouldn't. He would have to wait until their next chance meeting, whenever that might be. At the rate things had been going, it wouldn't be for another thousand years.

With a mix of frustration and annoyance, he realized he was checkmated. No matter what tactics he employed, she wasn't going to acquiesce, not with her child standing right next to her and the theater crowd now starting to exit the building in full force.

He considered tailing her, learning where she lived, who she lived with. But given her age and experience, she would likely spot him, and she seemed the sort that if he lost her trust it would take a lot longer than a millennium to win it back.

So in the end he smiled and gave her a small bow. No sense alienating her. After all, they *would* meet again. And he would be ready.

"Till next time, then," he said.

She smiled, relieved. "I look forward to it."

He started to turn away. In doing so, he saw Cara staring up at him, her face expressionless.

"Take care of your mom," he told her. She gave a single

sharp nod.

He climbed into his carriage and told Metaturk to take him home. He didn't look back.

Half an hour later, as the carriage pulled up in front of his mansion, he spotted Saffron's face glaring down from the bedroom window on the second floor. His head started to pound in anticipation of the impending confrontation.

"Cunt," he muttered, then wondered which woman he meant.

4

Colbon
3388 A.C.

Reynard stood at the living room window and gazed out at the Black Cathedral's four towers looming above the rooftops of downtown Colbon.

He could dimly make out his reflection against the dark towers and the slate shingles of the roofs and the gray clouds that filled the sky; and his expression was pensive, his eyes dark.

He was in a situation that he had never imagined he would be in, a situation that had seemed reasonable and even inevitable when he accepted it, but that now seemed absurd and terrible, a situation he vowed never to even consider again.

Marriage.

This was his fourth year of wedded life with the woman variously known as Kendria, Keilie Barrett, Tampipi Groz, Trixie Underhand, and a host of other names, but whom he always called Kay when they weren't on a job. He wasn't sure which, if any, was her given name. She insisted it was Kay, but she was a born trickster just like him, and he couldn't be sure she was telling the truth. He had never had a problem with that. Names, like all words, were lies anyway.

The marriage had made a sort of sense four years ago. With their similar talents and traits, they had seemed a perfect match, and it was all too easy to envision the two of them conning their way around Eridia, every Realm their plaything. He had assumed she would sustain his interest long enough that she would pass away before he grew bored.

He couldn't have been more wrong.

Somehow he had forgotten how quickly he wearied of things—of seeing the same sights, hearing the same stories, fucking the same vaginas. Thrills waned. New thrills beckoned. His decision to wed was inscrutable to him now. He wondered if she had conned him in some subtle way. Or if he had conned himself.

Getting out, alas, wasn't so easy. Insanely stubborn Kay would never consent to a divorce, no matter how chilly and uncomfortable the relationship got, and trying to trick her—faking his death, for instance—ran the risk of rousing her wrath if it failed. She had a cruel, vengeful side worse than any he had ever seen. So far it had never been directed at him, but if he hurt her too badly…

Well, sometimes he still had nightmares about what she did to that innkeeper in Cern. He had never imagined a screwdriver could be used like that.

The most logical solution was to disappear, head to some obscure village on the South Sea and snooze on a beach for a century or so, until he was sure she was dead and the marriage existed only as a handful of documents crumbling away in a file cabinet no one ever opened anymore. When you were immortal, time was your friend if you knew how to use it.

That, then, was his plan. Sometime soon in the dead of night he would slip out of their marital bed, then out of the house, then out of the city, and secretly make his way south, leaving no traces in his wake.

But before he did that, he had one last task to perform

here in Colbon: break into the Black Cathedral.

"Introspection is unlike you," Kay said behind him, giving him a start.

He turned, catching a glimpse of his somber expression morphing into a willed smile as he did so. Kay stood in the entrance to the study, one arm propped against the door-frame. She wore a white shirt unbuttoned and untucked over a tight orange sleeveless shirt, plus a pair of black slacks. (She never wore dresses or skirts unless a job demanded it. He was surprised at how much this had come to bother him.) She had unpinned her long, crow-black hair, and it hung sexily tousled around her angular face. Her lips were bent in that arrogant smile he had once found so irresistible. Her blue eyes probed his face.

"Just wondering if it'll ever rain, or if those clouds'll keep hanging there forever," he said as he crossed the room toward her, passing the many luxurious furnishings bought with the fruit of their scams: the ebony and ivory chessboard table; the black leather sofa and armchair; the bearskin rug; the antique Embarathan wall mirror; the silver-filigree dwarven carousel clock on the marble mantle above the fireplace. All of it had grown so familiar he wanted to scream. "You done in there already?"

"Yep," she said. "I have well and truly mastered Mr. Artemis Henn's signature down to the last pretentious cur-licue. All we need now is to whip up a bill of lading, and we're set."

He stopped in front of her and wrapped his arms around her waist. "Not only are you the best forger I've ever known, you're probably the fastest, too."

"I know."

"And so humble." He leaned in and kissed that smirking mouth, his own mouth twisted into a cocky lustful smile despite his secretly wishing he were anywhere else, with anyone else. At least he wouldn't have to maintain this charade much longer. The details of his journey south had been ironed out long ago, and he had had the necessary funds set aside for over a month, the money having been garnered from several solo scams he neglected to mention to Kay. All he needed to do now was figure out how to infiltrate the Black Cathedral. Once that was done, he was gone. Sure, he could just go now and wait a couple centuries before tackling the Cathedral. Seeing as how the building had been sitting there inviolate for thousands of years, the odds of someone else solving its mystery in the next two hundred were slim. But slim wasn't none. He refused to wait. He wanted the achievement all for himself.

"So," Kay said, "I was thinking: Since the weather's so bleak, maybe we could stay in this afternoon, snuggle in front of a fire, cuddle a while, fuck each other's brains out."

He nuzzled her earlobe. "Sounds good." Despite his weariness with her, with this life, his cock began to swell.

"Oh, good," she said, drawing back a little to look him in the face. "I'm glad. I thought maybe you'd prefer to slip out for a few hours and not tell me about it, the way you always do when I'm at work."

His heart jumped and ice filled his veins, but thanks to millennia of experience he managed to keep any trace of alarm from his face, offering only a baffled frown to the calm, keen gaze she was fixing on him in search of any telltale flicker of guilt.

Damn it. She knew. How much she knew, he wasn't sure. At the very least she knew he had been going out while she was at work at the East Belephon Shipping warehouse, where she had taken a secretarial position as part of their current scam. And she also knew he had been lying about it, answering her casual after-work questions about his day with bland tales of naps, or fencing practice, or reading the latest government legislation in search of amusingly exploitable loopholes. But did she know he actually spent most of his time taking long walks near the Cathedral, watching, analyzing, thinking? Worse, did she know the whys and wherefores behind it all?

Her calm face told him nothing. Despite her relative youth, she was almost as good at veiling her thoughts and feelings as he was. She once told him that as a teenager she had spent countless hours in front of a mirror mastering control of her facial muscles till she could adopt any expression at will. She had then worn that cool, cocky smile of hers until it became habitual, her default expression.

Maintaining his puzzled frown, he shook his head. "I'm not really sure what it is you're getting at."

"You're not fucking someone else, are you?" she asked, her calm, collected manner never wavering.

"Of course not," he said, letting his relief that she hadn't learned the truth manifest as a burst of laughter. He was pleased to see a flash of surprise in her eyes before she slammed her mask back into place. He appreciated her dilemma: He seemed to be telling the truth, but given his masterfully tricksterish ways, how could she know for sure? And if he wasn't fucking someone else, what *was* he doing when he headed out on those afternoon excursions he always lied about?

They regarded each other in silence a moment as they weighed conversational gambits like chess masters running through potential sequences of moves.

Kay found a move first. Her smile widened while her eyes narrowed, and she opened her mouth to say something he could tell she expected to be decisive and devastating.

There was a knock on the door.

"I'll get it," Reynard said, glad for the distraction. It was likely nothing important—a solicitor or a wrong address—but it gave him a chance to figure out what to tell Kay.

He opened the door, and there stood Solace, a polite smile draining away beneath her wide, stunned eyes.

"Reynard?"

"Solace?"

"Friend of yours?" Kay said, gliding into place beside Reynard, her arms crossed, one sleek black eyebrow arched, a deceptively friendly smile on her face.

"Yeah," Reynard said. "Old, old friend. Haven't seen her in years."

Kay's smile wavered briefly. No doubt she was wondering if the comment meant Solace was an immortal like Reynard. He had told Kay about his immortality shortly before their marriage—immortals were more widely accepted these days, and in many quarters Elders were virtually worshipped—and although on the whole she seemed comfortable with it, she sometimes showed signs of insecurity and envy, as if being mortal were something she longed to overcome the way she strove to overcome every other trait she saw as a failing. Thus, the notion that this beautiful woman might share with Reynard that remarkable gift which she—Kay—would never possess or fully understand had to be like a splinter deep in her soul. Immortality was an arena she simply couldn't compete in. Not that she would let it stop her from trying, of course.

"Well, any friend of my husband's is a friend of mine," Kay said with a warm, congenial smile. Reynard knew she had phrased it that way just in case Solace didn't already know Reynard was married.

Which Solace didn't, of course. Her eyebrows flew up in

amazement. "Oh! That's—I had no idea! Congratulations to both of you."

"Thank you," Kay said. Then to Reynard: "Well, don't just stand there; invite her in."

"Oh, um, yeah, come on in," Reynard said, backing up and opening the door wide.

Solace stepped in, took a quick glance around the room, then fixed a smile on Reynard. "Well, I certainly wasn't expecting to find you on my route."

"Route?"

"I'm here for the Census." She tilted up the clipboard in her hands to reveal an orange-and-green "Colbon Census" logo on the back.

"Ah." Reynard nodded. The Greater Colbon Census was all the news lately. It was the first census in the area's history, and the way the government and various civic organizations had hyped it up, you'd think it was the answer to all the world's problems. Reynard had been eagerly awaiting the census taker's visit, planning to answer every one of his or her questions with outrageous lies. Now, though, that didn't seem so feasible. Not with someone he actually knew. Especially not another immortal.

"Please, sit," Kay said to Solace, directing her to the black leather chair.

"Thanks." Solace sat down, smoothing out the seat of her long blue dress with one swift sweep of her hand as she did so. She took another, longer look around the room while Reynard and Kay seated themselves on the couch. "Nice place you have here."

"Thanks," Reynard said. "I had no idea you lived in Colbon. How long have you been here?"

"Six years now. I like Colbon. It's pleasant." She glanced at Kay. "What about you two?"

"We've only been here about nine months," Reynard said. "Before that we lived in Cern."

"What brought you here?"

"The usual merchant business. There were some opportunities here I thought were too good to pass up."

"Ah."

Reynard sensed Kay shift a little beside him, a shift no doubt due to sudden relaxation. If Solace didn't know Reynard's true profession, then the two of them couldn't be all that close, which surely came as a huge relief to Kay.

"What have you been up to lately?" Reynard asked Solace. "Aside from the Census, I mean."

"Honestly, there isn't anything else right now. I'd been doing some minor work for the regional government, mainly clerical stuff, and I was getting pretty sick of it. Then I heard about the Census, which sounded a lot more interesting, so I decided to switch over to that. It really is a full-time job. Going into it, I don't think any of us grasped the magnitude of what we were getting ourselves into. There are far more people living in this area than anyone thought. Did you know there's a weird offshoot group of the Pith living in a system of caves deep in Erstwood? Apparently they hunt and forage for all their food, and they've even set up a small-scale mining operation to get the metal to make their swords and armor. Nobody had any idea they were there. It's incredible what we're finding out."

"What'll you do when the Census is over? I mean, this can't be a very permanent job…"

"It's longer-lasting than you probably think. Not only will it take us several more months to finish the basic data collection, but then we'll have the task of collating and analyzing all that data. We'll be working on this stuff another couple of years, at least."

"Wow."

"So where do you two know each other from?" Kay asked.

"Oh, we met a long, long time ago in a little place called New Portland," Reynard said. "Way up to the northeast, near the Wilds. Not all that far from Mickelberg, actually, where you and I spent a certain quiet, rainy evening on our way to the coast." He smiled lovingly and patted Kay's knee.

Not one word of which told Kay what the question had really been intended to ascertain: namely whether or not Solace was an immortal. Kay didn't dare ask anything too direct, since exposing Reynard as an Elder to the wrong person could end up garnering the couple far more attention than a pair of con artists were comfortable with. Likewise, Solace couldn't be sure Kay knew about her husband's immortality, and hence would avoid saying anything that might blow his cover. Reynard was curious to see how long he could keep the two women tiptoeing around the subject of Elderhood before the truth emerged (if it ever did).

Kay, of course, couldn't help but notice the evasiveness of his response.

"Of course I remember," she said, bestowing upon him a smile which, though warm and loving on the surface, harbored in its depths an entire winter's-worth of frost.

Solace cleared her throat and took a pencil from a holster at the top of her clipboard.

"We'd better get down to business," she said. "I mean, I don't want to be brusque, but I have a certain number of streets I need to cover today, so I can't really linger in one place for too long, much as I'd like otherwise."

"Perfectly understandable," Reynard said.

"Okay…" Solace scanned the topmost sheet of paper on her clipboard. "First of all, the address is Number Two,

Francis Street, correct?"

"That's right," Kay said.

Solace nodded and made a small notation with her pencil. "Two residents only?"

"That's right," Kay said.

Another nod. Another notation. "Full names?"

"Reynard Kitson," Reynard said. "No middle name."

Solace penciled this in, then looked at Kay. "And you?"

"Kay Liana Kitson."

"Oh, Liana's such a lovely name."

"Why, thank you."

"Now then, the part everyone hates: your ages." With a reassuring smile, she held up a hand, palm out. "Please be honest; no one's passing judgment here."

"I'm thirty-one," Reynard said.

He had been a little afraid she would react in a way that made it obvious she knew he was lying: raising her eyebrows in disbelief, for instance, or glancing at Kay to check her response. But Solace merely nodded once again and wrote down his answer. He should have known that anyone thirty-five hundred years old—even an utter Pollyanna—would have long since gotten dissembling down to an art finer than a pinpoint. For all Kay's wiliness and mirror-gazing, she was an absolute tyro in comparison.

"You?" Solace said, glancing up at Kay.

"Thirty-four," Kay said.

Solace wrote it down.

The rest of the questions passed without incident or, to Reynard, interest. Species, gender, marital status, length of residency in Colbon, occupation, blah, blah, blah.

"That's that," Solace said as she reholstered her pencil. "Fast and painless." She unclipped the topmost paper and reinserted it at the bottom of the stack.

"I expected more for some reason," Reynard said.

Solace smiled. "Most people say that." She stood up. "Well, like I said, I have a lot more territory to cover before the end of the day, so alas, I must go."

Reynard and Kay saw her to the door.

"It was delightful and certainly unexpected to run across you like this," Solace told Reynard. "And it was a pleasure to meet you," she said to Kay.

"Likewise."

"Since we're both living in Colbon," Reynard said, "we'll have to keep in touch."

"Yes!" Kay exclaimed as if she found this a wonderful idea. "Perhaps we could have you over for dinner sometime."

"Oh, thanks," Solace said, "but I wouldn't want you to go to any trouble…"

"No trouble at all," Kay said. "Are you free Sunday evening?"

"Um…not this Sunday, no. Maybe the following Sunday?"

"Splendid," she said. "We'll plan on dinner around six. If there's any trouble with that just send us a wire." She laughed blithely. "You have our address, after all."

"Thank you," Solace said. "I look forward to it." She started to turn to leave.

"Just out of curiosity, who's next on your route?" Reynard said, grabbing hold of the top of Solace's clipboard and tilting it toward him so he could read the topmost sheet. "Number 6?" He looked over his shoulder at Kay. "That's old man Festal, isn't it?"

"I think so, yeah," Kay said. She was eyeing Reynard's face closely, no doubt wondering the reason behind his sudden interest in Solace's route.

"Watch out for his dog," he told Solace, all seriousness now as he let go of the clipboard. "It's bitten people before."

"Oh!" she said. "Thanks for the warning." She opened the door and backed out into the hall. "Well, thanks for everything, and I guess I'll see you two the Sunday after next."

"We look forward to it," Kay said. "Bye."

The door closed. Kay and Reynard looked at each other.

"She's nice," Kay said.

"Isn't she sweet?"

Kay headed back toward the couch.

"So, is she an Elder?" she asked in a bland, conversational tone. "I couldn't tell for sure."

"She—oh!" He stooped and pretended to pick up Solace's pencil, which he had been hiding up his sleeve ever since he palmed it when he took a peek at her clipboard. "She dropped her pencil."

Kay froze, her back to him, then looked at him over her shoulder, her face unusually still.

"Excuse me?" she said.

"Her pencil. I'd better hurry and get it back to her."

"I'm sure she has extras."

He already had the door open. "Well, just in case she doesn't." He frowned at her, as though puzzled by her chilliness. "She *is* an old friend, after all. Geez." He shut the door on Kay's rising left eyebrow.

He caught up with Solace as she was just ascending the steps to Mr. Festal's place.

"Hold up," he called.

She turned, surprised, and watched him trot up to her.

"You lost this." He held out her pencil.

She blinked at it, then checked the holster on the clipboard.

"Thanks," she said. She took the pencil and slid it into its proper place. "That's odd. It's never fallen out before."

From inside Mr. Festal's place came three sharp barks. A moment later there was a faint scrabble of claws on tile, and something heavy slammed against the front door.

"I see what you mean about the dog," Solace said.

"Yeah, so, hey, I was wondering," Reynard said, talking fast so he could keep the encounter short enough for the returning-a-pencil story to remain plausible, "what time's your lunch break tomorrow?"

"Uh, about noon, but—"

"Great, that's what I figured. See, I'll be in Estover Park around that time tomorrow, and I was thinking, if you're free, you're welcome to join me. I'll be at the bench on the south side of the pond, you know the one?"

"Um, yeah, but—"

"Great, well I'll be there, like I said, and if you have the time, you are more than welcome to join me." He leaned in toward her and in a lower voice said, "Besides, there's something I really need to tell you."

She cocked her head, intrigued. Before she could think to ask why he couldn't just tell her now, he said, "Well, sorry to hold you up like this, I know you're in a hurry, and actually so am I, so I'll get going now, and hopefully I'll see you tomorrow."

He turned and strode away without awaiting a reply, sure she wouldn't be able to resist the mysterious "something" he needed to tell her.

When he returned to the apartment Kay was in her rocking chair reading a book. She didn't say a word or even look up as he entered, and she responded to his questions and comments with frosty politeness, an attitude she maintained the rest of the evening. She retired early with no explanation.

The lack of further questions about Solace left him more worried than relieved. Kay hadn't forgotten; she never forgot a thing. More likely, she was deferring her next move until she had thought things through more carefully.

She wasn't the only one. Solace's reappearance had led Reynard to completely reconsider his own plans. Perhaps he shouldn't be in such a hurry to crack the mystery of the Black Cathedral and split Colbon. After all, he had been aching to bang that sexy brown body for over three thousand years. Of course, now that she knew he was married, seducing her would be tricky. But not impossible. Impossibility was only a failure of the imagination.

At quarter to noon the next morning Reynard sat on a bench on the south side of the pond in Estover Park, tossing bread crumbs to the ducks and smiling at the frenzied quacking and splashing that ensued. The ripples generated by the ducks' greedy antics radiated out across the water and made the Black Cathedral's inverted reflection waver and break.

He glanced up and down the gravel paths. There was no sign of anyone anywhere, and he wasn't at all surprised. It was a dreary day for park-going, the mid-autumn nip in the air exacerbated by a thin drizzle that had been falling intermittently all morning. Right now there was no rain, but the leaden clouds suggested that could change at any moment. He hoped the bleak weather didn't keep Solace away. It was still a good fifteen minutes before he would know for sure, though, so rather than fret—always a waste of energy—he turned his eyes and thoughts once again to the dark, hulking structure that reared above the trees lining the pond's far shore.

Predating the Cataclysm, the Black Cathedral was an enigma, its builders unknown, its purpose unknown, its interior and contents a mystery because no one had ever gotten inside. In truth, no one was even sure it *was* a Cathedral. It simply resembled one in many ways, with its soaring black granite walls; its massive buttresses; its quartet of towers, one at each corner. And yet there were no other ornaments, no signs, no carvings, and most notably no doors or windows anywhere.

Muddying matters further was the Cathedral's best-known yet most perplexing feature: the weird gonging sound it emitted every day around noon. It had been doing this without fail since the Cataclysm, over three millennia earlier. No one had any idea why or how.

The absence of entrances led some to speculate the Cathedral was the kind of place that was never meant to be entered—a tomb, perhaps, or a prison for some terrible being. More hopeful speculations made it the treasure vault of an ancient race of conquerors, its rooms packed wall to wall with gold, gems, fantastic weapons.

Aware that speculations were so much bullshit, no more than projected hopes and fears, Reynard refused to hazard any guesses as to what might lie inside. For all he knew, the interior might consist of nothing more than a bunch of empty cobwebbed rooms. But there was no way he could leave town without finding out. It was a challenge he couldn't resist.

He was certain there was a way in, for during his initial research on the Cathedral a few months ago, he came across the curious, mostly forgotten case of the aeromage and thief Gidard Smyes, who in 1555 had used his inborn power of flight to investigate the Cathedral's upper reaches. An associate on the ground had watched Smyes float up along the structure's west side, probing the stone wall as he went, then disappear from view around the northwest corner to inspect the north side. No one ever saw him again.

But Smyes had to have gone somewhere. And the only logical place was inside.

Since then, Reynard had devoted most of his waking moments to finding the way in. While Kay was at work, slaving away in pursuit of an elaborate con Reynard had long since lost interest in, he took long walks around the Cathedral, pretending to be enjoying the spacious park the residents of Colbon had built as a verdant buffer between their homes and businesses and the square stone plaza in the midst of which the Cathedral sat. He strolled past its sheer walls, watched its towers from the various benches stationed around the park, and spent a week posing as an artist and painting the Cathedral at an easel he set up on the east side of the plaza.

Alas, for all his efforts he hadn't found a single chink in the Cathedral's dark armor. Not even underground, as at one point a brainstorm had led him to hope: City records showed that no subterranean lines or tunnels of any kind were known to exist under the plaza. Everything circumvented it. The Cathedral sat alone, untouched, seemingly untouchable.

Footsteps sounded on the gravel path. He looked around and saw Solace striding toward him, her face cool, cautious, the Census clipboard and a tangerine-colored umbrella tucked under one arm. He raised one hand in a wave. She lifted her chin in acknowledgement, her expression never changing. Despite her reserved demeanor, he felt a surge of pleasure and accomplishment. She had come after all. What's more, this was the first time they had managed to have a second meeting. It was a momentous occasion.

She came around the bench and stood next to him but made no move to sit down.

"So what's on your mind?" she said, watching his face carefully.

"Have a seat," he said, gesturing at the stretch of empty bench beside him.

She glanced at the bench, then at his face again, and then with a barely audible sigh she perched herself stiffly on the edge of the seat as though not intending to stay more than a moment.

"I don't really have a whole lot of time," she said. "So what's this big secretive thing you have to tell me about?"

He drew in a deep breath and let it out in a long, deliberately shaky exhalation.

"Look, it's about yesterday. It's..." He looked down at his hands, which were fiddling with the hem of his coat in an excellent imitation of nervousness. After a moment he swallowed and looked back up at Solace. "Things aren't well between Kay and me."

Her expression softened a minute amount, though he couldn't tell if it was genuine. "I'm sorry to hear that."

"Thanks. In fact, things have gotten particularly bad lately..." He trailed off and gazed at the pond as if he needed to pause a moment before continuing to discuss such a painful subject. The ducks were bobbing about in silence as they digested the bread, and the Black Cathedral's reflection was whole once more upon the surface of the water. "Kay's grown...cruel. Malicious. I don't even know why. Sometimes I wonder if she's got some kind of mental illness or something. But whatever the reason, the fact is, her invitation to dinner was not made without ulterior motives. I don't know exactly what she has in mind, but given the way she's been behaving lately, it won't be anything good."

He glanced at Solace and was pleased to see that her face had grown a few notches more sympathetic. And more curious. Despite her reservations, he had managed to suck her into his story, to get her involved. Nobody could resist a good story.

"Yeah," she said. "I thought I detected some tension between the two of you."

He nodded. "I guess it's kind of obvious. I just felt that I should let you know the truth. I'm really sorry you had to get caught up in the middle of this. I'll understand if you decide not to come by for dinner after all. In fact it'd probably be best for you to avoid us altogether. This really isn't the best time to get involved with me again."

She tutted. "I'm a big girl. I can handle myself."

"You don't know Kay. You don't know what she's capable of. She can be…" He shook his head, his eyes dark with worry that was only half feigned. "She can be very, very nasty."

"Oh, please. I'm not intimidated one bit." She waved a hand dismissively and settled back onto the bench, all her qualms and stiffness gone. He had done it again. Why was it that women invariably advanced with renewed vigor whenever you tried to push them away?

"Maybe you *should* be intimidated," he said.

"Reynard, I'm over three thousand years old. However bad she is, I'm sure I've dealt with worse. Heck, I've probably *done* worse."

"I sincerely doubt that. You're a nice person."

She tutted again. Reynard suppressed a smile. Most people hated being called nice. It made them feel bland and weak. It made them want to do naughty things to dispel any whiff of boring niceness.

She gestured at the small cloth pouch in his lap.

"What's that there?"

He held it up so she could see the bread crumbs inside.

"For the ducks," he said. "Care to try?"

"Sure!" She took the bag, scooped out a handful of crumbs, and tossed them into the pond. There was a brief flurry of splashes and honks, and the Black Cathedral's reflection dissolved into slivers.

"Honestly," she said, turning back to him, "what you're going through sounds remarkably similar to what I went through with Joshua."

"Joshua?"

She waved her hand back and forth as if to erase something. "No, I mean—you didn't actually meet him, did you? That was my husband the last time we met, remember?"

"Ah. Yeah. I don't think you mentioned his name at the time."

"Didn't I?" Her brow buckled into a small frown he couldn't interpret. Then it was gone. "Well, at any rate, that was a total mistake. It was a complete disaster."

"Really?"

"Absolutely," she said. "I mean, it was wonderful for a while, but at some point he or I or both of us changed too much, and by the end we couldn't even stand to be in the same room together. We were doing and saying all these ridiculously petty things to each other." She shook her head and almost absentmindedly flung another handful of crumbs at the pond, glancing away from him just long enough to make sure she was aiming in the right direction. "The funny thing is, even then, I still loved him on some level. But it was just such a horrible, horrible mess."

"Sorry to hear that."

She shrugged. "It was a long time ago. It's all way in the

past."

"Your daughter," he said. "Cara. Did she age normally?"

"Yes. She did. I…" She stared down into the bag of crumbs. There was a long pause. Apparently not everything was way in the past.

"You know," she said, not looking up, her voice so soft he could barely hear her, "I loved her more than I've ever loved anyone else. And if I had a choice, painful as it was watching her speed through her little life, get old and sick and die so quickly, even then, I'd do it all over again, just for her, just so she would exist, because the world—*my* world—was a better place with her in it."

There was a sound like the crash of a giant gong but with the bass boosted and the whole thing somewhat muffled. The ducks took flight, quacking madly, drops of water trailing behind them. By the time the ducks had shrunk to dots in the sky, the noise had faded.

"I've lived here six years," Solace said, gesturing at the Cathedral, "and I'm still not used to that."

"Yeah, same here."

She looked at him with a thoughtful smile. "I have to admit, I'm surprised to run into you here, of all places."

"Why?"

"Colbon just doesn't strike me as your kind of place. Too…languid. I figured somewhere like Peridor or Shandar or even Quontoon would offer much better opportunities for someone in your line of work."

He shrugged. "Every place has its own unique opportunities."

Footsteps sounded once again on the gravel path, but this time the steps were much too loud for the average foot. It was as if someone were pounding the gravel with mallets: *Chash chash chash.* Reynard and Solace looked at each other, then twisted around to look up the path in the direction of the sounds.

Round the bend came an old woman, hunched and thickset and clad in a frayed, shapeless gray overcoat draped with a grimy white shawl. On her feet was a pair of blocky wooden shoes. The narrow blue eyes in her wrinkled, scowling face were fixed on the path ahead of her, as if she expected to find traps or obstacles in her way.

Reynard and Solace shared a baffled glance. Wooden shoes, never common to begin with, were unheard of these days. And the cut of the coat and shawl matched no fashion Reynard was familiar with.

"Hello," he said, his curiosity roused.

The woman's head jerked toward him, though she didn't actually look at him. She made a grunting sound that might have been reciprocation.

"Miserable day, isn't it?" he said.

The woman's head returned to its previous position, and she continued stomping along in silence. As Reynard started to turn back around, feeling a little disappointed that she was ignoring him, the woman worked her mouth as if chewing something, then snapped, "Not if you're young."

Surprised by the woman's undisguised hostility, Reynard and Solace watched her vanish around the bend in the path.

"Well," Reynard said. "She sure showed us, didn't she?"

Solace continued staring at the bend in the path, silent, eyes distant and thoughtful.

"You okay?" he asked. Something about her expression gave him a sinking feeling.

"We're not young," she said. She shot him a pained look. "We're older than she is."

"Um, yeah."

"We've lived hundreds of times longer than her."

"Uh-huh. We probably had sex with ancestors of hers."

She started to say something in continuation of her previous comment, but then his words sank in and she frowned.

"What?"

"Just saying."

"I'm being serious here."

"Sorry." He gestured at her to proceed. "Be serious. I'm curious to hear where this is going."

"Where it's going?"

"Yeah."

"What is that supposed to mean?"

"It simply means that I'm not sure what your point is."

She looked at him indignantly. "My *point?* My point is…" Her shoulders slumped. "I guess I don't really have a point. Except, I don't know, I think we should help her."

"What?" He couldn't see a connection between being surprised the old woman had thought them young and helping her. "Why?"

"Because she looks like she needs it. She was wearing rags!"

"She looked healthy, though. Plump and healthy. She certainly wasn't starving."

She clucked her tongue. "That's a terrible thing to say!"

"Sorry. It's just, I'm not sure what you think we can or should do."

She studied his face as if searching for any hint of mockery, then looked away with a sigh.

"I don't know," she said. "I just think we should help her."

He could tell she wouldn't be satisfied until they had done some token something, so he said, "Well, why don't we follow her and see where she lives. Then maybe we can figure something out."

It was a vague and pointless plan, but she seized it with glee.

"Yes!" she said. "That's a good idea. Let's go."

Solace handed the cloth pouch back to Reynard, who cinched it tight and stuffed it into his jacket pocket. Then the two of them rose and set off along the path.

The path ringed the pond, with side paths radiating from it at intervals like spokes. Trees ablaze with autumn colors lined and overarched the paths, an arrangement that on a sunny day would have lent the paths the appearance of fiery corridors. Today, however, the gloomy weather killed the effect.

It took a few seconds of brisk walking to bring the old woman back into view. She was far ahead now, just a small dark shape in the distance. She must have picked up her pace after passing them.

They bustled along. The old woman slowly grew larger, closer, clearer. By the time Reynard and Solace reached the north side of the pond, they had halved the distance between themselves and the woman. Suddenly the woman turned down a side path that led straight to the plaza in which the Black Cathedral sat. She slipped from sight behind the trees.

"Hurry, we don't want to lose her," Solace said. She quickened her pace until she was almost running. Reynard did likewise.

When they reached the side path, the old woman had already entered the plaza and was angling northwest across it toward the Cathedral. No one else was in sight.

"That's one fast old biddy," Reynard muttered as they rushed down the side path. Before long, the clopping of the woman's wooden shoes on the plaza's flagstones became audible.

When Reynard and Solace entered the plaza, the woman

was already two-thirds of the way down the Cathedral's east side and proceeding north at a rapid clip. She was so close to the structure that her coat brushed the outer edges of the buttresses as she passed.

"Come on," Solace said. They hurried forward. The sound of the woman's shoes was lost beneath the clacks of their own boots upon the stones.

They had just entered the Cathedral's shadow when the woman reached the building's northeast corner and turned left, disappearing from view.

Reynard and Solace broke into a trot. When they got to the corner less than ten seconds later, there was no sign of the woman anywhere, just a bare expanse of damp flagstones stretching from the Cathedral to the trees and bushes that lined the plaza's north side. Given how fast Reynard and Solace had run, there was no way the woman could have made it across the plaza, even at a sprint.

"Where'd she go?" Solace asked.

Reynard shook his head.

They strode down the length of the Cathedral's north side to make sure the woman hadn't hidden behind one of the massive buttresses. They found nothing.

"Huh," Solace said. "Maybe she was a mage, or a mutant. Maybe she teleported or something."

"Or she could've turned invisible and is standing here right now silently laughing at us."

She shot him a frown as if he had said something mean. Then she glanced around a little nervously.

"Or," he went on, "maybe she was a manitou, or a ghost, or a manifestation of one of the Twelve. In this crazy world, the possibilities are endless."

"Very true," she said, and sighed. After a pause, she gave Reynard a vaguely guilty smile. He realized what was coming even before she said it.

"I have to go," she said. "I have two more blocks to do for the census before the end of the day."

"Are you going my way? I could walk you back." He jerked his thumb to the west, in the direction he and Kay lived.

"Thanks, but I'm not in that area anymore. Today I'm covering the Dandridge neighborhood." She gestured north with her clipboard.

"Ah. Okay. But before you go, I'd like to thank you for taking the time to meet with me and listen to me go on about my problems. It's nice to know I have someone I can talk to."

"It's my pleasure."

"Would you be interested in meeting again tomorrow? Same time, same place?"

She hesitated a moment, eyes probing his, then nodded. "Sure. That would be nice. See you tomorrow, then."

"See you."

She turned, crossed the plaza, and strode down a path that led due north. He watched her for a minute, then turned to look at the Cathedral, his eyes roving over the building's north side. The dark stones were blank and silent, as always.

With a grunt, he ambled home.

Sometime around midnight he sat up in bed and stared at Kay's slack and faintly snoring form for over a full minute to make sure she was asleep. He would be amazed if she weren't, considering the three-hour bout of makeup sex they had had after she got home from work and expressed her deep, deep remorse at everything that had happened. Which didn't mean that a single one of their issues had been resolved, of course. In fact, he suspected the détente was a fakeout, the opening gambit to some crafty and elaborate plot.

When he was sure she was asleep, he slid out of bed, got dressed, and crept out of the house. Sticking to back alleys and unlit streets, staying out of sight of anyone and everyone, he made his way to the Cathedral. The plaza and park were empty, just as he had expected; even the city's roving gangs of pre-teen thugs avoided this area after dark. Overhead the clouds had dissipated, and a full moon shone, turning the sky around it a deep, dark blue and lighting the plaza enough for him to do his work.

While it was possible the old woman possessed remarkable powers, a simpler explanation for the biddy's disappearance was far more likely. Just because there were no visible doors in the Cathedral, that didn't mean there were no doors at all.

Starting at the building's northeast corner, he examined the north wall for even the minutest irregularities. Twenty feet from the corner he found a section of stones about six feet high and three wide that looked different from the surrounding stones in some manner he couldn't precisely identify. They were the same color as the other stones, the same texture, the same cut. They even smelled the same. Yet they were different. It was almost as if the light weren't reflecting off them in quite the normal fashion.

Grinning, sure that he had found the way in, he carefully explored the whole section, starting at the perimeter, then working his way in, peering, poking, pushing, prodding. When he reached the center of this area without result, he worked his way back outward.

He was grinding his teeth in frustration when he spotted another stone that possessed the same indefinable peculiarity as the ones he had been examining. This new stone sat alone, about six feet west of the larger group and five feet off the ground. He hurried over to this stone and pushed it. It didn't budge. He tried to slide it up, down, side to side. It didn't budge. He stood back and eyed it critically. What was he missing?

After a good twenty minutes of thought, of pondering possibilities of geometry, geology, masonry, temperature, color, wind pressure differentials, and moisture, he was about to give up entirely. But then he remembered the most incongruous and hitherto inexplicable feature of the old woman.

The wooden shoes.

The *noisy* wooden shoes.

And a Cathedral that emitted an inexplicable gong every day.

It was all about sound. It had to be. It fit all the facts.

Quiet as a cloud, Reynard made his way to Grannie Goodie's Bakery on Queen Street two blocks west of the park. The shop was locked and dark at this hour, of course, so he swiftly picked the lock, slipped inside, and emerged a few minutes later with a wooden spoon, a cutting board, a rolling pin, and five wooden bowls of different sizes, all of which he carried back to the Cathedral's north side.

He rapped the various objects against the pavement near the two anomalous areas on the wall, methodically varying the number, speed, and strength of the raps. He soon found that the clack of the bowls sounded most like the noise the woman's shoes had made, and he subsequently focused his attention on those. Not long thereafter, when he tapped the smallest, shallowest bowl against the pavement thrice in rapid succession, there was a sudden sharp crack from the smaller of the two anomalous patches of stone.

"Yes," he hissed. As he rose, the crack sounded a second

time, and when he inspected the stone he saw nothing.

He tried again, responding faster this time: squatting, rapping the bowl three times, then springing back up before the first crack had finished sounding. A look at the stone showed it had sunk half an inch into the wall.

Knowing it would swiftly return to its original position, and not sure what else to do, he thrust out a hand and pushed against the recessed stone.

It sank back another inch, and a louder crack sounded to Reynard's left. Glancing that way, he found that the larger section of anomalous stones had likewise receded into the wall.

He rushed over and pushed against it with both hands. With a low grating rumble, it sank farther into the wall, pivoting as it went and soon providing a space just wide enough to admit a full-grown man. Exultant, heart racing, Reynard slipped through. Just in time, too; the moment he cleared the door, it began to rumble back into place.

The dim light from outside showed he was in a narrow corridor that ended in a blank wall ten feet ahead. After he had taken a couple of steps toward the wall, the stone slab clicked shut behind him, plunging him into pitch blackness.

He shuffled forward, groping blindly, until his fingers touched the cool stones of the far wall. He planted both hands firmly against the wall and pushed. The wall pivoted open just like the section in the Cathedral's outer wall. Stepping through, he found himself in a corridor that ran perpendicular to the one he had just exited. The walls, floor, and ceiling were bare gray stone. High on the walls, cubic stone sconces that contained some unwavering light source Reynard couldn't see from the ground flung fans of pale yellow light toward the ceiling.

To his right, the corridor extended a few hundred feet

before making a sharp left turn at the Cathedral's west wall. To his left, it made a sharp right turn at the much closer east wall, only twenty feet away. In neither direction did he see anything that looked like a door.

He slunk toward the nearer bend. When he got there, he flattened himself against the south wall and peeked around the corner.

As expected, he found a corridor stretching the length of the east wall. It looked the same as the corridor he was in now—same stone blocks, same stone sconces—except that halfway down, the wall on the corridor's west side was broken by an open space about four feet wide and eight high. From where he stood, he couldn't tell if it was an archway or a niche or something else.

He rounded the corner and inched toward the opening. As he did so, he realized that though he had hitherto believed the Cathedral's interior to be dead silent, there was indeed a sound, but one so low it was on the very threshold of hearing. It was a deep, steady hum, as of some massive machine miles underground.

The sound troubled him in a vague, atavistic way. He found himself thinking of Gidard Smyes, who had disappeared while investigating the Cathedral and was never seen again. Smyes, he recalled, had vanished on the building's north side, the very side where Reynard had found the hidden door...

Oh, fuck Smyes, he told himself; he would succeed where that pathetic nobody had failed. After all, Reynard had lived thousands of years, thanks as much to wit and talent as to anything else. Smyes hadn't even made it halfway through one normal human lifespan.

As he neared the gap in the wall, he detected a smell just as odd and disturbing as the hum. It reminded him of many things—snow, metal, parsley, mothballs—while matching none of them. The fact that he couldn't even classify the smell as organic or inorganic made his hackles rise high.

He crossed the last few feet to the gap as cautiously and soundlessly as he could. As he did so, the hum grew a fraction louder.

When he reached the gap's edge, he paused, looked up and down the corridor to make sure he was still alone, then peeked around the corner.

The gap, it turned out, was an archway that led to a large flagstone courtyard above which white stars winked in a black sky. In the courtyard's south wall was a similar archway. The north wall was blank. He wasn't sure about the west wall because the bulk of it was obscured by a monolithic stone that towered over the courtyard like a menhir erected by giants. It was even taller than the Cathedral's towers. Which meant, of course, it should be visible from outside. Yet it wasn't.

He waited. Nothing stirred. He heard no sound save the hum. The mystery smell was stronger now and was almost certainly coming from the courtyard, possibly from the huge stone.

He found his eyes returning again to the stars. Something about them bothered him, but he couldn't figure out what. After taking another quick glance around to confirm his solitude, he stepped into the archway for a better look at the stars. A few moments of scrutiny made him realize he couldn't identify a single constellation. These were not the stars that shone in the night sky of Colbon or any other place he knew.

An icy rill of fear trickled down his spine. Somehow he had entered the Cathedral and found himself in a place that wasn't where the Cathedral was. Except it was still inside the

Cathedral.

"It makes your head hurt, doesn't it?" said a voice behind him.

He whirled, his heart slamming up into his throat. A few feet away stood the old woman from yesterday, barely recognizable now. She had swapped her rags for a clean gray robe with a gray wimple. In place of the wooden shoes she wore soft gray leather slippers. Her back was straight, her movements sure and steady. Her face was younger and less lined, and her surly, bitter look had been replaced by a calm and unpleasantly knowing smile. Her eyes, much brighter and cannier than before, fixed on his with almost hypnotic intensity.

"It was unwise to enter here, young man," she said.

He snorted out a laugh he didn't really feel. "I'm not so young."

The woman's smile widened. "Oh, but you are. Compared to me, you are. Compared to this place, you are."

Her words and tone made it clear she knew exactly how old he was, and was not the least bit impressed by it. He suddenly felt certain that she had known who he was and what his plans were when she passed him and Solace in the park yesterday, that she had intended him to follow her, that the whole thing had been a test, or a trap.

"Don't be silly," he said, swallowing back his fear and giving her his best roguish smile. "You look far too ravishing to be a day over two thousand."

She said nothing, didn't budge a muscle.

"So what is this place?" he asked, then waggled his eyebrows lasciviously. "And more importantly, where's the bedroom?"

She simply continued staring. The moment he opened his mouth to speak again, she took a step toward him. Instinctively, driven by some powerful, primitive back-brain fear, he took a corresponding step backward. She took another step. He stepped back again. After half a dozen steps in this manner he realized that the quality of the light had shifted from the hazy yellow sconce-light to light that was dimmer and faintly silvery.

Starlight. She had herded him straight into the heart of the courtyard.

He looked over his shoulder. The monolith loomed above him like a cliff. Now that he was closer to it, he saw that its gray surface shimmered as if it were glazed with melted mica. The hum was louder now, too. Like the weird smell, it was almost certainly coming from the monolith. On the heels of this realization came the strange surety that the monolith wasn't merely a piece of stone; it was a machine.

The woman stopped advancing. Reynard took two more steps backward, then stopped as well.

"This," the woman said, "is not a place."

"So what is it, then?" Reynard asked. "A person?"

The woman's gaze rose over his head to the stone/machine/whatever, then dropped back down to him again. She took another step forward. Mustering every last scrap of courage, Reynard did not step back. The woman cocked her head and regarded him with narrow eyes, her smile widening even further. She seemed pleased.

"Sound cannot exist without time," she said. "A three-dimensional object can exist without time, but it will never move. It will be height, width, and depth without time and thus without change and thus without motion. And without motion there is no sound. Silence reigns below the fourth dimension. Sound is a byproduct of time happening."

"Oh, dear," Reynard said. "This really *is* a church, isn't it?"

Her smile tightened, growing less amused. Her eyes glittered in a way that made Reynard think of snakes.

The hum loudened, while the light in the courtyard grew brighter and more silvery. His shadow manifested long and fuzzy on the flagstones before him.

Heart quickening, mouth suddenly dry as pumice, he spun around. The monolith was glowing like a full moon, its glazy surface glimmering. At times small areas flashed brightly, perhaps denoting cryptic inner processes at work, like chemical reactions, or thoughts.

"What the fuck?" he muttered.

"It's time happening," the woman said behind him, raising her voice to be heard above the steadily loudening hum.

Reynard became aware of a barely detectable change in the light, but it wasn't the monolith's radiance that was changing. It was something else. He looked around, confused, then up.

The stars were moving slowly in the sky, circling through the blackness like sluggish fireflies.

The hum swelled rapidly, like a whale streaking up from the ocean depths toward the sunlit surface. Everything began to thrum: the floor, the air, his skin, his bones.

"Stop!" he screamed, clenching his eyes shut and clamping his hands over his ears as the hum blossomed into a skull-bursting boom, a boom which in the outside world, he realized, would be the gong heard around noon every day.

Somewhere deep beneath this terrible sound, he heard, or thought he heard, the old woman laugh and say one last thing about time.

He ran toward the archway in the south wall. At first he kept his eyes closed, but after a dozen steps his fear of slamming nose-first into a wall compelled him to open them to see where he was going.

What he saw made him stumble to a stop, his jaw hanging wide. The whole room had become a frozen blur, as if he were inside a wax building that had begun to melt and spin before solidifying again. It wasn't hard to discern what each blur represented: the wide swaths of gray were the walls and floor, of course; the black smears were the archways; the complex gray shape with the pale patches had to be the old woman; the white arcs and circles in the blackness above were the stars. The only thing that wasn't blurred was the monolith, which stood in the center of this chaos, clear and bright and glimmering.

The sound suddenly ceased, and some unseen force yanked Reynard through the air toward the monolith like a stone flung from a catapult, too fast for thought or prayer or pleas. And then…

For one vertiginous instant he thought that he had somehow fallen *into* the monolith, that its stoniness was an illusion and that its surface was actually brittle, powdery.

But no. The monolith wasn't white. Or wet.

Reynard sat up. He was in the middle of a snowy field with white-capped mountains all around him and a gray winter sky above. There was no sign of the Cathedral. Or Colbon. Or civilization of any kind. The snow in the field was pristine and unbroken save for the Reynard-shaped hole in which he sat.

He pushed himself to his feet. The wind picked up, reminding him he was dressed for temperate climes.

"This is why I never go to church," he said through chattering teeth as he stomped through snowdrifts in what he hoped was the right direction.

*   *   *

After nearly freezing and starving to death, he finally chanced upon a small rustic village nestled in a sheltered mountain valley. Though no one spoke his language, he was fed, draped in a toasty yet moth-eaten bearskin, then given a ride in an ox-cart to a town ten miles distant, where he learned from a polyglot alderman that the town was Ropertino in the country of Latravia, nearly three thousand miles north-northeast of Colbon. What's more, the year was now 3599, over two hundred years after he had entered the Cathedral.

"Well now," he said once he had collected his wits enough to speak. "I guess my problem with Kay is pretty much taken care of." Then he cackled in a way that made the alderman murmur something about having other business elsewhere and hurry away.

After a moment it struck Reynard that Solace had once again slipped from his grasp, and he let his head flop back with a groan.

"Unbelievable," he muttered at the ceiling, then started laughing again, harder than ever.

5

Shandar
4904 A.C.

He awoke to the smell of lavender.

Which was puzzling because he hated lavender. It was an old woman's smell. It reminded him of hominess, good citizenship, death.

Underlying that smell was the smell of leather, which, along with the faint creak he heard as he moved his head, led him to conclude he lay on a leather-upholstered surface. Given how long and soft it was, most likely a couch.

He opened his eyes. Mostly. One of them wouldn't open more than halfway, and the flesh around it felt tight and puffy. He wormed a hand out from under the unfamiliar blue blanket that draped him, and felt the swelling around the eye. The resulting sting made him wince.

What in Yango's name had happened to him? And more importantly, where was he?

Facing him was a wall of black leather. The back of the couch, no doubt. Beneath him, a cream-colored sheet covered the seat of the couch. A few smears of dried blood stained the fabric.

He started to roll over, then stiffened and sucked in air between his teeth as bolts of pain shot through his chest. Either a cracked rib or some hardcore bruising. He also felt pains in his knees, hips, arms, and...

He raised his hands in front of his face. The knuckles were bandaged. Very professionally, too. Irregular spots of blood dotted the gauze. The skin beneath the bandages felt raw and bruised.

It looked like he had dished it out as well as he had received. Must've been one hell of a fight. Too bad he didn't remember any of it.

What *did* he remember?

His name was Reynard. He was over seven thousand years old. He currently lived at 2121 Wain Street, Apt. 3, in the Chalk Hill neighborhood of Shandar, a city-state on the coast of the South Sea. He had recently moved to Shandar with the intention of seducing Isabel d'Argent, a beautiful young painter and heiress to the d'Argent fortune. It wasn't Isabel or even her family's fortune he was really after but access to her father's vast collection of rare maritime maps, amid which, he had reason to believe, was one that contained coded directions to the fabled lost treasure of the infamous pirate Blackhand Benedict. The most entertaining way to the map, he had decided, was via lovely Isabel.

Posing as Renny Zoro, an expressionistic portraitist, he had inserted himself into Shandar's art scene, and in three short weeks, he had not only won the heart and loins of Ms. d'Argent but enjoyed several visits to the d'Argent mansion in Shandar's posh Bayside District, though he hadn't been able to wangle a look at the maps. Caution was essential in this con; Isabel's father, the shipping magnate Salvador d'Argent, was notorious for his ruthlessness and sadism. He was also one of the few people whose claim of descent from Blackhand Benedict was based on valid genealogical research (which wasn't to say the other several hundred claimants were wrong; Benedict had had quite a fondness for the ladies, a fondness he pursued to its seedy conclusion even when the ladies weren't interested).

To complicate matters further, d'Argent, like his infamous ancestor (and like a lot of Shandar's elite, for that matter) owed the bulk of his prosperity to illicit activities, including but by no means limited to piracy, smuggling, extortion, bribery, and almost certainly murder. He was smart, cunning, and could smell bullshit through a steel wall. A private army protected his mansion round the clock, and d'Argent himself was constantly at the center of a swarm of bodyguards led by d'Argent's right-hand man, a scarred, muscle-knotted ex-con named Belgar Scurve.

Despite all that, Reynard hadn't been too concerned. He had handled scams far more dangerous than this a thousand times before, and he felt sure that his performance as Isabel's love-struck suitor was convincing enough to fool even the canniest eye. The map, he had no doubt, would be in his hands within one month, tops.

Could he have been wrong? Had he been found out?

What had happened?

He closed his eyes and cast his mind back to the last thing he could remember.

It had been evening, around six p.m. He had been walking from his apartment to the Black Galley Gallery where Isabel was meeting with the owners about an upcoming show of her work. Once the meeting was over, he and Isabel planned to go out to dinner, then head back to her place for a night of "horizontal waltzing" (her favorite euphemism for sex).

He cut down an alley that ended directly across the street from the gallery. Ahead of him, framed in the alley's mouth, he saw Isabel's cherry-red Arnko Cruiser parked along the curb. One of the new horseless vehicles that the dwarves were producing in their factories in the Silver Mountains, the

Cruiser was a large boxy contraption made of steel and titanwood with Syrkranian gum tires and a large blackglass panel in the hood, beneath which lay the barrel-sized solarite crystal that powered the whole thing. It had been a birthday present from her father, and she drove it everywhere, basking in the awe and envy it aroused. Reynard, however, wasn't particularly impressed. These new vehicles looked grand, but traveled barely eight miles an hour, which wasn't substantially faster than a horse and carriage. One day, he was sure, the technology would improve and they would become worthwhile tools, but at this point they were primarily a status symbol, a new toy for the wealthy to flaunt.

His musings on Isabel's car had been interrupted by a sudden shuffle from behind a stack of crates he had just passed. As he started to turn, a hand seized the back collar of his crimson Jezebaran magistrate's jacket, and then…

That was it. Nothing else. He had no idea who grabbed him, what happened next, or how he ended up here. Or even where here might be.

Time to find out.

He rolled all the way over, the blanket sliding off him in the process, and discovered he was in a tastefully decorated living room, its small size suggesting it was part of an apartment rather than a house.

In front of the couch was a dark walnut coffee table bearing a copy of the Shandar Free Press, a mug with a smear of lipstick on the rim, an abstract metal sculpture he thought resembled a pair of copulating stick figures, and a candlestick carved from what looked like giant-oyster shell. The pale green candle in the candlestick was scented: Sniffing, Reynard caught a quick whiff of *athelas*.

Against the far wall sat a rocking chair and a small table on which sat a white ceramic solarite lamp shaped like a whale, a green cut-glass dish filled with individually wrapped candies, a stack of books, and a spiral-bound notebook with a pen clipped to the front cover.

Behind and above the chair was a window, its thin white curtains bright with daylight. The faint, steady murmur of city life percolated in from outside. A framed print of Üster Hamaman's *The Cloud and the Wave* hung on the wall beside it. Overhead, silent and still, was a black ceiling fan.

This was all he could see without sitting up. The couch's armrests blocked everything else from sight.

The lavender smell he had detected earlier was coming from somewhere beyond the armrest by his feet, as were the occasional faint sounds of fabric rustling and footsteps padding across a carpet.

The evidence suggested he was in a woman's apartment. But what woman? He was sure he had never been in this room before, and—

He caught a trace of another scent and froze.

It was Solace.

Ignoring the yowls of pain from nearly every portion of his body, he sat up and looked around.

To his left was the front door, a sliding closet door, a framed sketch of a city street, and a side-table with an empty basket on it. To his right, at a right angle to the couch, was a matching leather chair, its seat heaped high with half a dozen pillows, which seemed odd and excessive until he realized that the pillows had no doubt been cleared off the couch to make room for him. Beyond the chair was a bookshelf crammed with books, a small attached kitchen whose wooden counter was being used primarily as extra shelf-space for books and various papers, and an archway that led further into the apartment. The sounds of movement and the scents of Solace and lavender were coming from beyond the archway.

Teeth clenched against the pain, he swung his legs around to the front of the couch and pushed himself to his feet. The movement made blood bang in his head and dark purple blotches strobe in his vision. He swayed in place, arms outstretched to keep his balance, eyelids beating hard to blink away the lightheadedness.

As the sensations passed and he checked himself over to make sure he hadn't opened a wound or left a piece of himself behind on the couch, he noticed that he was still wearing what he remembered wearing last night except that his boots and jacket had been removed. Another, more careful scan of the room revealed his boots sitting on the hardwood floor next to the couch. Of his crimson jacket there was no sign.

"You're finally awake," Solace said behind him.

He turned. She stood in the archway, regarding him with a small, tentative smile, as if she weren't sure he was well enough for a smile to be appropriate. She wore a black vest over a white silk shirt, and a black skirt over rainbow-striped toed tights. Her black hair was long and loose and had a pink streak running down the left side.

"Hi," he said, returning her smile, marveling at how natural and unremarkable it felt to see her. Though he had barely thought of her since their last encounter so long ago, everything about her—her face, her voice, the way she moved—remained as familiar to him as if they had just parted last week. He felt a sense of continuity, a thing he wasn't used to in this ever-shifting, all-too-mortal world. By now Solace had become a periodic body in his personal solar system, like one of those comets whose vast orbits brought them within sight of Eridia once every thousand years, regular as clockwork.

"How do you feel?" she asked.

"Like someone used me to break rocks with."

Her smile flickered and her eyes darkened as some troubling thought or memory surfaced. Dread slithered in his gut. What had happened? What had she seen? What did she know?

"Well, it's good that you feel well enough to crack jokes," she said. "Are you dizzy?"

"Nope."

"Any nausea?"

"No."

"That's good," she said with a small nod, not even remotely looking like someone who thought something was good. Her expression was now completely blank.

"Uh, thanks for…" He held up his bandaged hands. "Whatever exactly you did. All and everything."

"Mm-hmm. Let me take a look." She examined his hands, his swollen eye, his bruised cheeks. As she did so, he watched her face for any trace of anger or disappointment or anything else she might be feeling about whatever had happened, but her expression remained perfectly neutral.

"You're healing fast," she said. "Are you hungry? I could get you something to eat."

He considered this. "Actually just a glass of water would be fine. I'm not really hungry, and I think my mouth's too sensitive to chew right now anyway."

She briefly closed her eyes and gave a small sigh. Then she headed into the kitchen for the water. He sat back down on the couch.

After a minute, she returned and handed him a mug that sported a picture of a galleon and the words "Shandar Maritime Fest 4900 A.C."

"Thanks," he said.

Without a word or nod in response, she sat down in the rocking chair and started rocking gently. For a couple of minutes the only sounds in the room were the sips and gulps of Reynard's drinking and the rhythmic cricks and creaks from the chair. When the mug was empty, Reynard set it on the coffee table and settled back on the couch.

"Thanks again," he said, hoping to elicit some response.

He thought she might have nodded, but the constant rocking motion made it hard to be sure. Either way, her gaze remained fixed on his face, her own face perfectly blank. Uncomfortable with the scrutiny, he pretended to examine his bandages and fiddled with their edges as if they demanded minor adjustments. Outside a carriage rattled past, the horses' hooves clopping sharp and loud on what sounded like cobblestones. The presence of cobblestones didn't tell him much about his location; half of Shandar was paved with the things.

Suddenly the rocking chair's creaks stopped. Reynard looked up to find Solace staring at him with eyes that glimmered with tears. Her lips were compressed into a thin, trembling line.

"What's wrong?" he said.

"I thought you were fucking dead!" she snapped. The tears quivered in her eyes, but none broke free.

He shook his head, completely at a loss. Did she mean recently, or when he disappeared on her in Colbon? "Uh, when?"

She rolled her eyes. "Last night! When the bloody fuck else would I mean?"

"I don't know," he said, a little more testily than he intended, her anger having precipitated his own.

She shook her head and dropped her gaze to the carpet. "There was blood everywhere. There were puddles…" After a long pause, she heaved a shaky sigh and swiped away her still-unshed tears with the forearm of her shirt. After another, longer, pause she looked back up at him.

"You don't even remember how you got here, do you?" she said.

"Uh, well, no."

She nodded, and then, after taking a long, deep, calming breath, she proceeded to tell him.

At around nine-thirty the previous night, as she was walking home alone down Medallion Street after dinner and drinks with a friend (whose gender she avoided specifying), she spotted a man lying supine on the sidewalk in the mouth of an alley up ahead. She cautiously approached and found it was Reynard. He had been beaten so badly she almost didn't recognize him.

She knelt down and felt his neck for a pulse. She couldn't find one. Nor did he seem to be breathing: His chest did not rise and fall, and no sounds emerged from his mouth or nostrils. He appeared quite dead.

Just as she was about to let go of his neck and stand up, she felt a faint flutter beneath her fingers. An instant later his chest rose and a thick, unpleasant rattle came from his throat, startling her so badly she yelped and jumped back, nearly falling.

She called his name. He didn't respond, though he was visibly breathing now. She looked around in search of potentially helpful passersby, but the street was empty except for a few carriages rolling past on Nackle Avenue three blocks north. She saw a trail of blood stretching away into the alley's shadowy depths; it looked as if he had dragged himself out onto the sidewalk.

She called his name again. This time his eyelids fluttered and he made a faint, incoherent sound.

She squatted and pulled open his right eyelid. The pupil contracted, then the eye swiveled toward her face. The other eye opened a crack.

"Whuh?" he said.

"Reynard."

He blinked. A clot of blood was gumming the lashes of his left eye together and preventing the eye from opening very far. Solace swiped the clot away with her thumb.

"Reynard, how do you feel? Can you move?"

More blinking. Then his eyes focused on her in a way they hadn't before.

"Sullis?" he said.

"Yes. It's me. Can you move?"

"Uh?" He frowned as if the question were beyond understanding.

She stood up again, looked around again, saw no one again, then sighed in frustration.

"I'm going to go find someone to call a biomage," she told him.

"Nuh!" He shook his head hard enough to make himself grimace in pain.

"What? Why not? Reynard, you need a biomage."

His only response was to repeat, "Nuh."

She stood there, indecisive. She glanced up and down the street once more. Still no signs of life except the distant traffic. When she looked back down at Reynard, he was squirming about as if trying to walk with his buttocks and shoulder blades.

"Are you sure you should be moving?" she said.

"Needa gedda shelder," he said.

She squatted beside him again, wobbling precariously on her high heels. Annoyed, she plucked off the shoes and stuffed them into her purse, not letting herself care that she was now standing in his blood in only her stockings.

"What hurts?" she said. "Be specific."

He stopped squirming and considered the question, eyes drifting in and out of focus as he did so. Finally he met her gaze and with a trace of a smile said, "Ev'rything."

"I'm serious, Reynard."

"So'm I."

She looked around one final time, hoping against hope that a last-minute appearance by a conveniently passing biomage would wrest the decision from her indecisive shoulders, but there was only the street, the silent buildings, the streaks and puddles of blood gleaming faintly orange in the glow of the street lamps.

"Helb m'up," he said, extending a blood-streaked hand toward her.

"Reynard…"

"C'mon."

She heaved a sigh that was equal parts uncertainty and irritation, then stood up, grasped his forearm, and pulled. He weighed a good forty pounds more than she did, and since his feeble efforts to raise himself did little to help, his mostly dead weight caused her to slide in his blood. Her feet skidded toward him, gaining speed by the second. She felt the soles of her stockings begin to abrade away against the pavement.

"Damn it, Reynard!" she snapped, her fear of falling manifesting as anger. "Help me! Push!"

He saw what was happening and redoubled his efforts, though with a clear cost to himself: As he levered himself up, his face bunched in pain, and a groan was torn from his throat.

But it worked. There was a complex blur of motion, and before Solace knew what was happening, she was steady again, and he was upright. At least for the moment: He swayed about as if trying to decide which way to fall.

Before he could, she swept an arm around his shoulders and draped one of his arms over her own shoulders.

"Come on," she said. "Walk slowly."

He did, frowning with great concentration at his feet as he moved them forward, first one, then the other, down one block, then the next, then turning right.

And it was there, at the corner of Medallion and Crater Lane, that he suddenly stopped. Not noticing, she continued moving forward until his inertia wrenched her to a halt. She turned, and was puzzled to find him just standing there with his lips pooched out and his mouth working as if he were tasting fine wine.

He turned to one side, leaned over a little, and spat out a bloody wad. Solace thought she caught a glimpse of something white inside the wad, and was sure she heard a faint clack as it splatted on the pavement.

"By the Twelve, Reynard," she said. "What happened to you?"

He made a mumbly noise and shook his head.

They arrived at her apartment five minutes later. While she fished her keys from her purse, he slumped against the brick façade, his eyes half shut, leaning over every now and again to spit out more blood. He seemed unwilling to look at her.

Inside, she helped him climb the stairs to her apartment. He sat on the toilet in semi-conscious silence while she treated his numerous wounds. Then she led him to the living room and put him to bed on the couch. He fell asleep (or lapsed into unconsciousness) almost instantly. She stayed awake for over an hour to make sure he would be okay. When she couldn't keep her eyes open any longer, she shuffled off to bed.

"Do you remember anything at all about what happened?" she asked him now, her expression closed, unreadable, all trace of her tears long gone.

He shrugged. "Not much. I remember I was on my way to meet a friend, and as I cut down the alley, someone grabbed me from behind. That's all I know. I guess it was just an especially brutal robbery." He gestured at himself. "I mean, they took my jacket. My wallet was in it."

"No, I hung your jacket in the closet. Your wallet was still inside. I didn't open it, but it looked…pretty fat."

"Oh," he said. "Huh. I guess…I don't know, then…"

"It looked to me as if someone was trying their hardest to kill you. Can you think of anyone who would want to do that?"

He shook his head, beginning to feel annoyed by her cool, remote manner. It was like being questioned by a judge. "I know a few people who don't like me very much, but not so badly they'd want to rearrange my face. It was probably just some crazy street person hopped up on devil grass or something."

"Hm. Maybe." She regarded him thoughtfully for a moment. "Maybe we should report this to the Watch, if only to—"

"Oh, no no no," he said, trying to sound blasé. "I wouldn't bother. I mean, I can't give them any real information about anything, so I'd just be wasting their time. Besides, I heal fast. It's okay."

One corner of her mouth curled up in a sort of sad, bitter smile. She looked almost disappointed. He had to resist the urge to squirm.

"What have you been up to, Reynard?" she said.

"What? I—"

"Why didn't you want me to call a biomage?"

"What?"

"You heard me."

He shook his head with a slight frown, as if the rationale behind the question mystified him.

"I don't know," he said. "I don't remember *what* I was thinking at the time."

Her left eyebrow rose.

"I was half dead," he protested. "I mean, who knows what kind of weird nonsense was burbling through my brain?"

She continued staring at him for a moment. Then with a tiny sigh, she shifted her gaze to a spot on the floor to his left.

"I guess that makes sense," she muttered. She resumed rocking, keeping her eyes fixed on the floor.

Reynard cursed himself for not having handled this better. Normally he would have come up with smoother responses to her questions, maybe concocted a fantastic story to account for every detail and seeming discrepancy. But right now his head was fuzzy, his thoughts sluggish. Which wasn't surprising: Given his condition when she found him and the amount of time that had passed since then—and hence the amount of healing he had done—he must have been in worse shape than he had ever been in before. He suspected he had indeed been technically dead for a short time.

After watching her rock in silence for a minute, Reynard craned his head forward and squinted a little till he could read the spines of the books on the table beside her.

The Shen Mystery Scroll: Complete and Annotated, edited by Sha Iodreppia. *In Plain Sight: The History of the Shen Mystery Scroll* by Salima Turnival. *The Shen Mountains: An Illustrated*

Journey by Cloot vip Skederwold. *Ghosts of Mount Benta* by Mastrid Angelo. *Authors Unknown: A New Interpretation of the Shen Mystery Scroll* by D. R. Hunter. *Full of Secrets: The Scroll Unveiled* by Viggo Platz.

"A fan of the Scroll, eh?" he said.

"They're for a class." Her eyes never wavered from the floor.

"You're taking classes?"

"I'm *teaching* classes."

"Oh." He blinked at her, surprised for some reason. Perhaps sensing this, she finally deigned to look at him, her eyes cool, perhaps even a little hostile.

"I teach Age of Chaos Literature at the University," she said.

"Nice," he said. He waited until she had returned her gaze to the floor, and then, trying to keep a smile from his face, said, "So, what do you think about the poems in the middle section? I know a lot of people dismiss them as being too trite, but while that's true, I think they're very important to the work as a whole because they demonstrate the poet's growing mastery of various poetic forms. In fact, I'd even go so far as to say that while their content is rather bland and clichéd, on a strictly technical level those poems are arguably the best in the scroll."

By the time he was done speaking, Solace had stopped rocking and was staring at him as if he had just yanked his head off his neck, bounced it against the wall a few times, then stuck it back into place.

Finally she frowned a little and said, almost grudgingly, "That's…a good point. I didn't realize you were much of a reader."

"I read a lot, actually." And that was true. He never used to read, regarding it as a complete waste of time; he felt the world was far too interesting and full of possibilities to live vicariously. But a few centuries ago he had had to familiarize himself with as much ancient literature as he could as part of a scam against a scholar. He had been shocked by how much he enjoyed reading. But he supposed he shouldn't have been. Had he stopped to think about it, he would have realized that stripped to its core, most writing was merely the stringing together of words and ideas to influence the mind of another person. In other words, it was a con.

"I have to admit, I'm a little surprised," she said. "I mean, it's not that I don't think you're intelligent. It's just... you don't seem the bookish type."

"Well, I'm not one of those people who surround themselves with books. I don't read for the mere sake of reading. I'm...selective."

"I see," she said quietly, frowning. He sensed cautiousness about her, as if she were reluctant to pursue the conversation further. Maybe she was afraid it would soften her attitude toward him when she wanted to remain a frigid hardass.

"So what's your favorite?" he asked.

"My favorite what?"

"Poem. From the Scroll."

She opened her mouth to answer, closed it, then shook her head like someone trying to snap themselves out of a trance.

"Look, Reynard," she said, "much as the Scroll is one of my favorite subjects, I'm just not in the mood to discuss it right now."

"You don't want to discuss anything with me, do you?"

She gasped in exasperation and rolled her eyes. Without looking at him, she snapped, "Look, I'm sorry if I'm not in a particularly chatty mood, okay? Running across someone half dead and drenched in blood and then having—" She cut herself off, perhaps to prevent herself from saying something she would regret, and sat very still for a moment, eyes closed, lips pressed tight. Then, very quietly, she took a deep breath and said, "Why don't I get you something to eat."

"I'm not really very hungry."

"Even so, I'm sure your body could use the nourishment. You haven't eaten anything in over twelve hours."

"But—"

But she was already rising and heading to the kitchen. "I have some shnozzberry sauce. That stuff's packed with vitamins and minerals. It's just what you need."

In silence, he watched her pour out a bowl of shnozzberry sauce from a jar in the refrigerator, plunk a spoon into it, and carry it over to him.

"Seriously," he said. "I'm really not hungry."

"You need to eat," she said flatly, holding the bowl in front of him with a stubborn expression that made it clear she wouldn't budge until he took it.

He took it. The moment the first spoonful touched his tastebuds, his stomach clenched with hunger, and he devoured the rest in huge swift scoops. After giving him the bowl, Solace had moved off to straighten up a few things that needed no straightening, and the minute he finished, she came back and took the empty bowl. Without being asked, she brought him another bowl of sauce, which he wolfed down the same way.

While Solace washed the bowl and the spoon, he probed his mouth's ridges and crannies with his tongue to clear away the bits of shnozzberry skin before they could get wedged too deeply in the numerous small wounds in his gums, lips, and cheeks, including the tender wet hole where one of his teeth had been. Judging by past experience, it would be a decade or two before a new tooth grew in.

Solace shut off the water. He expected her to return to her seat, but instead she vanished through the archway without even glancing at him and thumped about in other rooms for awhile.

He had started to doze off when she returned.

"You can use the shower if you want," she said, her face and voice once again artfully blank. "I imagine you probably need it. I set out some spare towels, along with bandages and some stuff to treat your injuries. The bathroom's through there." She gestured at the archway.

"Thanks," he told her, surprised by the offer. He pushed himself to his feet, exaggerating the difficulty a little, hoping she would offer to help him to the bathroom and then, if he played this right, help him undress and shower and who knew what else, but she moved past him to her chair without another glance and sat down.

He hobbled to the archway. Beyond it was a short hallway with three doors. Two of the doors were shut tight. The third led to the bathroom.

He stepped inside, flicked on the light, and shut the door. The bathroom walls were light blue, and a canary yellow rug sat in the middle of the black-and-white tiled floor. The white shower curtain was decorated with cartoon frogs leaping about or perched on lily pads. On the toilet tank was a bowl full of potpourri, the origin of the lavender scent he had been smelling since he woke up. Given how strong the scent was, she must have set it out fairly recently, no doubt after she realized she had an unwanted guest on her hands who might—heaven forbid!—smell the normal odors of human habitation. Indeed, a look in the trashcan next to the sink revealed the potpourri's wrapper and a receipt dated this morning. She had spent a whole two decans on him. How sweet.

After examining the items Solace had laid out—a red towel and washcloth, a roll of gauze, antibiotic ointment, rubbing alcohol, and cotton balls—he dared a glance into the mirror.

He winced at the sight of his face. The skin around his left eye was swollen and shiny and the color of an eggplant. Both cheeks and most of his jaw were bruised and pocked with small angular marks. The skin had split down both the middle of his right eyebrow and the right side of his upper lip, and though these wounds were mostly healed, they still looked raw and ugly.

Leaning in over the sink, he examined the weird pock marks more closely in the mirror. A few of them, the clearest ones, were perfect triangles with round indentations in the center. Why did that seem so familiar? He wasn't sure, and knew from experience that trying to force the memory probably wouldn't work, so he set the matter on his mental back burner for the time being.

He stripped off his clothes to discover that his body looked as bad as his face. His entire torso was mottled purple and yellow, except for a few spots his assailant(s) must've forgotten to punch. The outer layers of skin on his knees and elbows had been abraded away as if he had been dragged across concrete. He peeled the bandages off his hands and marveled at the scab-caked knuckles beneath. Thank the Twelve he healed fast; if he were a normal man he would still be dripping blood everywhere. No, wait; if he were a normal man, he would be in the morgue.

Showering was an unpleasant adventure. When the hot water hit his various scrapes and sores the brief flare of pain was so bad he couldn't breathe for a second. And it took him forever to wash himself; most of his body was still so sensitive he had to dab on the soap with gentle pats of the washcloth.

It was while he was toweling off, again with gentle pats, that he remembered where he had seen that triangular pattern before. It was from a ring, a silver ring with a small round emerald set in its triangular face, a ring worn by Belgar Scurve, Salvador d'Argent's chief bodyguard. Scurve never wiped his butt without his boss's say-so, which meant d'Argent himself had almost certainly arranged the assault on Reynard.

No, not just an assault. This had been an attempted murder. It *would* have been murder if Reynard had been a normal man, but thankfully no one in Shandar knew that Reynard was an immortal.

He glanced at the closed bathroom door.

Well, almost no one.

He set to work hatching a new plan to acquire d'Argent's map. This plan wouldn't be as oblique and harmless as the old one. No, this one would do maximum damage. This one would bring d'Argent's whole world crashing down around him like a cheap chandelier.

As ideas arose and changed and coalesced in his racing mind, he finished toweling off, then treated his wounds, repeatedly choking back gasps at the rubbing alcohol's deep, sharp bite. The tube of ointment, which started out half full, ended up squeezed flat and in the trash.

He slowly dressed, wincing as fabric scraped across his body's more sensitive spots, then just stood there a while, staring soberly at the closed bathroom door, at the approximate spot where Solace sat in her living room.

He couldn't stay, he realized. He wished otherwise, wished he could take the time to thaw her out, to melt her heart and ultimately other, more interesting body parts. But he couldn't afford to right now. He was about to effectively wage war on a major crime lord, and while there was no way of knowing for sure how events would play out, things would likely get quite brutal. No one around him would be safe. If d'Argent learned about Solace, he would use her as leverage or worse against Reynard. And Reynard couldn't allow that to happen.

Maybe when everything was done and the dust had settled he could get back in touch with her. Maybe. But for now, he had to just go, before anyone could connect Solace with him.

When he returned to the living room, she sat in the rocking chair with *The Shen Mystery Scroll* open in her lap.

She shut the book and placed it atop the stack beside her.

"How do you feel?" she asked.

"Much better. Thanks." He paused before her chair, noting the way she stiffened a little as he did so. "I appreciate your helping me. I really do. That's twice I owe you."

"Twice?"

"You did save my ass in New Portland, remember."

"Oh." She waved a hand dismissively. "I'm not really keeping track."

"At any rate, one of these days I'll pay you back for all you've done. But right now I need to get going."

"Oh!"

He savored her brief look of surprise. She hadn't been expecting that at all.

"Um…" She shrugged. "If you're sure. You're not really fully healed yet, you know."

He suppressed a rueful smile. He could tell this feeble protest was merely for politeness' sake. Deep down, it was clear she was glad he was going.

"I'm fine," he said as he put on his boots. "People like us, we're hearty. We heal fast."

"True."

He headed to the closet for his jacket. When he saw the tattered, blood-stained mess hanging at the far right side of the rack, well away from Solace's own outerwear, he sighed, then yanked it off its hanger, rolled it up, and tucked it under his arm. That had been his favorite jacket, too.

He shut the closet door and turned to Solace, who had risen to see him out.

"Thanks again," he said.

"Not a problem. People are supposed to help each other. Um…" She frowned, glanced at the couch. "Are you absolutely sure you're well enough to—"

"I'm fine. Trust me. I've already imposed more than enough. I'm sure you have a life to get back to, and to be honest, I have some important business to take care of that'll keep me occupied for quite some time. Which means that while I'd love to stay in touch, I'm afraid it's not really doable right now."

She studied his face a moment as if suspecting a trick. Then, finding no evidence of one, she smiled with obvious relief.

"Well, maybe things'll be more propitious next time around," she said. "I hope things work out okay for you."

"I usually land on my feet." He smiled, remembering what had happened last time they met. "It's just, sometimes I land a few thousand miles from where I started out."

She gave him a puzzled smile, not understanding the comment but feeling obliged to return the good humor.

He opened the door, stepped through, looked back. "Take care."

"You too."

She shut the door.

He stood in the hallway a moment, listening. He heard no sounds from the apartment. No creak of floorboards. No rustle of fabric. He knew she was standing there on the other side of the door, listening just as he was. It crossed his mind that the next time they met, the rocking chair and the couch and the books and the frog shower curtain and maybe even the building itself would probably no longer exist.

With a grunt, he headed off to make ready for war.

6

Peridor
5989 A.C.

Reynard peered through the air vent in the ceiling of Room 304 of the Toy Box, Peridor's swankiest brothel. On the silk-sheeted bed below, a stocky male dwarf was being orally serviced by a morbidly obese human woman, thus validating the well-known stereotype that dwarves harbored a BBH (Big Beautiful Human) fetish.

Alas, Reynard wasn't as amused by this spectacle as he might have been, because the duo's position was such that the dwarf was lying on his back with his hairy face pointed straight at the vent. Currently his eyes were squinched shut in ecstasy at the prostitute's clearly expert ministrations, but that could change at any moment. And if it happened to be the moment that Reynard's body was moving over the vent, then a truly monstrous shitstorm would ensue.

But Reynard couldn't wait. He checked his watch. The pulsed interrupt signal he had sent into the brothel's security system would disperse in less than three minutes. If that happened before he reached Room 310, the system would reactivate, the currently dark sensors stationed every ten feet along the duct would glow red once again, and the presence of a foreign body in the ventilation duct would be detected. And then one more person in the brothel would be getting fucked really hard, only this time in a purely figurative sense.

He took a deep breath and pushed himself across the vent as fast as he could without banging around too much. There were no sudden gasps or exclamations from the room below, so presumably no one saw him. He couldn't stop to make sure, though.

As he neared the next vent, about twenty feet farther on, he heard the creaks of a bed being put to heavy use, accompanied by animalistic growls and a woman's steadily loudening moans. He was pretty sure he knew what he would see before he saw it.

Indeed, when he reached the vent and carefully peered through the slats, hoping none of the boudoir's occupants were gazing ceilingward at the moment, he saw that the noisemakers were a chubby redheaded human woman and a wiry, brown-haired kokoroo, one of the bipedal coyote people from out near the Akai desert.

The kokoroo was most likely one of the brothel's many male prostitutes. The Toy Box was renowned for catering to every possible sexual taste, and in a world that contained dozens of sentient species of every shape and size, as well as robots, undead, mutants, mages, and a host of other remarkable entities, the possibilities were almost literally endless.

The kokoroo lightly clamped his fangs on the side of her neck. She squealed in delight. The kokoroo snarled and picked up the pace. He was pounding her from behind, Reynard noted. Doggie-style. Of course.

Fortunately doggie-style meant that they couldn't see Reynard, so he wriggled on his way.

The next room in line, number 308, was currently being used by an older silver-haired gentleman who was chugging away at a rather plain-looking woman whose vacant gaze and pale skin and complete lack of movement suggested she was a zombie. Though the woman's glassy eyes were pointed roughly in the vent's direction, they clearly weren't seeing anything at all. Still, it was with some trepidation that Reynard crawled over the vent. Thankfully nothing happened.

With his watch informing him he had only slightly more than a minute left, he arrived at the vent for Room 310. When he peered through it, he was confronted with the sight of Optimo Bargeillian, chief of the Peridor Watch, vigorously ass-fucking Prestin Blush, the pouty-faced lead singer of the flux-pop band Upsy-Daisy.

Or at least it *looked* like Prestin Blush. It was actually Reynard's friend and occasional partner-in-crime Zezora Miglia, nicknamed Zezzy, an adult human female metamorph who put her talents to extremely lucrative use as a prostitute here at the Toy Box.

Zezzy/Prestin's tanned and slender legs were draped over Bargeillian's fat, hairy shoulders as the Watch chief pumped away, Zezzy having maneuvered the fascistic bastard into anally drilling her in the missionary position, as planned. This allowed Zezzy to watch for Reynard in the overhead vent.

When she spotted him, she let go of her client's sweaty red arm long enough to flash Reynard a single finger, signaling him to wait a moment.

Wait? Was she mad? There wasn't time to wait. He glanced at the still-dark sensors in the air duct's wall, then checked his watch again. He had forty seconds left. Stupid bitch.

Bargeillian stopped thrusting and let out a low groan. It wasn't a groan of orgasm, though. No, this was one of those little troubled groans people make when they're suddenly not feeling well. Bargeillian swayed back on his knees, his penis popping out of Zezzy/Prestin's anus, which briefly gaped in accord with the size of Bargeillian's fairly average member before slowly sliding shut.

Reynard rolled his eyes. He really hadn't wanted to see that.

"Whoa," Bargeillian said, his voice thick and woozy. "I don' think…"

Whatever it was he didn't think, he didn't have time to articulate it before letting out another, louder groan and keeling over sideways hard enough to make the bed's baroquely carved black walnut headboard bang against the pink-painted wall.

"It's clear," Zezzy called out. Her trim young man's body was swiftly growing less trim and less mannish as it morphed into her usual form. "You can come out now."

He hadn't had to be told; the moment Bargeillian's fall began, Reynard had pushed open the vent cover and started to maneuver out of the duct, feet first. He hung from the open vent a moment, then let go. Then he immediately leaped back up and swatted the vent cover hard enough to make it snap back into place.

His watch beeped, which meant that inside the vent the sensor lights had started glowing red again.

"That was fucking close," he growled at Zezzy.

She shrugged. She had fully reverted to the form she adopted most often when she was in Reynard's presence: a short, chubby young woman with pale skin and long blue hair. He suspected this really was her true form (except perhaps the blue hair). After all, if it were an assumed form, why wouldn't she make herself look stunningly beautiful? He knew *he* would.

"Don't blame me," she said. "I slipped him the chimmin over five minutes ago. I'm not exactly happy about it myself, you know. I was really kinda hoping to avoid anal with the fat little turd this time around. Besides, everything worked out okay, right? You're in one piece."

"For now." Reynard grabbed Bargeillian and propped him upright against the headboard.

"Muggle muh…" Bargeillian mumbled. His eyes rolled whitely, unseeing. A saliva bubble expanded at the corner of his thick lips. He wasn't unconscious but at the same time he wasn't aware either. Chimmin, the drug Zezzy had slipped into his wine, turned people into suggestible automatons, little better than the zombie the old guy in Room 308 had been screwing. Anyone under the effect of chimmin would answer any question truthfully, perform any action requested of them, and not remember a single thing if you told them not to. Naturally, a drug of such potency was a Class A Restricted Substance, and the illegal usage or ownership of it had penalties so severe even the Cagliostro Cabals wouldn't touch the stuff. To get some, Reynard had had to go straight to the source: Maxipettle, the South Seas island that was home to the chimmin plant. And when he got back, he had had to spend the better part of a week sweet-talking Zezzy into going along with his plan. Despite her initial flat-out refusal, he finally managed to convince her that the scheme's potential rewards so far outweighed the drawbacks that refusal to do it was tantamount to insanity.

Which wasn't to say she still wasn't apprehensive about the whole thing.

"Let's hurry this up," she muttered, glancing at the door. "He only paid for half an hour, you know."

"Yeah, yeah," he said. He looked her up and down, then gestured at the old-fashioned archer's outfit she was now decked out in, complete with green tights, a green leather vest, and a green peaked cap with a hawk feather in it. It wasn't real clothing, he knew. It was her own body morphed into the appearance of clothing. "By the way, what's the deal with the outfit?"

"I don't know. I just like it. You got a problem with that?"

"No, I mean, why make yourself appear clothed? You were naked just a minute ago. What's the matter, you don't want me seeing you naked?"

"I was naked as Prestin Blush. It's not the same thing."

"It's not?"

"No!"

"But—"

"Besides, we do not have that kind of relationship."

"What if I were to pay for your services?" he asked with a smug smile.

"Then I would refuse."

"Why?"

"Because I would. We don't have that kind of relation-ship."

"Fine," he grumbled. "Have it your way, Ms. Modesty." He looked at Bargeillian. The Watch chief's porky form was slumped against the headboard, his arms limp and heavy at his sides, his head drooping forward, his chin on his breast. A shining string of drool now connected his lower lip with his bloated belly. Farther down, nearly concealed beneath the rolls of gut-fat, his limp penis glistened with lubricant.

"Mr. Bargeillian," Reynard said. "I want you to sit fully upright."

Instantly Bargeillian's back stiffened, his shoulders squared, and his head rose, snapping the string of drool. He now sat as erect as a teacher's pet on the first day of class.

"Good." Reynard glanced at Bargeillian's flaccid penis, then with a frown grabbed one of the bed's robin's-egg blue pillows and placed it over Bargeillian's crotch. Big improvement.

"What's the matter?" Zezzy asked with a playful smirk. "Penises make you uncomfortable? You got some issues you need to deal with, maybe?"

He scowled. "Knock it off. Maybe you like seeing fat guys' ugly dicks waving in your face, but it's not something I particularly care for."

"Hey, I don't *like* it, okay? It's just a job, that's all."

Reynard returned his attention to the Watch chief. "Mr. Bargeillian. Optimo. Can I call you Optimo? Tell me I can."

"You can call me Optimo," Bargeillian said in a voice so clear and lucid it was startling.

"Pick your nose and eat it."

"Oh, come on!" Zezzy said.

Bargeillian inserted his right index finger into his right nostril, twisted it around a little, and withdrew it with a clot of snot on the end. He pinched the snot off with his teeth and swallowed it.

"That's disgusting," Zezzy said.

"More or less disgusting than seeing his shriveled little dick with ass-tainted lube on it?" Reynard asked.

"Oh, shut up," she said. "Shouldn't we be getting on with this? We have a time limit, remember?"

"Yeah, yeah."

Reynard grabbed the pink velvet–upholstered chair in the corner, set it next to the bed with its back to Bargeillian, then sat down straddling the chair's back, his arms crossed atop the headrest. After studying Bargeillian's still-rigid form a moment, he shook his head with a marveling grin. He had never used chimmin before, but damn, this shit was incredible. The chief of the Peridor Watch, one of the toughest, gruffest, most feared men in the whole city-state, had been reduced to a witless puppet. It was a beautiful thing.

"Now, then, Optimo," Reynard said, "I have a few questions I need to ask you. First of all, you recently confiscated a shipment of black-market ISR bots, correct?"

Bargeillian's mouth opened but nothing emerged except a thin squeaking sound.

"Optimo?"

The squeak was replaced by a low, buzzing voice, which issued from Bargeillian's open mouth without his lips and tongue moving so much as a millimeter: "Unauthorized tampering of subject detected. Countermeasures activated."

Reynard frowned and glanced at Zezzy who was likewise frowningly glancing at him.

"What does—" she began.

Bargeillian's head exploded, showering Reynard and Zezzy and everything else in the room with blood, wads of skin, and blobs of brains. A small shard of the Watch chief's skull thwacked Reynard on the cheek.

Reynard tried to scramble to his feet but got one foot tangled in the chair's legs, and he and the chair crashed to the gore-spattered carpet. Meanwhile Zezzy was backing toward the door screaming, "Fuck! Fuck! Fuck!"

His eyes flew wide when he saw her extend one hand behind her for the doorknob. In her panic she was going to stumble out into the hall, still screaming, and bring everyone—the Toy Box's employees, the customers, Bargeillian's bodyguards waiting downstairs, and ultimately the Watch itself—down on their heads.

"Zezzy, don't!" he shouted, thanking Vävel that the Toy Box's bedrooms were soundproof.

She didn't seem to hear him. Her groping hand found the doorknob. Her fingers closed around it. She started to turn toward the door.

He kicked the chair aside so hard one of its legs snapped

off, and then started to spring up. His left foot skidded in the blood with a short sharp sound that reminded him of a zipper zipping, and he crashed back down to the floor.

Just then Zezzy paused in her turn, blinked three times, then leaned to the right and vomited.

Reynard scrambled to his feet and rushed toward her before she could recover enough to open the door. By the time he got there, he saw he didn't have to; when she turned to face him, her eyes were scared but free of the panic that had held her in its grip a few seconds earlier.

"What the fuck just happened?" she said.

"His head exploded."

"No shit! But why?"

"I don't know. That voice said something about unauthorized tampering."

"It sounded like a robot. Do you think he was a robot?"

Reynard turned and studied the wet red meat that crowned the ex-Watch chief's shoulders.

"No, but maybe he had an implant or something. I know the URWA's been experimentally implanting some of their agents with tracking devices and stuff like that."

"What the fuck are we gonna do?" Zezzy asked.

Good question. Reynard looked around. From the costume cabinet next to the door to the ornate gilt-framed mirror on the wall beside the bathroom, the entire room was spattered with bits of Bargeillian's head. There was no way they could clean or cover this up in the fifteen minutes they had left before the session expired. Besides, what would they do with the body? There was nowhere to hide it. The only option was to flee. If they could get themselves cleaned up in time, he and Zezzy could stroll right out the front door. Sure, Bargeillian's guards had seen her when she led their boss upstairs, but she could transform herself into anyone, so…

Wait.

"Could you transform into Bargeillian?" he asked.

She stared at him uncomprehendingly for a moment, then glanced at the gory mess on the bed.

"Yeah. Sure."

Her body swelled up and out, her features shifting, her blue hair shortening and turning brown, her archer's outfit morphing into a black business robe with a Peridor Watch logo on the breast. The blood and bits of brains remained, but their relative positions shifted as they rode the trans-muting flesh like bits of debris on ocean swells.

"Hold on, it'll take me a couple seconds to get his voice right," she said, her voice starting out as a deep manly rumble then slowly modulating as she spoke, coming closer and closer to Bargeillian's more raspy tones. "Is this about right?"

"A touch higher."

"What about now?"

"Perfect."

She spread her hands. "What good will this do, though? We've still got a body, and it's not like I can start a new career as the chief of the Peridor Watch. So what now?"

"I'm not sure."

She goggled at him. Or rather Bargeillian goggled at him, an effect that looked weird and dissonant; it was an expression Bargeillian would never have made, except maybe when he was a child. The man had been totally unflappable and tough as troll hide.

"What the hell does that mean, you're not sure?" she said, reverting to her normal feminine voice, which, coming from Bargeillian's fat, jowly face, was even more dissonant than the goggle had been.

"It means I'm considering options."

She rolled Bargeillian's beady brown eyes and flapped his flabby arms. "Well, shit, I don't think we really have much time for fucking consideration of all our lovely fucking options."

"Stop getting hysterical."

"I am not getting fucking hysterical!" she shrieked.

He ignored her, then eyed the corpse on the bed.

"Does that look like Bargeillian to you?"

She blinked at him, her eyes morphing back to her usual green ones though the rest of her stayed the same. Then she turned and studied the corpse.

"Yeah," she said.

"But would it if you'd never seen him naked?"

"Well, the body type's the same…"

"Lots of older men have bodies like that."

She shook Bargeillian's head. "What are you suggesting, exactly? It's not like we can sneak the body out of the room." She paused, frowned. "Can we?" Before he could answer she forged ahead: "And if we leave it here it'll be found by Lorelei."

"Lorelei?"

"Yeah, the next girl. Bargeillian was my last client of the day." She folded her arms across her chest with a doleful sigh. "Probably my last client *ever.*"

"Now, now. We'll find a way out of this."

"How?"

"I'm working on it. But whatever the plan, I need to clean myself off first." He turned and made his way toward the bathroom, trying not to step on any of the larger clots of brain matter as he went.

"Yeah, me too," Zezzy said, heading after him.

He paused in the bathroom doorway and turned toward

her. "No, actually, you should stay just the way you are."

She stopped in mid-stride and glared at him, her body swiftly morphing back to her own. "Ex*cuse* me? What in Nün's name is that supposed to mean?"

"It means you might need to keep the…" He gestured at her crimson-spattered body. "The evidence on you. You might need it later as an alibi or something."

Her glare collapsed into a gawp. "Oh."

"But like I said, I don't actually have a plan yet. Or at least not…uh…"

He stopped talking, stopped thinking, able only to stare at what was now transpiring on the bed behind Zezzy. Seeing his reaction, Zezzy whirled, then screamed.

Emerging from Bargeillian's neck stump was an eight-legged mechanical creature that vaguely resembled a large metal scorpion. Its long, spidery forelegs gripping Bargeillian's clavicles for leverage, it pulled itself up and out through the meat and sinew with a thick, wet tearing sound. On its front end was a small pulsing red light.

"What the fuck is that?" Zezzy screamed.

"I…I have no idea. Some kind of robot, but…"

But what was it doing inside the chief of the Peridor Watch? Was this the origin of the weird robot voice they had heard right before Bargeillian's head blew up? It seemed more than likely. Unless, of course, there was a whole nest of those things in there.

When it had pulled itself free of Bargeillian's neck, it perched atop the stump a moment, front end slightly raised as if sniffing the air.

Reynard had a sinking feeling he knew exactly what was going to happen next…

Indeed, the creature swiveled toward the duo in the bathroom doorway, its ominous blinking light pointed straight at them.

Zezzy swallowed. "Is it—"

Fast as a centipede, the creature raced down Bargeillian's corpse and streaked across the bed toward them.

Zezzy screamed again, this time so loud Reynard's eardrums throbbed with pain.

Reynard grasped her shoulders and yanked her with him into the bathroom even as the scorpion-thing launched itself off the bed straight at them. The moment the two of them were fully inside the bathroom, Reynard flung out a leg and kicked the door shut. A millisecond later something slammed into the door, then dropped to the carpet.

"What the hell is going on?" Zezzy asked in a choked whisper as they watched the creature's shadow move back and forth along the narrow gap under the door.

"Well, this scorpion robot thingie came out of a corpse whose head just exploded—"

"I fucking know that, dumbshit!"

"Well, I don't know any more than you do. I guess the chimmin activated something that was already inside him. But I don't have the slightest idea what that something is."

"Well, then, what the fuck are we gonna do?"

Good question. Reynard glanced around the bathroom. No other doors. No windows. There was a fan above the queen-sized tub, but it was way too small for him to climb through. If they could get the grille off, Zezzy might be able to shrink small enough to get inside, but there were no doubt motion sensors in there, and in any case, he didn't trust her to come back for him, so he didn't even mention the idea. What else was at hand? Toilet. Towels. Wastebasket. Mirror. Broken glass? No, sharp objects usually didn't work so well against metal. But the tub! Water! Maybe they could short-circuit it.

A series of cracking sounds from the door made him whirl back around. The shadow had stopped moving, and judging by the noises and the way the door was vibrating in synch with them, the creature was now tearing through the wood.

Reynard grabbed the wastebasket and started filling it with water from the faucet in the tub.

"When I give the signal I want you to open the door, fast," he said.

"You're kidding, right?"

There was a louder crack, and the door jolted violently. Several smaller shadows fell around the main one as chunks of wood from the door came loose. At this rate, the creature would be through in less than a minute.

"If you can think of a better idea, I'd love to hear it," he snapped.

"Okay, okay!"

The wastebasket nearly full now, Reynard shut off the water and took up a position to one side of the door, one hand gripping the wastebasket's rim, the other supporting its bottom. With his head he motioned for Zezzy to open the door.

She laid a hand on the knob, winced when the door trembled again as the creature tore out another hunk of wood, then took a deep breath and pulled the door open, staying behind it as if it were a huge wooden shield.

The instant the door began to open, the creature darted inside. It paused for the briefest instant before detecting Reynard to its left and swinging toward him, but a brief instant was all Reynard needed to unleash the whole waste-basket's worth of water upon the creepy insectoid robot.

The force and weight of the water sent the thing flying back against the open door, and that impact, combined with the sudden surge of water pouring under and around the door, made Zezzy yelp in surprise. The creature caromed off the door and spun into the center of the bathroom, underbelly up, legs crooked and stiff like those of a dead spider.

Reynard suspected the creature had been short-circuited, but he wasn't about to hang around to find out for sure. He slammed the wastebasket upside-down over the creature's still slowly spinning form, trapping it (though if it was still alive, or activated, or whatever, the wastebasket wasn't even remotely heavy enough to hold it for more than a second or two), then grabbed Zezzy and fled the bathroom, slamming the door as hard as he could behind him.

For a moment the two of them just stood there, panting, watching the door, surveying the deep, wide gouges in its base and the heaps of splinters on the carpet before it. No sounds came from the other side.

"Did you get it?" Zezzy asked.

"I guess so. It—"

Two short, faint beeps sounded from the bathroom, followed by a third, longer beep.

Reynard and Zezzy looked at each other.

"Do you think that means it's shutting down?" she whispered.

He shrugged. "I—"

There was a loud *whoomp* from the bathroom followed by the sound of the wastebasket banging off the edge of the tub.

Reynard and Zezzy slowly backed away from the door, eyes fixed on it all the while. Dimly Reynard could make out the faint clicks of the creature's metal legs on the bathroom tiles as it skittered about. It seemed to be turning this way and that, as if assessing its surroundings.

The clicking paused. Reynard and Zezzy froze, not even

breathing.

There was a rapid series of clicks as the creature scuttled to the door, and then the door trembled and the sound of splintering wood resumed anew.

Reynard grabbed the heavy oaken table that stood near the bathroom door, flipped it on its side, and rammed it top-first against the door.

"That'll keep it busy a little longer," he said.

"What do we do now?" Zezzy said.

"Personally, I think leaving would probably be a good idea at this point."

She looked at him as if he were insane. "How? They'll see us! If the Toy Box's security guards don't, Bargeillian's bodyguards will."

"What are *you* whining about? You're a shapeshifter. You can morph into the friggin' owner if you want."

"I'm covered in blood, dumbass!"

"So morph into the owner wearing a blood-colored costume…"

Costume. Of course.

He strode to the costume cabinet and flung open the doors. Inside was a dizzying array of fetishwear: rubber suits, maid outfits, man-sized diapers, butcher's aprons, military uniforms, mage robes, mummy wraps, and dozens more. But the one Reynard selected, partly because it would cover his whole body and partly because it amused him, was a full-body GO GO DREAMY costume. The creation of Acme Enterprises, GO GO DREAMY (always spelled all in capitals) was a white cartoon elephant that had somehow become the most popular cultural icon in the United Realms, its round white face with its little black oval eyes, floppy ears, and short, stumpy trunk (it had no tusks or mouth) gracing every object imaginable, from notebooks to cars to vibrators (adults loved GO GO DREAMY just as much as, if not more than, children). GO GO DREAMY was a multi-billion decan industry. Some people half-jokingly said it was the most powerful entity in the history of the United Realms.

Grinning, Reynard pulled the costume off the rack.

"What are you doing?" Zezzy asked.

He scanned the hanging outfits for something for her, something that wouldn't take her long to put on.

Another crack sounded from the bathroom door, this one the loudest yet.

"Here," he said, grabbing a multicolored mage robe and a mask that resembled a fat, rosy-cheeked baby. "Put these on."

She stared at the proffered outfit for a moment with an almost disgusted look, as if one or both of the items held unhappy memories for her, but then with a sigh she snatched them and started to put them on.

There was a loud sharp bang from the bathroom door. With only one leg inside the pants of the GO GO DREAMY costume, Reynard twisted around and saw that the bathroom door was split nearly all the way up its middle. The table he had shoved against the door had been knocked an inch or two out of place.

"Shit," he hissed. He jammed his other leg into the pants, then hurried to the bathroom door, having to take long, high strides in order to run in the suit's big puffy feet. As he passed the bed, he swiped the blood-soaked sheet from it, careful not to let it touch the outside of the suit.

Peering over the edge of the upended table, he saw the creature's forelegs poking through a narrow hole near the base of the door. As he watched, the legs prized free another chunk of wood, widening the hole, revealing a glimpse of the robot's sleek silvery body on the other side. He stuffed the sheet into the crevice between the table and the door, then slammed the table against the door again. After a brief pause, the splintering sounds resumed. By then, Reynard was halfway to the costume cabinet again.

Already fully disguised, Zezzy waited impatiently, her nervous breaths muffled and echoey inside the baby mask, while Reynard pulled on the top half of the GO GO DREAMY suit, then buckled the large, round mask into place. The moment it was on, he realized this might not have been the best choice of costume after all. Not only was he already starting to sweat, but his range of vision was reduced to a pair of narrow ovals. Alas, it was too late to change.

"Now what?" Zezzy asked. "We just run out of the building? You think no one'll ask what we're doing and why we're dressed like this? By Vävel, this was a stupid plan."

"Now, now. Don't be so negative. We could always—"

There was a loud, sharp bang, and the overturned table juddered half a foot across the carpet.

"Uh-oh," Reynard said.

The creature scuttled into view around the edge of the table.

"Shit!" Zezzy cried. She whirled around to open the door while Reynard tensed, ready for the creature's advance.

But it didn't advance. Instead, with a complex series of high, quick whirs and clicks, each section of its jointed legs telescoped to an incredible degree, lengthening and lengthening until the creature's body was suspended six feet off the carpet by an angular network of needle-thin rods.

"Well, I'll be fucked," Reynard said. Beside him, Zezzy glanced back over her shoulder as she pulled open the door, and let out a yelp at the sight of the new-and-improved robot monster.

A compartment beneath the blinking red light on the creature's front end popped open, revealing a row of tiny silver pellets inside. An instant later one of the pellets shot out straight at them.

"Down!" Reynard hollered, flinging himself atop Zezzy and sending the two of them toppling out the open door and onto the elegant red-and-gold carpeting of the hallway beyond.

The pellet sailed over their falling bodies—missing Reynard's back by centimeters—streaked across the hallway, and struck the opposite wall, where it exploded with enough force to leave a hole in the plaster the size of a man's head. Reynard stared at the hole through the haze of dust and smoke, and muttered, "Oh, lovely." A direct hit from one of those pellets would probably be an instant kill-shot even for an immortal like himself.

Reynard sprang to his feet, pulling Zezzy up with him, and galumphed down the hall as fast as he could in the ridiculous, ill-chosen costume.

Already doors up and down the corridor were opening and frightened faces were peeping out to see what all the noise was about. A naked elf girl stepped out of Room 305, a quizzical frown on her face, which along with her hair and chest was coated with a pearlescent film of semen. Drops of it oozed off her and plopped to the carpet.

"What's happening?" she asked Reynard and Zezzy as they raced past.

"We're under attack!" Reynard cried, deepening his voice so as to eliminate any possibility of a positive vocal identification during the now-inevitable police investigation. "Get to cover!"

As if to underscore this, there was a loud crash down the hallway behind him. An instant later a woman screamed.

The elf girl gave one terse nod and ducked back inside. You had to love those unflappable elves.

They came to an intersection. Reynard paused, unable to recall which way the main exit was.

Zezzy knew, though, and not bothering to wait for Reynard to recollect correctly or ask, she veered right, yanking him after her, he stumbling and nearly falling in the GO GO DREAMY costume's huge feet. As he rounded the corner, he chanced a quick glance down the corridor they were vacating and saw the scorpion-thing scurrying after them thirty feet back. About fifteen feet behind it, a man's nude body lay in a spreading pool of blood. Judging by the body's white hair, it might have been the corpse-fucker from room 308.

This new corridor, Reynard saw with dismay, was long and straight. They would be sitting ducks (or rather, running ducks) if the creature fired any more missiles. Even if it didn't, at the rate it was running it would catch up with them long before they reached the hallway's end.

But what else could they do? Fight it? Duck into one of the rooms? None of the rooms on this floor had windows, and as had already been amply demonstrated, doors and walls offered little protection against this thing.

Screams rang out behind them. A door slammed. Reynard heaved a frustrated sigh, wishing the costume allowed him to turn his head so he could keep periodic tabs on the creature. He hated not knowing what was happening.

Thankfully Zezzy was keeping tabs, and the next time she glanced back, her eyes went huge. She threw herself against Reynard, driving him toward the right wall just in time to avoid another missile, which went zipping on down the corridor straight at the team of silver-suited, heavily armed security personnel who had just rounded the corner at the corridor's far end.

Reynard missed the ensuing calamity because Zezzy's shove had sent them hurtling straight toward a door marked 329, a door that just happened to open as they hurtled toward it, with the result that the two of them crashed into the red-haired woman in the chainmail bikini who had opened the door. The three of them tumbled to the floor in the room beyond.

Down the hall there was an explosion, then screams and the bark of small arms fire. Bullets whicked past the doorway. As soon as he had gathered his wits Reynard disentangled himself from the women and pushed the door closed.

Everyone stood up. At least everyone who had been in the doorway stood up; the skinny naked middle-aged man on the bed merely struggled against his manacles and made squealing noises through his gag.

"What the heck's going on out there?" asked the red-haired woman, her nervous, whiny voice somehow at odds with the chainmail she wore and the rack of whips and canes next to the bed.

"There's a killer scorpion robot-thing on the loose," Zezzy said.

The redhead peered at her. "Zezzy? Is that you?"

"Uh-huh."

"Is there any other way out of this room?" Reynard asked, once again deepening his voice.

"Um, no," the redhead said. She stared at Reynard's masked form a moment then turned to Zezzy. "Who's this? I thought you had Bargeillian."

"She did," Reynard said. "But we lost track of Mr. Bargeillian in the confusion. We believe the robot was sent to assassinate him and anyone associated with him. Which means we have to get Ms. Miglia here to safety."

"Oh, I see." The redhead nodded, her doubts quelled and her fears eased by his confident, authoritative manner. She probably assumed he was with Bargeillian's bodyguard team or the local Watch or the URWA or some other lawful agency. Sooner or later she would wonder about the GO GO DREAMY costume, of course, but by then he hoped to be long gone.

The man on the bed shrilled against his gag. Everyone ignored him.

More gunshots rang out. Reynard tensely watched the thin shadows of the robot's legs moving about at the bottom of the door. Every now and then the legs clicked and scritched against the door itself, though it was hard to tell if the robot was probing the door for access or simply seeking purchase against the hail of bullets.

"So what do we do now?" Zezzy asked.

"For now, wait and see," Reynard said.

The man on the bed shrilled again.

"Shut up, Herman," the redhead called over her shoulder.

The gunfire intensified, more guards having apparently joined the others at the end of the corridor. The creature advanced against the onslaught, and the spindly shadows passed out of sight beyond the right side of the door. A moment later there was another explosion down the hall, followed by more screams, some of which lingered on and on. After a brief lull, the gunfire resumed, less intense now, though not by much. The door to the room shuddered as a stray bullet thwacked into it.

Suddenly there was a high-pitched whining sound from the corridor, a sound that reminded Reynard of an overloaded machine that's about to burn itself out. He hoped that was what it was—that the robot had been damaged or had exhausted its power and was now seizing up.

But then one of the guards shrieked, "Holy fucking shit! What the fuck is it—"

The succeeding cacophony of mechanical squeals, groans, and whirs drowned out the rest of his statement. The cacophony sped down the hall toward the guards, many of whom screamed in what was clearly horror rather than pain. Some of the screams swiftly decreased in volume as the screamers took cover or ran away.

"Let's go," Reynard told Zezzy. "If we go back the way we came, we can still get around to the exit, right?"

"The long way, yeah, but—"

"Well, I'm going. You can stay if you want."

Ignoring her protests, he opened the door and peeked out in the direction the scorpion-thing had gone. The end of the hallway was thick with haze amid which faint shapes moved. The largest and strangest shape resembled a cross between a giant tumbleweed and a Thüselanyan torture device. This could only be the robot. It had sprouted dozens more wiry appendages, which with frightening speed and precision flailed, stabbed, and slashed at the shadowy shapes of the few guards still standing upright. Now and then gunfire flashed bright orange amid the murk, but it didn't seem to be doing much good.

"Come on." He grabbed Zezzy's wrist in one fat, three-fingered GO GO DREAMY hand and pulled her down the hall in the direction they had come.

At the intersection they turned right and joined the stream of panicked whores and johns who had likewise chosen to take the longer and currently safer route toward the Toy Box's main exit.

On every side naked breasts wobbled. Penises bobbed.

Flabby asses jounced. A purple-haired male gnome covered head-to-toe in whipped cream raced along shrieking loud as a tweenage girl, specks of cream flying off him to spatter the walls, the floor, and the faces of everyone in his wake. The morbidly obese woman Reynard had seen through the vent in room 304 puffed along as best she could, the dwarf she had been servicing clutched so tightly to her ample bosom it was a wonder the little fellow didn't get smothered amid the rolls of pink flesh. At one point Reynard collided with a middle-aged human woman who wore only a leather harness and a collar with a leash trailing behind, and it was only after the woman had mumbled a distracted apology and sprinted away that he realized she had been Derry Kellio, the Kansian ambassador to Peridor.

The stream of evacuees turned right, then left, then right, then right again, and finally came to the wide marble staircase leading down to the Toy Box's grand lobby with its crystal chandeliers, burgundy chaise longues, and gilt-framed erotic art. Trying to make their way up the stairs against the frantic tide were six of Bargeillian's bodyguards and a dozen of the Toy Box's security personnel.

Across the landing at the top of the stairs, another corridor stretched away. This was the last stretch of the route he and Zezzy had originally planned to take, the route down which the creature had stormed toward the security guards.

It was also the route the creature was close to the end of, judging by the screams, gunfire, and smoke coming from a side-corridor that met up with the main corridor about fifty feet past the staircase. As Reynard watched, wondering just how close the creature was, the top half of one of the guards, loops of intestines trailing behind him like the world's worst prolapse, shot into view from the side corridor, slammed into the wall of the main corridor, leaving a huge expressionistic blotch of blood and viscera on what appeared to be an original Zogodogo oil painting, and tumbled to the floor.

This gruesome spectacle sent everyone on the staircase into more of a frenzy than ever. Shrieking louder than banshees, they stampeded forward, driving the bodyguards and security personnel back toward the lobby.

Reynard and Zezzy were almost halfway down the stairs when a mechanical whir grew audible behind them, and the screams of the crowd's rearmost members rose several notches, shifting from fear to pure pants-shitting terror. Reynard twisted around as best he could in the clumsy costume just in time to see the creature emerge from the main corridor and step onto the landing.

The robot had changed so much Reynard thought at first he was looking at an entirely different entity. Its body was now larger than an adult man and bristled with a scrotum-tightening array of deadly appendages, including jointed arms tipped with blades, flexible whip-like rods, a pair of huge metal lobster claws, and over a dozen gun barrels that could swivel about to point in nearly any direction desired. What's more, the aperture below the blinking light (which had turned purple, oddly enough) was still there, only now it was the size of a Rottweiller's open mouth and contained a row of missiles the size of cigars.

"Oh, come on!" Zezzy cried. "How can it have gotten that much bigger? Hasn't anyone told this thing the laws of physics?"

The guards down below opened fire. Some of the evacuees on the stairs wisely ducked. The others, too panicked to notice the gunfire, continued trying to flee and wound up tripping over those who had ducked. A few also got hit by friendly fire and collapsed limp and bleeding onto the stairs. Their fallen, twitching bodies of course tripped up still others, and so on and so on until all progress was brought to a halt.

After hunkering down with Zezzy against the stairwell's railing, Reynard dared another glance back. The creature, seemingly oblivious of the bullets denting its metal hull, had paused upon the landing and was sweeping its front end back and forth across the crowd. Suddenly it froze, and the purple light blinked faster, as if in excitement. It was pointed right at Reynard and Zezzy.

"Fuck!" Reynard seized Zezzy's hand. "We're out of here."

Without even bothering to look over the edge to see where they would land, Reynard hopped the railing with Zezzy in tow.

And not a moment too soon: As they plummeted toward the lobby fifteen feet below, gunfire strafed the section of staircase they had just vacated, filling the air with blood and screams and chips of marble.

Reynard landed feet-first on a chaise-longue. Zezzy missed it by inches and crashed to the floor with a pained yowl.

"Fuck!" she screamed, rolling back and forth on the gold-and-green Briéskan carpet and clutching her left shin. "My fucking ankle!"

"Can you move at all? We kinda need to hurry."

"No shit. Help me up." She stretched out a hand. He took it and pulled her to her feet. Or *foot*, rather, since she kept her injured foot in the air.

Reynard glanced up at the staircase, half afraid he would see the creature clambering over the railing toward them. There was no sign of it. The guards' gunfire had intensified, he noticed. Perhaps that was distracting the creature. Perhaps the guards would continue distracting it long enough for him and Zezzy to make their escape.

Half a second after he had entertained this hopeful thought a massive explosion rocked the bottom of the stairs where the guards were. Chunks of marble and bits of people showered down all over the lobby. A hand still clutching a gun hit the ground a few feet away from Reynard and Zezzy.

Reynard took a quick look around, assessing his options. The Toy Box's main entrance faced the stairwell, so that was definitely a no-go. More promisingly, behind the stairwell, at the rear of the lobby, hallways extended to both the left and the right. People were fleeing down each of them in equal numbers.

"Where do those hallways go?" he asked Zezzy. Behind them, the remains of the security team resumed firing at the creature, while far away in the distance the wail of Watch van sirens grew audible. "Is there a back exit?"

"Um, yeah," Zezzy said, her voice thick and slow. "We come into work that way. We, uh…I think…um, I think I'm not…uh…" She swayed on her foot. Through the eyeholes of the baby mask, he saw her eyelids flutter and her eyes roll up, then she toppled sideways. Somehow he managed to catch her before she cracked her head open on the marble floor.

"Fuck," he muttered. This just got worse and worse. He stared at her limp body in his arms. He supposed he could just leave her here…

But no. She could finger him. Besides, he kind of liked her.

He slung Zezzy's limp body over his shoulder and made his way as fast as he could to the rear of the lobby. There, he waffled a moment, torn between the two hallways, which appeared pretty much identical: wood paneling, brass lamps, numerous doors, and a right-angle bend about fifty feet down. He finally chose the left-hand hallway for no particular reason, and joined the press of bodies therein.

While the lobby continued resounding with explosions, gunfire, and screams, the bottlenecked evacuees advanced slowly down the corridor. Too slowly for Reynard's comfort. Unlike the rest of the cattle in this chute, he knew exactly what the creature was after, and hence knew it was only a matter of time before the damn thing made its way back here. Alas the cattle were too tightly packed in the corridor for him to be able to shoulder his way through, so he just glowered at the witless heads in front of him and silently exhorted them to move faster. In doing so, his gaze fell upon a woman a few feet ahead of him and to his right. She had shoulder-length black hair and light brown skin, and wore a pink-and-white outfit reminiscent of a nurse's. Though he could see her face only in one-quarter profile, he was sure it was Solace, a surety that was confirmed a few seconds later when she glanced back, clearly worried about the creature's current whereabouts. Her eyes settled for a moment on Reynard—or rather, on the GO GO DREAMY costume, for she had no way of knowing who was inside it—and her eyebrows rose a fraction in surprise. Then her eyes moved on, and she turned back around.

Reynard, on the other hand, couldn't stop staring at her. What was she doing here? Was she a prostitute? A client? More likely the former, given the cute little nursey outfit she was dolled up in.

Damn! He never would have imagined her working a job like that. If this place stayed open (an admittedly dubious prospect at this point), he would have to return for a private session.

The crowd inched forward. The right-angle turn up ahead drew closer. A gust of cool fresh air blew through the

GO GO DREAMY mask's eye-holes, stirring the stuffy air within and partly drying the sweat on Reynard's face. At the same moment, he heard clear, unmuffled sounds from outside—shouts, Watch sirens, passing traffic. There had to be an open door not far past the corner, then. Thank the Twelve.

An explosion boomed behind him. He turned. There was now a smoking hole in the back wall of the lobby with shards of wood and plaster and twisted fragments of broken bodies strewn around it. Other, less broken bodies lay screaming and burning nearby. One of Bargeillian's black-suited bodyguards backed into view at the end of the corridor, his teeth clenched with determination as he fired round after round at something just out of sight in the lobby. He kept firing even as a metal tentacle tipped with something that looked like a meat cleaver whisked out and neatly lopped off his head. The head and the body toppled away in opposite directions, blood geysering, the body's spasming hand firing off two more shots, one of which disappeared into the neck of an extremely fit naked man at the back of the crowd in the hallway. Blood jetting from what was likely a severed artery, the man made a gargling sound and sank out of sight. An instant later the robot appeared at the mouth of the corridor and peered down it, its purple light blinking rapidly. The damn thing was now the size of a horse.

"Shit!" Reynard hissed. He whirled back around and began pushing harder than ever against the evacuees ahead of him. Fortunately everyone else had the same idea, and the crowd surged ahead.

He was only five feet from the bend when the gunfire started. The hallway filled with screams. Reynard felt a brief tug at the top of the GO GO DREAMY mask and saw a few bullet holes appear in the wall ahead of him. Gritting his teeth, he drew upon some hitherto-untapped reserve of strength and muscled forward, sending heads knocking and bodies tumbling. In what seemed like no time, he found himself at the corner, with Solace right beside him. He seized her around the waist with one puffy white elephant arm, causing her to yelp in startlement, then pressed her to him and continued barging forward, carrying her and Zezzy to cover around the corner.

Though the gunfire ceased the moment they were out of the creature's sight, though he was wheezing for breath from the weight of the two women, though so much sweat was pouring off him his feet were squishing in the costume's boots, he didn't stop or slow down. He just kept on shouldering forward because he felt sure he knew exactly what the robot was going to do next.

He had made it to within an arm's length of the open double doors at the end of the corridor, finally in sight of the outside world—the blue sky, the white clouds, the Toy Box's green manicured lawn across which evacuees were sprinting away while a crew of Watch officers sprinted forward—when a missile exploded at the bend in the corridor behind him. The resultant shockwave flung the entire mass of evacuees forward, sending Reynard, Zezzy, and Solace straight through the open doorway to collapse amid a heap of others on the sidewalk outside.

Slowly the mass of groaning, shell-shocked bodies unsnarled themselves and rolled away or rose shakily. Ears ringing, flesh still vibrating from the blast, Reynard pushed himself to his feet, re-slung the still-unconscious Zezzy over his shoulder, then helped Solace up. Drops of blood gleamed in her hair. Thankfully the blood didn't appear to be hers. She looked back through the open doorway at the heaps of unlucky evacuees who had been too close to the explosion and now lay in mangled bloody piles inside.

"By the Twelve…" She looked at Reynard. "You…you saved my life."

Not wanting to risk speaking even in a funny voice—he wasn't sure he could pull it off in his current state of spacey exhaustion—he extended one GO GO DREAMY arm and stuck up one fat GO GO DREAMY thumb.

Solace just blinked at him, looking bewildered. Then her eyes shifted to something over his shoulder and widened in horror. At the same time mechanical whirs sounded from the corridor at his back.

Not even bothering to look, he shoved Solace as hard as he could into the bushes next to the sidewalk then raced away in the opposite direction. Behind him, the Watch officers on the lawn opened fire. The creature opened fire in return.

After he had gone about fifty feet, Reynard paused to look back and was relieved to see one of the officers leading Solace and the rest of the survivors away from the melee. The other officers' fusillade was keeping the creature contained in the doorway for now, and more officers were racing across the lawn to join the battle, many of these newcomers equipped with more powerful ordnance: grenade launchers, zonar cannons, rapid-fire rail guns.

Reynard turned and ran on, soon ducking behind a row of hedges to get out of sight of the creature and the officers, then following the hedges toward the property's outer wall.

On his shoulder Zezzy stirred and moaned.

"You awake finally?" he said.

"Uhhh." A pause, then: "Ow! Put me down!"

"What about your foot?"

"It's not my foot. I just healed that."

"You what?" He slipped her off his shoulder, glad to be free of the weight.

"I healed," she said, twisting around to look at her backside. "My ankle was broken. I knitted it back together. I'm a Level 4 metamorph, remember? I can do that with my body."

"Nice trick."

"Yeah. It's not as easy getting bullets out of my ass, though."

"Bullets?" He craned around her body for a look at her rear end. Indeed, in the seat of her red mage robe was a small round hole, the fabric around it stained a darker red. "Sorry. I didn't even notice that."

"It's okay," she said, voice tight with exertion. "You got me out of there, so it's cool. Besides, I can fix it; it's just not easy. I have to make the flesh sort of harden and flow around the bullet, pushing it back toward the surface and knitting the wound closed behind it as it goes. I did it once before when..." She gasped. "There we go." She stepped to one side, revealing a bloody bullet on the grass.

"You're full of tricks," he said.

"You have no idea."

There was a deep, reverberating boom powerful enough to make nearby trees shake and Reynard and Zezzy totter on their feet. In the sound's wake came the roar of part of the Toy Box collapsing. That hadn't been one of the creature's missiles. That had been a Crux implosion bomb. Apparently the Watch had felt the situation was dire enough to resort to scorched-earth methods.

Reynard and Zezzy watched a cloud of gray smoke rise up over the tops of the hedges.

"It seems kind of soon to be using something like that," Zezzy said.

"Unless someone at the Watch already knows what they're dealing with. That thing came out of their chief's body, after all."

They stared at each other a moment.

"We'd better get *way* the fuck out of Peridor for a long, long time," Zezzy said.

"Agreed," he replied. "But first let's find somewhere to ditch these clothes and get cleaned up."

It wasn't until that night, as they drove west toward Quontoon in Reynard's Blissmobile PurplePurr, that he broached the subject that had been nagging at him since the Toy Box's back hallway: "So, um, I saw a woman while we were escaping. One of the prostitutes, I think."

Zezzy glanced at him but said nothing. She had been abnormally quiet and surly ever since they hit the road. He wasn't sure if she was exhausted, if the horrors of the day had finally caught up with her, or if she blamed him for the loss of her job, friends, etc. Maybe all three.

"I think I know her," he went on. "She has, uh, black hair, light brown skin. Kinda thin. Nice teeth."

Zezzy rolled her eyes. "That could be one of, like, ten billion people. Besides, are you sure she wasn't a client or something?"

"No. But she was dressed in this sort of pink-and-white outfit like a nurse."

"Oh! You're talking about Consuela. She's the resident clinician."

"Clinician?"

"Sure. By law every brothel has to have an onsite clinician. You know, someone to check the workers for diseases, make sure everyone's up to speed on health issues, distribute contraceptives, shit like that."

"Ahhhh." Reynard nodded. Yep. That made a lot more sense than her being a prostitute. "Any idea what her last name is?"

She sighed wearily, as if the question were an enormous imposition. "I don't know. I hardly ever dealt with her. If you're that curious you could try contacting the Toy Box's management."

"Uh, think I'll pass."

"Figured as much." She gazed out the window at the starlit surface of the Saros River for a moment, then turned to look at him again, her expression pinched with what looked like jealousy despite her repeated protestations that their relationship was strictly professional. "So where do you know her from anyway? She's not a con, is she? She always struck me as a total square."

"No, she's not a con," he said. Then he chuckled. "She's just someone I always happen to run into when there are killer robots on the loose."

Zezzy's eyes narrowed, and she sank down into her seat with her arms folded across her chest.

"Fine, don't tell me, jackass," she muttered.

7

The T-Net
6692 A.C.

Telepathic Network, Strain 23X: Archive (General): Psionic Transcript of the QuatWorld Lounge, June 21, 6692; 8:34pm-9:11pm:

berrylady8: Hey, everyone!

shiransbadassdeathstick: Howdy.

snarkygirl: Hey.

heliz: Zangin'!

berrylady8: Did everyone read my post yesterday?

snarkygirl: I did indeed.

heliz: Ain't had time.

raman(00): Hey, Berry. Yeah, read it. Found it interesting.

darner25: Hello. New here. What was the post?

berrylady8: I'd love to hear everyone's opinions on the subject, if you'd care to discuss it. And darner25: Nice to meet you; the post is here: QUATWORLD: BRANCH-15 (DISCUSSION): TWIG-11902 (PLEASE READ!). I'd love your input as well.

raman(00): FWIW, I think it's a logical extrapolation, though the one Quat went with in the movie seems just as valid. Given what (admittedly little) we know about the government of Drell back then, they may well have had a special squad devoted to seeking out the Database. Or not. Without any real hard evidence, I can't endorse either extrapolation. All I can say is they both seem valid.

grandpa-heppel: Greetings, berrylady8. I read it with great interest, and you present quite a cogent argument. As raman(00) said, it does lack the dramatic punch of Quat's version, but that does not make it any less plausible, and in fact may well make it moreso. In its own way, your theory is quite original. I don't believe I've ever heard anyone propose that the Database was located right in the heart of the city. Most (like Quat) put it outside the limits of Drell proper or in the elaborate and probably mythical sewer system.

snarkygirl: Or in a glittery undersea grotto filled with cute widdle starfish!

berrylady8: Yeah, well, the less said about Kebel's rather *unique* extrapolations the better.

shiransbadassdeathstick: Crud, I didn't even know there was a posting.

heliz: It's just the usual extrapolatory whackiness. I'm not really into that hypothetical stuff. I just liked the movie.

berrylady8: That's fine too, Heliz. I don't expect everyone to share my rather geeky interest in history.

heliz: Hey, you know me—I just come on here to talk about the sex scenes!

snarkygirl: Yes, we're all painfully aware of that.

raman(00): I have to admit, I think I like your take on it better than Quat's, berrylady8, but only because yours is more realisitic and seems more probable. That said, the extrapolation Quat used in *Covert* was more entertaining and made for better film-making. No offense.

berrylady8: No offense taken, raman(00).

snarkygirl: raman(00), probability itself is no good reason to believe something, despite what legions of math nerds say. If we believed things only according to their probability, then we would have no choice but to disbelieve that the War of Unification occurred, that Lal and Ralaro Omroth died simultaneously, that Element Man returned, and that the Cataclysm happened. Which is not to say that berrylady8's theory is incorrect, of course.

darner25: Okay, I read it. Very interesting theory. Very sensible. I think I'd side with it over Quat's extrapolation.

berrylady8: Thanks for the support, darner25.

shiransbadassdeathstick: I read it too. Well, skimmed it. No opinion. Sorry. I side with heliz on things like this. Well, not that I'm all about the sex scenes (not that they're bad) but all those annotations make my head hurt. I like Quat for his artistry—his technique, his sense of pacing, his use of sound and music. That's what jolts *my* nads. But if you must have an opinion, I think it's kinda unlikely the Database would be right in the middle of the city, just a few blocks from the government buildings and everything. You can't keep something like that secret in a location like that for hundreds of years!

heliz: I think he's got a point, berrylady8.

snarkygirl: On the contrary. Drell was a *city*. Cities are huge, complex places with so many nooks and crannies and hidden alleys and sub-sub-sub-basements that not even the most determined urban explorer could find them all. I, for instance, live in a city, and though I've lived in the same apartment for over a decade, I couldn't tell you the first thing about the interior or contents of the building right across the street. For all I know, it could be full of ghouls. Or, worse, professional movie critics.

grandpa-heppel: I second snarkygirl's comments. In fact, I'd go one further and say that the location posited by berrylady8 is ideal for the Database: far enough (relatively) from the government buildings to ensure that no one from said government would stumble across it by accident, yet not so far as to be outside the limits of the city proper and thus prey to the countless monsters abroad at that time. And by putting it near an area full of taverns, it helps explain any suspicious traffic at odd hours.

heliz: Yeah, while also risking exposure to tavern traffic at odd hours!

snarkygirl: Yes, because those late-night drunks are such keen-eyed observers. Hm. The more I think about it, the more and more I like berrylady8's theory. It doesn't require us to swallow something as inherently ludicrous as Quat's battle-scholars grimly saving heaps of old scrolls from parchment-hungry wyverns.

grandpa-heppel: Ha! Well put, snarkygirl. And amusing to boot, as always.

shiransbadassdeathstick: Geez, I thought the two of you liked the movie!

snarkygirl: I can't speak for g-h, but I absolutely adore the movie and think it's a brilliant piece of art. But that doesn't mean I believe it's literally true.

grandpa-heppel: I concur. I can respect a man's opinion, and even find great eloquence in his utterance of it, without sharing that opinion myself.

shiransbadassdeathstick: Okay, I admit Quat's "battle-scholar" thing was over the top (though in a fun way), but I still think having the Database just a few blocks from the government buildings, including the freaking *military barracks*, and not only that, but having security that wasn't much better than a secret password, is going to the opposite extreme. This was Drell we're talking about, remember. They had one crazy weapon-hoarding, monster-hating government.

darner25: Yeah, and they were too busy looking for weapons and using those weapons to kill monsters to go rooting around for musty books and artifacts they considered practically worthless. I'll wager the government simply forgot about the Database after a couple of centuries. If so, it doesn't seem likely the Database would need much more security than a big, badass dude named George.

heliz: Fucking har! George! Love it!

shiransbadassdeathstick: I don't buy that. I just can't see the Database folks thinking like that. I mean, if you were dealing with something of great value, wouldn't you wanna protect it better?

grandpa-heppel: I would surmise that they likely adopted an extremely paranoid and secretive attitude at first, but as decades passed without incident, their guard slackened. Consider the time-span we're talking about, and then consider the differences that transpire simply between one generation and the next. What the elder group deems of vast importance, the younger dismisses as trivial. The Database existed through dozens of generations, and the attitudes of those generations surely shifted.

heliz: Yeah, so maybe there were a couple generations that went all battle-scholar.

snarkygirl: Actually that raises an interesting point: Are we sure the Database was in the same place during all those hundreds of years?

raman(00): Probably. Have you ever tried to move a warehouse full of material?

snarkygirl: It would be a massive undertaking, I'm sure. But not impossible.

shiransbadassdeathstick: More or less possible than sitting unnoticed right under the government's nose for umpty-hundred years?

snarkygirl: More, I'd say. A lot more. Then again, that's assuming the estimates of the Database's size are accurate. What's your take on that, berrylady8 (if you're still around)? You seem to have done a considerable amount of research into the Database.

berrylady8: I'm still here. I'm just following the conversation with keen interest. As for the question of the Database's size…well, it would change over time, of course. We know how large it was when the government handed it off to Lummy Hood. It was surely many times larger than that by the time of the fire.

heliz: Lummy Hood. I don't know why, but that name always makes me giggle.

shiransbadassdeathstick: That brings up another point. If the Database grew so much, where did it grow into? If they didn't move it, they would've had to knock down walls or fill up an entire building or something. That's one advantage of Quat's theory. Since he puts the Database outside the city proper, it could sprawl out as far as it needed to. But inside the city? How big could it grow then?

berrylady8: I would imagine they did exactly as you suggested: Knocked down walls or filled a whole building.

grandpa-heppel: Also, it seems more than likely that Lummy Hood and the other early caretakers of the Database took its future growth into account when they chose a location. Though they lived long ago, it does not follow that they were less intelligent than us.

darner25: Excellent point.

heliz: Okay, that's the second time Lummy Hood's been mentioned. Good place to quit. I'm off to bed. Got an early morning tomorrow. Night all.

snarkygirl: Nightie-night.

berrylady8: Good night.

shiransbadassdeathstick: Hh. So I guess everyone's on board with the idea that the Database was in the middle of a busy city?

raman(00): I wouldn't say I'm "on board" with it. Like I said before, I find it a bit more logical than Quat's notions, but I'm a practical sort of fellow, so I can't really get behind any theory when there's a total lack of evidence.

snarkygirl: As they say, lack of evidence is not evidence of lack.

raman(00): No, but it's not proof of anything either.

darner25: Well, I have to say I find berrylady8's theory completely logical and realistic. And though Quat's an entertaining director, logic and realism aren't always his strong suits. I mean, just look at *Stray*.

raman(00): Whoa! Don't say that too loud! Them's rumble words round here! That film has a rabid fanbase!

snarkygirl: Don't worry. The new guy'll learn fast. Especially if he says something like that when quatbitch182 is in the Lounge.

raman(00): Oh, yeah! That'll ignite a firestorm as bad as the one that destroyed Drell!

shiransbadassdeathstick: I think people get too worked up about the factual details. Quat's awesomeness as a director is based on his entertainingness.

grandpa-heppel: No one disputes that. His status as the UR's greatest living director is well merited, in my opinion. But when one's extrapolations get as wild as his, people will notice. And talk about it. Alas I think we've reached the point where the film industry demands such wildness. People have come to expect wilder extrapolations. Without such excess, a film can't find a wide audience.

berrylady8: I know, and that's sad. I dislike such sensationalism.

grandpa-heppel: As do I. In Quat's case, however, his brilliant artistry makes his sensationalism more palatable.

shiransbadassdeathstick: If he was going only for sensationalism, he woulda made the movie about the Peridor Archives instead. I mean, the Archives had that whole crazy history, what with all the Elders involved, and the Ox Kings, and all those ten-year-long voyages all over the place, and everything.

raman(00): The Archives have been done to death, though. And with a few obvious exceptions, Quat clearly prefers to bring to light obscure backwaters of history, like in *Bitter* and *Blackout*. Hardly any filmmakers have dealt with the Database.

snarkygirl: Yeah, well, now a whole shitload of third-rate filmmakers will deal with exactly that in a parasitic effort to cash in on this film's popularity.

shiransbadassdeathstick: So sad, yet so very, very true.

darner25: Well, maybe one of them will be wise enough to adopt berrylady8's ideas.

snarkygirl: Wow, suckup much?

darner25: Not at all. Just able to recognize quality and intelligence when I see it.

berrylady8: Why thank you, darner25. It's lovely of you to say so.

darner25: I mean it. I have something of an interest in history, including the Drell Database, and I think your ideas fit the facts perfectly. Seriously. I've spent a long, long time thinking about these things.

berrylady8: A long, long time, eh? What are you, an Elder? ;)

darner25: ;)

snarkygirl: Oh, for Vävel's sake, get a room already.

raman(00): Squee! Name the baby after me! I'm out for the night, my SO's home! Bye all!

darner25: Good night, raman(00). Nice to meet you.

berrylady8: Night, raman(00). And snarkygirl: You are rude. Like usual. :)

snarkygirl: Hey, the name was chosen for a perfectly good reason.

berrylady8: So, darner25, what other avenues of history are you interested in? I'm something of an amateur historian myself.

darner25: Oh, a whole city's worth of avenues, actually. For instance, lately I've been reading up on the Shen Mystery Scroll.

grandpa-heppel: Ah, now there's a fascinating subject. So much so, in fact, that it retains its fascination despite having been so heavily extrapolated about.

berrylady8: Indeed. I've done a fair amount of reading into that myself. Which theory of its origins do you prefer, darner25 (if any)?

darner25: I've always been partial to the idea that it was an elaborate hoax.

snarkygirl: Oh, not *that* old chestnut!

darner25: I'm not saying I believe it. I just think it's fun to think about. At this late date, I doubt the real truth about the Scroll will ever be known.

berrylady8: Hm. We'll have to agree to disagree about that, then, for I'm convinced it's exactly what it appears to be:

a batch of brilliant love poems hidden away during the Age of Chaos to protect them from harm.

shiransbadassdeathstick: Bleh. I'll take hoaxes over slobbery romance any day.

darner25: Oh, I enjoy them both in equal measure. :) On that note, sadly, I must go. I had a busy day today. It was nice meeting you all. I'll definitely be back tomorrow. This is too much fun.

snarkygirl: Bye, darner25. Ah, another nut for the mix. Just what we needed.

grandpa-heppel: I rather liked him. He seemed a good deal more mature than many of the kids on here lately.

snarkygirl: Yeah, the release of the movie really lowered the Lounge's IQ.

berrylady8: Why are we calling darner25 a he? Do you guys know this for a fact?

shiransbadassdeathstick: He's a he.

grandpa-heppel: Oh, I know nothing for certain. It was merely the impression I got based on darner25's attitude and so forth.

snarkygirl: Yeah, same here. Just the impression I got. Sometimes you can just tell, you know?

berrylady8: Very true.

Telepathic Network, Strain 23X: Archive (General): Psionic Transcript of the QuatWorld Lounge, June 22, 6692; 6:15pm-6:37pm:

berrylady8: You're back already!

darner25: Yup. Can't keep away.

berrylady8: Have you been here long? Has anyone else been in here today?

darner25: I've been here since around 5. Somebody named

reaperman was here when I first entered, but he left shortly thereafter.

berrylady8: I'm sure that must have come as quite a relief. Har.

darner25: Yeah, well, I hadn't wanted to say anything in case reaperman was a friend.

berrylady8: I don't think reaperman has any friends. I think he actually prefers it that way.

darner25: Good thing.

berrylady8: So…since it's just the two of us, why don't you tell me a little about yourself.

darner25: Only if you tell me about you in return.

berrylady8: Hmmm. How about this: I ask you three questions, then you can ask me three questions.

darner25: Why do I have to answer first?

berrylady8: It was my idea. First question: Are you a man or a woman?

darner25: A man. You realize, of course, you have no way of verifying anything I say.

berrylady8: I trust you.

darner25: Your final mistake…

berrylady8: I don't think so. Second Q: How old are you?

darner25: Older than you think.

berrylady8: Not fair. That's not a proper answer.

darner25: I said you could ask, I never said I'd answer.

berrylady8: Hmm…so cagey about your age. Maybe you're really a woman after all. :)

darner25: Har.

berrylady8: Third Q: Have you ever been to New Portland?

darner25: Solace?

berrylady8: Reynard! Yes! I knew it!

darner25: This is unbelievable!

berrylady8: Not really. Both of us have, shall we say,

specialized knowledge of the Drell Database, so it's inevitable we'd be drawn to something like this.

darner25: True. Hey, tell you what…why don't we exit the Lounge and continue this via T-mail. In private. I mean, we don't want to attract attention with info on…you know.

berrylady8: I was going to suggest the exact same thing. Here's my T-mail address: solace34*brask.

darner25: And mine: kaleidoscope999*bandernot. Talk to you soon.

T-mail transmission:
*From: Solace Tenant <solace34*brask>*
*To: Reynard Fuggs <kaleidoscope999*bandernot>*
June 22, 6692; 7:09 PM:

Hey, Reynard,

Wow, this is weird, isn't it? It's been, what, about 2000 years or so since we last saw each other? We've got a lot of catching up to do. The world has completely changed since then.

I can't wait to hear what you've been doing. As for me, the last time we met, I was a teacher, I believe. I've continued to do that from time to time. Mostly, though, I don't really hold any job. Over the years, I've managed to arrange my finances so that I don't have to work. If I do any work, it's because I want to. I've talked to a few other Elders over the years, and most of them do the same. It's pretty easy to get rich when you live this long.

Most of my free time is spent reading, traveling, writing, a few other things. And before you ask, the writing's mainly just a hobby. I've written many many things, and they almost always wind up in drawers, then thrown away after a few decades or centuries. All I've ever published is a few poems, and like most of my writings, they were pretty terrible.

But enough about me. Tell me something about you.

—solace

T-mail transmission:
From: Reynard Fuggs <kaleidoscope999*bandernot>
To: Solace Tenant <solace34*brask>
June 22, 6692; 7:59 PM:

Dear Solace,

You're right, this is quite weird. But then, it seems that our whole history of meet-ups and partings has been pretty weird, no?

Yeah, you were a teacher last time we saw each other. How could you forget that last meeting? I bled all over your couch and you were mad at me for being less than forthcoming about what had happened. I don't blame you. I would've done the same. I put you in an awkward spot, and I apologize. Water under the bridge, right?

I bet you're actually a really good writer and you're just being unnecessarily modest about it. Writing seems like something that would come easily to you. Any chance I'll get to read some of your work someday?

Since when is your last name Tenant? Is that a pseudonym? Or is it really your last name? Heck, I didn't know you *had* a last name, and at the risk of sounding jerkish, I never thought to ask. Then again, given how brief many of our previous meetings were, there wasn't usually a lot of time for questions.

Like you, I've managed to set myself up pretty well financially, so I do whatever strikes my fancy. A lot of what I've been doing lately falls under the broad heading of entertainment—stuff like juggling, acting, and so on. Not really theater work. More like street art, I guess you'd say. I enjoy it way too much to think of it as work.

In fact, that's what I'm off to do right now. Mail me back soon. I'd love to hear more about yourself and your life of late.

—Reynard

T-mail transmission:
*From: Solace Tenant <solace34*brask>*
*To: Reynard Fuggs <kaleidoscope999*bandernot>*
June 23, 6692; 9:23 AM:

Good morning, Reynard Fuggs!

Ha, I didn't know you had a last name, either.

Or do you? Is this a pseudonym? Mine is. Kind of. It's based on my real surname: 10-NT. Yes, back in Interon, my technologically advanced home reality, we had computer-assigned names composed only of numbers and letters. It was functional but lacked poetry. I suppose in a way that's why I've always found poetry and art in general so fascinating—it's the opposite of the rather sterile culture I grew up in.

I must say, I'm surprised to learn that you yourself have an interest in the arts-and-entertainment field. Juggling? I never would have guessed, but I love it! Tell you what: if you juggle flaming torches for me, I'll share some of my embarrassing poetry with you. Deal?

As for what happened in Shandar all those years ago: It is indeed water under the bridge. Times change. People change. The past is gone. The future has not yet come. Now is the only time there is.

So let's enjoy now.

More about me? Why? Do you need to sleep? Honestly, I'm not very interesting. Sometimes I volunteer at various local charitable organizations. I help house the homeless and feed the hungry. But I don't consider that a big deal, and certainly not worth talking about. It's what any right-thinking person should do. I only look forward to the day when it's unnecessary, when the governments realize that society should be structured to take care of people who need it. To bring everyone up instead of pushing everyone down. After all, why else did we invent government? I'm glad the general trend of Eridian government is heading in that direction, though I have concerns about the URWA becoming too powerful.

It's interesting, isn't it, to talk about trends and suchlike when you get to watch them unfold over thousands of years? It makes me a little sad for all the people who don't live more than eighty or ninety years. How little they see.

Then again, much of what I—and no doubt you—see is just repetition. Or at best, themes and variations. Immortality is both a blessing and a curse. Like most things, I guess.

Just for making me talk more about boring old me, you'll have to tell me even more about you.

—solace

T-mail transmission:
From: Reynard Fuggs <kaleidoscope999*bandernot>

To: Solace Tenant <solace34*brask>
June 24, 6692; 5:55 PM:

Dear Solace,

Actually, I didn't originally have a last name. Hardly anyone in my homeworld did. Since last names have become the norm nowadays here in Eridia, I've gotten into the habit of using one—and changing it periodically, for privacy's sake. I'm not one of those Elders who loves the limelight. Some of us, I have to admit, are total attention-whores.

I'd be happy to juggle flaming torches for you! Then again, meeting up might be a problem. Where are you living right now? I'm in Altolinda, on the coast of Twai. It's not the most populous area or the most well-known, but it's scenic and it's quiet. I've got a large manor overlooking the ocean. I spend every morning lounging in a local coffee shop called The Diving Bell. The rest of the day is spent strolling about, working on whatever performance pieces I'm working on at the moment, having a Queen Pithylia at the local bar, and taking naps. For some reason, I've been really big on naps the last decade or so. Oh, and I've also developed a fascination with Acme gadgets. When the latest catalogue arrives, I put everything else on hold till I've read it, and I always wind up ordering a few new toys to play with.

Interesting views on government. My own opinion on the government is, the smaller the better. I think people can do fine on their own most of the time, without intrusive bureaucracies nosing about. But then, I try not to discuss politics with people. It usually ends badly. Everyone gets too riled up.

Okay, that's enough from me for now. Your turn.

—Reynard

T-mail transmission:
From: Solace Tenant <solace34*brask>
To: Reynard Fuggs <kaleidoscope999*bandernot>
June 26, 6692; 8:39 AM:

Good Morning Reynard,

Truth be told, I've never even heard of Altolinda, though I have of course heard of Twai. It sounds lovely, though. Hmm. Maybe someday I should visit the area. I do enjoy traveling.

And a visit to Twai would require much traveling indeed: I'm living in Basilond, a smallish city in Serobar. How I got here is a longish tale I don't really feel much like telling. Suffice it to say, there was a man who turned out to be an unfaithful fool, alas. I haven't mustered up the energy or the will to move just yet. Fortunately, he has. He moved away with the notorious *her*. If I sound glib, it's really just a cover. The whole thing's still rather painful, even though it's now nearly a year in the past. I guess relationships have always been a weak spot of mine. Ah, me. I can be quite a fool for love.

I must say how remarkable it is that though we live thousands of miles apart, we can communicate nearly instantaneously with the T-Net. We had something like this in Interon, except instead of telepathy, ours was run by electromagnetism manipulated by tiny wafers of silicon (or something like that; I never really understood the technical details all that well). To be honest, I find it a little creepy that at the heart of this T-box I'm typing away at is a wad of a telepath's cloned brain cells suspended in bio-preservative fluid. But I wouldn't trade it for anything. I grew so used to the privations of the post-Cataclysm world that I'd forgotten what it was like to have technology like this. It's marvelous! For perhaps the first time, this world is starting to feel like home.

Speaking of tech, I'd love to know what sorts of Acme gadgets you enjoy. I myself have a fondness for their products. They produce such a dazzling variety of things.

I don't know how you can stomach Queen Pithylias. They're nice to look at but waaaay too potent for me. I'll stick with simple martinis, thank you very much. That is, on the rare occasions when I drink at all. I've rather fallen out of the habit of late.

Yes, perhaps we shouldn't discuss politics too much, though I have to say I definitely do not agree with your thoughts on government. Agree to disagree, I guess. That's one of the few sure things I've learned from my many years of existence. If we were meant to be the same, with identical beliefs and behaviors, we'd be insects or lesser robots rather than people. We all hold such wildly conflicting views on anything and everything, and I always find it thrilling to experience brand new ideas. Alas, when you've lived this long, new ideas become increasingly hard to find.

Ugh, listen to me babble. Your turn. Tell me something good.

—solace

T-mail transmission:
From: Reynard Fuggs <kaleidoscope999*bandernot>
To: Solace Tenant <solace34*brask>
June 27, 6692; 7:34 PM:

Dear Solace,

Serobar, eh? Never been to Basilond (passed close to it once, back around 3000 A.C. or thereabouts) but I spent some time in other parts of Serobar. I didn't like it, to be honest. Too archaic and stuffy and overloaded with political pomp and ceremony. Everyone was very humorless and spoke in a very formal way. Admittedly, that was a long time ago (a *very* long time, har) and maybe I only happened to see the worst of it.

As for gadgets, I'm currently rather partial to the official Acme Telescoping Object-Retrieval Unit & Bottom Biter, if only for the name. Despite the silly nomenclature, it's very useful. Basically it's just a button-activated serrated clamp on the end of a telescoping arm. I once had to use it to retrieve a key that had fallen down a grate.

I have to admit, I get Queen Pithylias mainly because I like watching the flames. They *are* strong. The bartender at the Sodden Sponge (the bar I go to) once told me I'm the only person who ever orders them, aside from the occasional college kid wanting to show off how bold he is. What can I say? I'm a sucker for cheap thrills. Except, given the insane number of ingredients they take, they're not all that cheap.

Sorry to hear about your man troubles. But what do you expect from lowly creatures like us men? Don't let us get you down. Not one of us is worth a single tear from your eye. :)

Interesting about the T-Net and its similarities with your home reality. My own reality, if you'll recall, was a lot more primitive, so all this tech is brand new to me…and I have to admit, I love it. It's all so amazing and time-saving and convenient. It's gotten to the point where I can't imagine life without it.

Tell you something good? Hmm…

Okay, how about this: We've resumed contact. I doubt I'll be able to think of anything better than that.

Now it's your turn to tell me something good.

—Reynard

T-mail transmission:
From: Solace Tenant <solace34*brask>
To: Reynard Fuggs <kaleidoscope999*bandernot>
June 28, 6692; 8:30 AM:

Good Morning, Reynard.

I must confess, you're right about Serobar overall. Even today it's pretty staid and stiff, with an atmosphere opposite of what I prefer and with types of people I don't really feel akin to. I need to move, to go somewhere new. But where? It seems liked I've lived pretty much everywhere in Eridia already, in some cases more than once (and in one case—Peridor—nearly ten times!). I think the next year or so will see me doing a lot of heavy thinking about where I want to go and what I want to do. To be honest, during the eighteen years I was with my ex-lover, I just sort of existed for him, you know? I didn't live for myself. Embarrassing as it is to admit it, it wasn't even my choice to move here. I generally went along with what he wanted. I fell into that peculiar mortal-immortal relationship pattern that I and a few other immortals I've met (don't know about you) are susceptible to: Since I loved him and knew his life would be so tragically brief, I let him have his way in most things, even if it was at my own expense.

Yes, I've told myself innumerable times that men aren't worth my tears, but somehow they always manage to elicit them anyway. *sigh*

I, too, am happy that we managed to reconnect, so I think that will count for my "something good."

Let's try something a little different: Tell me something about yourself I don't know.

—solace

T-mail transmission:
*From: Reynard Fuggs <kaleidoscope999*bandernot>*
*To: Solace Tenant <solace34*brask>*
June 29, 6692; 9:59 PM:

Dear Solace,

Honestly, I can't say I'm familiar with the relationship pattern you mentioned. But then, I keep myself too busy for relationships most of the time, and on the rare occasions I succumb, I try to avoid relationships with mortals. They're too full of problems and grief to be worth it. I've always felt more comfortable with others like us. There's a sort of intellectual, emotional, and experiential connection that just isn't possible with mortals.

It's funny your mentioning places you've lived: Just the other day I realized I couldn't recall where I lived during most of the 3100s. I knew that in 3099 I was living in Caiaxia, and in the 3180s and 90s I lived in Pithkaron. But I had (and still have) absolutely no idea where I lived in between. My memory's normally excellent (not a boast, just a fact), but every now and then something like this crops up. Oh, the perils of age, even among those of us who don't actually age.

As for something about me you don't know. Hmm. I

guess the first thing that springs to mind is the fact that I was briefly the mayor of a small town. By briefly I mean about two days. It's a long and silly and frankly unflattering story, so I won't get into it except to say that it was all due to a case of mistaken identity and copious amounts of alcohol.

I've spilled my beans. Now it's your turn: Tell me something I don't know about you.

And, hey, if you're trying to figure out where to live, I recommend Altolinda. As I said before, it's scenic and quiet. Plus there's good company. ;)

I hope all is well...

—Reynard

T-mail transmission:
From: Solace Tenant <solace34*brask>
To: Reynard Fuggs <kaleidoscope999*bandernot>
June 30, 6692; 6:59 AM:

Good Morning Mr. Mayor,

I bet you made a decent mayor, even if it was for only two days. I would love to hear the more detailed version of the story of your mayorhood sometime.

And Altolinda, eh? It's certainly something to consider. I should probably visit it first, though. Hmm...

Yes, I know it's probably best to avoid relationships with mortals—trust me, I've told myself that about a billion times—but there are so few immortals in the world that it's almost impossible. I'm not like you. I can't keep myself "too busy" for things like that. To me, intimate relationships are one of the things that make life so rich and wonderful. And painful, too, yes; but the pain, I think, is worth it.

And don't get me started on the subject of forgetfulness! My memory isn't anywhere near as good as I made it sound. I've forgotten so much over the years. It gets to be quite depressing sometimes. I'm sure you understand. We live so very long, and we don't have room in our heads for everything. Inevitably some things slip away, and all too often we don't get to choose what those things are. What goes, goes. Once I nearly forgot my mother's name. It took me ten minutes of steady thinking to remember it. I had the feeling that if I didn't do it then, I'd never do it at all, and it would have been lost forever. Sometimes I don't think people were meant to live this long. Our bodies and minds weren't designed for it. But then I reflect that we are self-correcting organisms and can change the parameters of our lives if we're determined enough. With intelligence and will, nothing is impossible. We must rely on optimism, yes?

Okay, here's something about me you don't know: I lived for a year on a nearly deserted island in the South Sea about three hundred years ago. It was very pleasant. I meditated a lot, learned how to fish (and how to gut and clean and cook the fish), and discovered a lot about myself. I stayed too long, though. By the time I left I was sick of the island and it took me a decade before I could bring myself to eat fish again.

Let's try some more Q & A. It's fun.

What is one thing you've never done but always wanted to?

Eagerly awaiting your response.

—solace

T-mail transmission:
From: Reynard Fuggs <kaleidoscope999*bandernot>
To: Solace Tenant <solace34*brask>
July 3, 6692; 10:23 PM:

Dear Solace,

I can't imagine living on an island for a year. I'm not surprised you were sick of it by the end. There's no way I'd do that, myself. Not for love or money. Then again, I suppose it would depend on how much money we're talking about...

I hope you're not just kidding about visiting Altolinda sometime. I'd love to see you again. Trust me, there's a lot more to see and do around here than you might think.

Hm. Something I've never done but always wanted to. I'd have to say write a movie. Seriously. I've always toyed with the idea, but never felt competent enough to sit down and do it. Maybe I should try. After all, I lived through the whole history of Eridia, so I've got plenty of first-hand knowledge to draw on. The time period I'd be most interested in writing about would be the early Age of Chaos, maybe even the fall of New Portland! The strife and uncertainty of that period was pretty awful at the time, but it makes for exciting viewing thousands of years after the fact.

It might surprise you, but I'm quite the movie buff. I remember when the technology first appeared, I thought it was ridiculous that people would just sit there gaping at things that weren't real for hours on end, but over time I too got sucked into the darn things, and now I've become one of those folks who can name every Wasp House film Yar Michelleinian appeared in.

Your turn. Something you've never done but always wanted to.

Till next time,

—Reynard

T-mail transmission:
From: Solace Tenant <solace34*brask>
To: Reynard Fuggs <kaleidoscope999*bandernot>
July 4, 6692; 7:01 AM:

Good Morning, Reynard,

A visit to Twai (and you) is a definite possibility. I've been trying to think of something to do for my birthday—it's September 19th, and I always try to take a trip or do something fun. Perhaps a visit to the east coast would fit the bill. Hm. I'll have to think about it. It's a big trip and would take a lot of planning.

And, ah, to write a movie. I, too, would like to do that. As I told you, I've written quite a lot over the years—books, essays, and reams and reams of lousy poetry. But never a movie, though I've always wanted to. Even before the Cataclysm, I toyed with the idea of writing one. Yes, we had movies in Interon but in some ways they were quite different from movies here. Our movies were almost always fictional. I never cease to be surprised at how low-class and childish fiction is regarded in Eridia. I mean, I know I shouldn't be so shocked; with Eridia's vast, rich history, why would anyone need to make anything up? But it's not what I grew up thinking of as movies. The extrapolatory stuff often comes close—filling in historical gaps and offering various interpretations of ambiguities often merges into fiction (especially Quat's *Covert*, har har!)—but even then it's always built on a basis of fact.

Anyway, although writing a movie is definitely on my list of things I've never done but wish to, it's not at the top. No, at the top would be to ride a dragon.

Yes, I know it's ridiculous and I'm sure you're laughing at me right now, but I love the idea. I've actually had dreams about it: straddling the hard scaly back, feeling the dragon's muscles rolling beneath me as the vast wings flap, the earth spread out miles below, cool clear air streaming across my face and blowing my hair back, the clouds around me tinged pink and orange by the sun hidden behind them—or maybe we're so high up we're above the sun (I know it's unrealistic and physically impossible, but that's how it is sometimes in my dreams), and me unable to stop grinning at the joy and freedom I'm feeling.

You must think me rather silly. Ah, well. And yes, I know there is probably no dragon in all of Eridia who would consent to being the personal vehicle of a silly girlie like me—even if I *am* older than any of them.

How's the weather out your way? We're in the middle of a massive heat wave here. For the last two weeks the average daily temperature has been 98 degrees. People just sit around most of the day, too listless to do much. Some normally conservative folk have even temporarily turned nudist. (And no, I'm not one of them!) We haven't had a single drop of rain in all that time, either, and if things don't change soon, drought will start becoming an issue.

Okay, we should do more Q & A. I rather enjoy it. Hmm…

Ah. I know. What was the happiest moment of your life? (So far, of course; I'm sure the future will be full of moments even happier.)

—solace

T-mail transmission:
From: Reynard Fuggs <kaleidoscope999*bandernot>
To: Solace Tenant <solace34*brask>
July 6, 6692; 10:00 PM:

Dear Solace,

It's funny that we both want to write movies. Maybe we should collaborate on something. However it turns out, it'd certainly be the most historically accurate movie ever made!

And no, I don't think your fantasy of dragon-riding is at all silly. It sounds quite beautiful, actually. I wish my own dreams were half so nice. I'll bet somewhere there's a dragon you could befriend and sweet-talk into taking you for a little ride. (Though I'm fairly certain no dragon would be able to take you above the sun.)

The heat is everywhere, actually. It's here too. Not quite as bad as what you're describing, but close. At midday the sun is oppressively hot in a way I haven't felt in centuries. Then again, I think the last few centuries have been colder than usual. Ever since the mid-5000s, actually. It must have been a Little Ice Age, or whatever they call it. At any rate, it's definitely over now. I heard a forecast the other day that said the heat is likely to get a lot worse before it gets better!

Honestly, I'm not sure I can think of a happiest moment. In a life this long, there are tons of happy moments, and they're all happy in different ways, so it's hard to rank them. If I really had to pick, then sappy as this sounds, I'd have to go with the first time I kissed a girl. Funny thing is, I don't remember the girl at all. No idea what she looked like or even what her name was. All I remember is how it felt. I remember the delicious tension of anticipation as I leaned in for the kiss, a sort of pleasant tingly tightness throughout my entire body. And then our lips touched and for one brief, beautiful eternity, all of reality was concentrated on a two-inch strip of soft, pink skin. Afterward, I was smiling for hours, dazed and giddy and buoyant with joy. I'd dreamt of kissing a girl for so long—I was kind of a late bloomer, romantically speaking, though I thought about such things constantly—and now that it had happened, I felt as if I had reached some sort of personal apotheosis, as if I could just die right then.

But then I moved on and discovered sex, and relationships got all weird and complicated. In a way, it was nicer when all there was was kissing.

Your turn. I've revealed embarrassing truths about myself and my past. It's only fair for you to do the same.

And let me know if you decide you want to visit Twai. I can help you work out arrangements at this end. You're even welcome to stay at my manor. There's plenty of room. In fact, you can have a whole wing all to yourself!

I hope all is well.

—Reynard

T-mail transmission:
From: Solace Tenant <solace34*brask>
To: Reynard Fuggs <kaleidoscope999*bandernot>
July 7, 6692; 5:43 AM:

Good Morning, Reynard,

Wow, you were right about the heat getting worse. It's even hotter now than it was when last I wrote. The temperature's a constant 101 degrees. My air chiller hasn't shut off in days. I'm fortunate I have it. Every day I hear news reports about people dying of heatstroke. Thankfully the Serobaran government is in talks with an air chiller manufacturer in Djoteth to buy a huge quantity of air chillers at a bulk discount then distribute them to those who can't afford them. Even then, though, it probably won't be enough for everyone.

My, your happy moment certainly was evocatively written. I can tell it made quite an impression on you. I feel kind of sorry for the girl, since you don't even remember her name. Though in a way I guess she should feel flattered that she's being remembered in some form so many millennia after she's just dust. Most people don't get anywhere near that much.

And yes, alas, the discovery of sex really does complicate everything, doesn't it?

My own happiest moment, as clichéd and sappy as it sounds, was the birth of my daughter Cara. Sometimes even now I still dream about her and miss her very very much. And she's been gone so long. Well, except in my heart. But the birth was so easy and painless. I really thought it would be difficult and agonizing. That's what I'd been led to believe by my experiences in Interon; there, babies were conceived outside the womb with their parents' genetic materials and grown in special incubators called Gestation Units, partly to spare the mothers the pain and risks of pregnancy and childbirth. So I'd grown up thinking childbirth was something terrible. Of course, after the Cataclysm I saw plenty of natural births, some painful, some not; but in my mind I remained convinced that were I ever to give birth it would be a torturous and perhaps even fatal experience. But when it came time for Cara to be born, it was swift and easy, and before I knew what was happening I had this chubby pink baby in my arms. She wasn't even crying; she was merely regarding me with that concerned, bewildered look babies often have, the one where it looks like they want to understand what something is but lack the words and concepts to make sense of it. I broke down at that point, I have to admit, just started bawling my eyes out. And you know what? Cara didn't cry even then. Instead she made this tiny cooing sound. It sounded almost empathetic, as if she wished to comfort me. Oh, she was so good and beautiful.

But listen to me going on. I'm starting to make myself cry. Time, I think, for me to sign off.

Be well.

—solace

T-mail transmission:
From: Reynard Fuggs <kaleidoscope999*bandernot>
To: Solace Tenant <solace34*brask>
July 8, 6692; 8:54 PM:

Dear Solace,

Wow! I was deeply moved by your description of Cara's birth and its effect on you. It sure beats my happiest memory by a long mile. Even though I met her only once, and then only briefly, I remember Cara very well. She seemed like a remarkable girl, and I'll bet she became an even more remarkable woman.

And about the Gestation Units in Interon: We're sure heading in that direction here, aren't we? We've already got special incubators very similar to that. Though they're only for emergency situations, I can easily see the day when people shift over to them fully in the name of safety and comfort.

How's the heat there? Amazingly enough, it's gotten considerably hotter here. Even the fishermen in this, one of the most fishingest towns in the United Realms, have taken to going out only early in the morning and late in the afternoon, when the sun's low in the sky. The rest of the day, they'd simply bake out there on those little boats with the sunlight reflecting off the water as if it were sheet metal. Trade is faltering, and when that happens, you *know* things have gotten bad.

I hope all is well.

—Reynard

T-mail transmission:
From: Solace Tenant <solace34*brask>
To: Reynard Fuggs <kaleidoscope999*bandernot>
July 9, 6692; 6:22 AM:

Good Morning Reynard,

The heat here is still terrible. I keep hearing about how in some places the Syrkranian gum in people's shoes and car tires has been melting, though some say that's only because the companies that manufacture them cut corners by not treating the rubber with certain chemicals that make it more heat-resistant. Don't know if that's true or not, but…wow, it sure is hot!

On the sort-of-bright side, the weather forecasts are saying we'll get a massive thunderstorm soon, big enough to end the drought, though the heat might linger on.

Yes, those new incubators are indeed a lot like Interon's Gestation Units. It's incredible how quickly the innovations are coming these days. I mean, they've finally put folks on the Moon, and they're talking about permanent moon-bases. Those were old news in Interon, but Eridia's catching up fast! I think all the input from different species, with all their different ways of thinking and seeing, really helps to foster progress. It's a shame it took a few thousand years before they trusted each other enough to really work together.

Thanks for the nice words about my description of Cara's birth, and about Cara herself. She was indeed a remarkable person. Have you ever had children? I can't remember (or maybe you never told me). I do recall that you were married when we met in Colbon, but you told me you were thinking about splitting up with her. Then you vanished—though I'm sure you had your reasons. ;) Whatever happened with that girl? I mean, I know she's gone now, but how did things work out? I don't think we ever talked about that, did we? If this is too personal for you to discuss, I'll understand, and sorry in advance if it is.

Peace be with you.

—solace

T-mail transmission:
From: Reynard Fuggs <kaleidoscope999*bandernot>
To: Solace Tenant <solace34*brask>
July 10, 6692; 9:03 PM:

Dear Solace,

And the heat wave smolders on. Today it was 103 in the shade. The town is dead, the streets empty, the fields brown and dry, the sand too hot to touch with your bare skin, and unlike in Serobar, there's no chance of a thunderstorm anytime soon. Oh, what I wouldn't give for a Little Ice Age right now.

I wasn't sure if you'd remember my long-ago wife Kay. As for how it turned out…well, let's just say you weren't the only one I disappeared on. I am sorry about that. I truly am. It was not because I wanted it. It was entirely against my will. I'd tell you what happened, but for one thing, I'm not entirely sure I can explain it in a way that would make sense, and for another, even after all these years it's still hard for me to talk about. Let me just repeat that I didn't mean or want to just vanish on you (or on Kay) like that, and I am deeply sorry it happened.

Did you hear Gordon Quat's announcement that he's planning to make only one more film and then retire? He refuses to say what the movie'll be about, only that it's a small, focused piece a lot like his first film, *Bitter.* I must say, it'll be disappointing not to have any more new Quat films to look forward to. The guy's been churning them out like clockwork for almost fifty years. I know that's not really a long time to folks like us, but in some strange way it feels like Quat's been around a lot longer than half a century.

In honor of his impending retirement, let's try another round of Q & A: What's your favorite Quat movie, and why?

Hope all is well,

—Reynard

T-mail transmission:
From: Solace Tenant <solace34*brask>
To: Reynard Fuggs <kaleidoscope999*bandernot>
July 13, 6692; 5:11 AM:

Good Morning Reynard,

Well, they said we'd have thunderstorms, and thunderstorms we had. Or rather, thunderstorm. One storm, the like of which I've never seen. It wasn't so much the force of it that was so remarkable; it wasn't like those destructive storms you saw in the decades after the Cataclysm. No this was remarkable because it was one horrible storm that went on and on for over forty-eight hours without end. It did let up a little a few times, just enough that we all thought it was finally passing, but then it would redouble in force within an hour and we were back where we started. They're saying it was a combination of factors: One, the storm was gigantic, covering pretty much the entirety of the Irian Lowlands; and two, the storm stalled out due to some weird confluence of weather systems that they explained on the local weather site but that didn't make a whole lot of sense to me. The storm just hung there for over a day without moving, or rather moving a little one way then back the other. Apparently there were a couple of places on the edges of the storm where the rain would stop as the storm-system drifted away, only to resume a few hours later as the storm drifted back. But those of us in the heart of it had it the worst. Over fifty people were killed during the course of it due to lightning, flooding, falling debris, and in one case, a bridge collapse. It was awful. Hardly anyone went outside. The winds drove the rain almost horizontal and pushed even the heaviest people around as if they were made of straw. And then of course, there was the constant lightning. I turned out the lights and watched the bolts flashing as bright and rapid as fireworks. It was scary but spectacular.

Ah, well. At least it's over now. I'm sure that was far more info than you wanted. Sorry, but major weather like this, while frightening, always fascinates me. We had nothing like it where I came from. In Interon, the weather was artificially regulated.

Sorry that I keep mentioning Interon. It's weird—at this point, the vast majority of my existence has been here in Eridia yet I still think of Interon as home. You'd think as my life rolls on, and my experiences build up and the bulk of my memories originate from happenings here in Eridia, that I'd think less about Interon as time passes. But the opposite is true. As the years go by, I find myself thinking about Interon more and more. Or least what I can remember of it. So much is gone…

But that's a topic we've already covered. Time to move on to other things…

I'm sorry about whatever happened in Colbon. It must have been pretty bad if you're still reluctant to discuss it after so long. If you ever do feel like talking about it, I'm here.

Yes, I heard about Quat's announcement. It's not exactly a surprise; he's getting pretty old. I think it's nice he's ending his career with something like *Bitter*, which despite its novice-filmmaker's crudity was quite a touching film. It will indeed be a poorer world, movie-wise, without him.

My favorite Quat movie. That's a tough one. After tons of deliberation, I think I'll have to go with the obvious choice and say *When I Die*. Not only is the story of the Berenyi Seven inherently dramatic and moving—so much so that it has become a sort of cultural foundation stone of the UR—but Quat managed to infuse it with a level of artistry and emotional power light-years beyond what anyone else had ever done with it (and a lot of anyone elses have done a lot with it over the years; I think I read somewhere it's the most-adapted story in the history of movies). The movie is a true masterpiece and a cultural touchstone. I doubt anyone can think of the Battle of Berenyi Pass anymore without thinking of Quat's version. And perhaps the most amazing thing is that he managed to do all this without contradicting a single historical fact! (Well, except the details of Vonor and Mendheina's first meeting. But I only know about that because I was acquainted with them personally.) (And some of the fashions were completely wrong, of course, but that's to be expected.)

Oh, for Quilith's sake, I'm really prattling on this time, aren't I? Time for me to go.

—solace

P.S. I forgot to return the question: What's your favorite Quat film? And please don't feel compelled to follow my babbly example. Brevity is nice too, or so I'm told.

T-mail transmission:
From: Reynard Fuggs <kaleidoscope999*bandernot>
To: Solace Tenant <solace34*brask>
July 13, 6692; 9:09 PM:

Dear Solace,

That must have been one incredible storm. I remember those post-Cataclysm storms and while, yes, they were incredibly intense, they never really lasted all that long. They just blew through and then the sun came out. The one you had, though…wow, I don't think I've ever heard of a storm like that before. Is the heat still an issue? It is here, with no letup in sight. Weather control like you had in Interon sounds like a spectacular idea. That gets my vote for the next big tech breakthrough in Eridia.

I find that my own memories don't work quite like

yours. As time passes, I remember less and less about my home reality. That's probably because I don't *want* to remember it. It was crude and ugly and primitive. Frankly, I prefer Eridia and wouldn't go back to where I came from for all the money in the world.

I agree that *When I Die* is indeed a masterpiece, but my own favorite Quat film is probably his most controversial: *Heavenly Nobodies.* Admittedly, part of the reason I love it so much *is* the controversy. To make a film positing an elaborate deception behind the founding of Dodecism was a bold, bold move, especially for someone at that stage in his career, with so much to lose. You have to admire that. But I also love it on an intellectual and artistic level. I mean, the way each of the film's twelve parts corresponds to one of the Twelve in pretty much every way imaginable—from the thematic concerns to the colors to the pacing—is simply breathtaking. As far as craft goes, I don't think Quat ever managed to top himself after that. But who knows, maybe this mysterious final film of his will top everything so far!

Talk to you soon,

—Reynard

P.S. Have you given any more thought about a trip out to Twai for your birthday?

T-mail transmission:
From: Solace Tenant <solace34*brask>
To: Reynard Fuggs <kaleidoscope999*bandernot>
July 19, 6692; 6:56 AM:

Good Morning Reynard,

Yes, *Heavenly Nobodies* was quite a brilliant film. But then, most of Quat's are.

Sorry to hear your heatwave is still continuing. Thankfully, it seems to be over for us. Ah, cool air.

I hope all is going well.

—solace

T-mail transmission:
From: Reynard Fuggs <kaleidoscope999*bandernot>
To: Solace Tenant <solace34*brask>
July 20, 6692; 10:03 PM:

Dear Solace,

Glad to hear the heatwave's over.

Yes, all is well with me. What about with you? Not to sound nosy, but is everything okay? Your last message was terser than usual. You're not mad at me about something are you? If so, I'm sure I didn't mean it, whatever it was :)

I hope everything's okay.

—Reynard

T-mail transmission:
From: Reynard Fuggs <kaleidoscope999*bandernot>
To: Solace Tenant <solace34*brask>
July 28, 6692; 7:17 PM:

Dear Solace,

Seriously, is everything okay? Has something happened? Have you been busy? This long silence isn't like you. It's

kind of worrying. Please alleviate my worries, if only tersely.
:)
    Your friend,

—Reynard

T-mail transmission:
From: Reynard Fuggs <kaleidoscope999*bandernot>
To: Solace Tenant <solace34*brask>
August 10, 6692; 5:38 PM:

Dear Solace,
    I don't know if something's happened, or if you've de-
cided you don't want to talk to me anymore for some reason,
or what. But whatever the case, at least let me know if you're
okay.
    Please. I'm worried.

—Reynard

T-mail transmission:
From: Solace Tenant <solace34*brask>
To: Reynard Fuggs <kaleidoscope999*bandernot>
August 23, 6692; 6:00 PM:

Reynard,
    I'm sorry I just disappeared without an explanation. I
really am.
    So here's the explanation:
    Some things came up in our dialogue—things you said,
comments you made—that made me realize just how little

we really know each other. I am not going to tell you what, and I know how unfair that sounds, but I really don't want to restart a dialogue.

Just because we're both Elders and have run into each other a handful of times over the last six thousand years, we used that to foster a false sense of familiarity. We don't really know each other at all. The times we met added up to, what, maybe a few days? A few days out of six thousand years.

We are strangers. That's all there is to it. And I think it's best and healthiest if we stop deluding ourselves that we know each other in any significant or meaningful way.

I will, of course, cherish the time we spent together, both in reality and over the T-Net, and perhaps someday we will meet again. But right now, we must bid each other adieu.

I hope your days are plentiful and bountiful.

—solace

T-mail transmission:
From: Reynard Fuggs <kaleidoscope999*bandernot>
To: Solace Tenant <solace34*brask>
August 24, 6692; 3:13 PM:

Solace,

I think you're being unfair. You won't tell me what it was I said to upset you, and you won't give me a chance to defend myself. Instead of trying to talk to me, you just slammed the door in my face.

You have hurt me. Badly. I am sorry beyond words if I said or did anything to upset you. That was never my intention. Why would it be? I have nothing but the highest regard for you, both as a person and as a friend. Any harm or insult was purely unwitting.

Maybe we don't know each other as well as we liked to think. But it doesn't follow from that that we're strangers. Not at all.

You mean more to me than you can possibly know, and you have no idea how much this unfairness wounds me.

Please, Solace, talk to me.

—Your friend Reynard

T-mail transmission:
From: Reynard Fuggs <kaleidoscope999*bandernot>
To: Solace Tenant <solace34*brask>
September 19, 6692; 4:18 PM:

Solace,

I know you don't want to talk to me anymore, but the heck with that, I'm going to wish you a happy birthday anyway.

So Happy Birthday.

—Reynard

[Message returned as undeliverable: T-mail address no longer extant.]

8

Nioedo

7407 A.C.

Reynard's boots clacked on the white floor tiles as he side-stepped a puddle of blood in the main hallway of the Seldon Street Wellness Center in downtown Nioedo. A trail of red drops led from the puddle to Healing Room 5, through the cracked door of which he caught a glimpse of a green-unitarded biomage tossing a bloody towel into a SaniCan while a young woman reclined on the Healing Couch behind him, looking relieved. The neck of her pink shirt was soaked with blood, but the wound responsible was now gone, healed by the biomage's inborn abilities.

Before either of them could notice him looking, Reynard swiveled his eyes away and continued on down the busy hallway, passing biomages consulting T-pads, aides escorting patients to Healing Rooms, friends and family anxiously awaiting news. He kept his gaze fixed on the main entrance a hundred feet ahead. He had come here on illicit business—namely to access the Center's internal T-Net and learn the status of Ravenna Smodge, who had been brought here for treatment in the wake of last night's botched data-heist at the Hexagon—but while that business was done, he wouldn't be free and clear until he was off-site. Continually looking around to make sure no one was noticing you was the surest way to get noticed. You had to walk as if you owned the world yet had no time for it; when you did that, people stayed out of your way. His attire helped, too, the carefully chosen black-and-white unitard, silver boots, and silver FyberSteel headband giving him the appearance of a top-tier professional. People were always more likely to trust someone well-dressed.

When the aides station appeared on the left, Reynard acted as if its hivelike activity weren't worth his attention. This was the biggest obstacle. Aides were notoriously nosy. A large part of their job was to keep the Center running smoothly, which meant that everyone and everything here was their business.

He was nearly past the station, and already beginning to bask in the pride of yet another success, when a figure in an aide's purple-and-white unitard separated itself from the incessant bustle to his left and stepped into his path, hands on hips.

"Reynard!" Solace said with a huge delighted smile.

He stared at her a moment, then shook his head.

"I'm sorry, ma'am. I think you have me confused with someone else."

She jerked her head back slightly, her happy smile morphing into one of puzzlement.

"Your name's not Reynard?"

"No. I'm Halfor Harriman." Indeed, should anyone scan the Realms Chip in his forearm, it would tell them exactly that. Of course, he had figured out long ago how to hack a Realms Chip to make it say anything he wanted. He was always amused that people trusted those things so much.

There was a long pause. Solace's puzzled smile slowly vanished. Her eyes narrowed.

"I'm sorry," she said, her gaze never leaving his face.

"But you look *just* like someone I know." The way she said this suggested she still thought the resemblance was more than accidental.

"Well…" Reynard spread his hands and grimaced to show his regret at having to let her down. "I'm not. Sorry."

She blinked at him, her eyes assessing him anew. It wasn't that she was starting to believe him, exactly. Rather, she was starting to doubt herself. There was, in fact, a difference. He didn't think he could make her fully believe him no matter what he did; but he could definitely make her doubt herself. And that was the war won right there.

He sensed she was about to apologize and leave, but he didn't want this to end so soon, so he looked her up and down—quickly, of course; most women like a look as long as it's no more than a flick of the eyes; linger anywhere too long and they'll feel violated—then smiled a little as if he liked what he saw (which he did, of course; though he loathed the current fashions, he had to admit Solace's lithe figure looked fantastic in a unitard) and said, "Seeing as how I've told you *my* name, it would be only fair for you to tell me yours."

Her eyes narrowed in suspicion. He stiffened inwardly while ensuring his calm veneer never wavered. Had he said something that gave himself away? If so, he couldn't see what.

"You *are* Reynard," she said. There was a pause, during which he raised his eyebrows in a perfect imitation of surprise. Doubt again clouded her face. "Aren't you?" She squinted at him like a tough cop peering at a suspected crook. "You *sound* just like him."

"Wow," he said with a laugh. "I've heard people say everyone has a double. I guess now I know who mine is. My evil twin, perhaps." He cocked an eyebrow. "Is he evil?"

She laughed. "Sometimes."

He gave her a questioning look. "So?"

She shook her head, confused: "So…what?"

"Your name."

A pause. Her eyes narrowed once again, but only slightly, barely more than a twitch of the eyelids.

"I'm Santvana."

"Nice to meet you, Santvana," he said with a big grin, looking just like any guy glad to have acquired a pretty girl's name. Behind the grin, he was cackling to himself at the instant's shock that flashed on her face. She had put a lot of stock in her fake name trick, sure that the lie would garner a reaction. But he had anticipated that gambit the moment he saw her eyes narrow. He was the trickster here, not her.

"Um, nice to meet you, too." Her voice was quiet, distracted. No doubt she was mentally retrenching.

He gestured at her outfit. "So, you work here, huh?"

"Yeah."

"What time do you get off work?"

Another pause, then: "Five."

"Well, if you don't have plans after work, can I take you to dinner?"

She hesitated, mouth half open, and eyed him closely as if he had just made a perplexing move in a difficult and elaborate chess game.

Then her face cleared and, seemingly free of suspicion now, she smiled.

"Sure. Dinner sounds great." She said it just like any woman flattered to be asked out by a handsome stranger.

Damn. He couldn't tell if she had decided that he was who he said he was, or if she was just playing along. Not that he minded. On the contrary, the uncertainty of the situation thrilled him. A certain world was a boring world.

And he had a feeling he was in for one very un-boring evening.

They met for dinner at Bistro 27, a chic restaurant five blocks north of the Wellness Center where Solace (or "Santvana") worked. It occupied most of the first floor of one of the few pre-Cataclysm buildings left standing in that neighborhood after the massive destruction the city suffered during the Last Great War over seven hundred years earlier.

Reynard had dressed as befitted the place's poshness, choosing a black-and-silver SynthSilk unitard accessorized with a white NuPlat headband and a white three-quarter length cape with numerous pockets, two of them hidden. On his feet were the same boots he had worn to the Wellness Center earlier, though between then and now he had scrubbed them well to ensure they were free of blood and any other stray bodily fluids.

When he arrived, exactly on time, Solace rose from the red padded bench in the lobby and gave him a smile and a wave. She wore a sleeveless black singlet whose legs extended only to mid-thigh and whose collar was cut low enough to provide a tantalizing peep of cleavage, plus a green half-cape, a green pouch-sash to hold her necessities and valuables, and a pair of white high-heeled boots. She had braided her hair and intertwined the braids in an elaborate bun atop her head, a 70-year-old style called Layered Organic that had lately become trendy again. He thought it looked terrible on her.

"You look great," he said.

"Thanks."

"I hope you weren't waiting long."

"Only a minute. I just got here."

"Oh, good."

The maître d', a five-foot-tall robot with a variety of limbs and sensory apparatuses bristling from its pyramidal body, rolled out from behind the podium on eight puffy tires and spread a pair of pincered arms in welcome.

"Is this the entirety of your party?" it said in a soft, pleasant voice.

"Yes," Reynard said.

"Excellent. Please follow me."

When the maître d' led them through a low archway and into the restaurant proper, Reynard's jaw dropped in astonishment. The room looked enormous, its dimensions many times larger than those of the building containing it. As they walked on and he looked closer, however, he realized its size was an illusion: The steel walls were polished to a mirror-like sheen that reflected the diners and the candlelit tables and the potted giant flytraps and the reflections from the other walls and the reflections' reflections and so on and so on to make the room appear as vast as a city block, an effect the high, steep-vaulted ceiling helped accentuate. It wasn't until they were halfway to their table that he noticed the room's other distinctive feature: The floor was made of thick glass, and beneath it a complex configuration of gears turned, some as small and delicate as snowflakes, others big enough to crush a house.

"I read up on this place on the T-Net before coming here," Solace said, voice low as if she didn't want the maître d' to overhear. "Apparently that's the original pre-Cataclysm machinery that did...well, whatever was done here. No one's quite sure what the building's original purpose was."

"Wow," Reynard said. "It's hard to believe something so old is still going after all this time."

She glanced at him uncertainly. If he were Reynard, he would know about her immortality and thus the comment would harbor a double meaning. But she couldn't be sure of his identity, so her only response was a barely audible laugh and a "yeah."

After seating them at a table for two near the back of the room, the maître d' sped away to tend to new arrivals, and their server appeared, a young, wiry Ajin man clad in the red tuxedo suit assigned to all of Bistro 27's bipedal employees. He bowed, introduced himself as Yif, and handed them menus and a wine list. After a brief discussion they ordered a bottle of Vävelaran Pink, 7067.

"So…" Solace said once Yif was gone. "Malfort, wasn't it?"

He gave a strained smile. "Halfor."

"Oh, I'm sorry. I'm so bad with names." She tried her best to sound embarrassed, but he could tell it was an act. She had been testing him, seeing if he remembered the name he used this afternoon. "I remember faces forever, though."

"Don't worry about it. I'm pretty bad with names *and* faces. For some reason, I always remember clothes the best."

"Seriously?"

"Yep. No idea why."

She laughed. "That's…different. Now I'm worried I should have spent a little more time choosing my outfit."

"Trust me, you did fine."

She smiled with a mix of satisfaction and self-consciousness, then looked down to watch the gears beneath the floor. He did likewise. Their seat was situated at the center of the largest gear in the room, a gargantuan piece of metal twenty feet across. Watching its thick spokes and wide, toothed rim sweep in slow unending circles around them made him feel a little dizzy.

"Well," Solace said, picking up her menu, "I hope the

food's as good as the ambiance."

"You've never been here before?"

"No, but I've always wanted to come. This place always gets stellar reviews from the food critics. You?"

He laughed. "No. Actually, I just moved here."

"Where from?"

"Shandar."

"Oh! I've been there. It's a lovely place. What brought you all the way to Nioedo?"

"New job. It's a big move, but it was way too good an opportunity to pass up."

"What is it you do?"

"I'm a financial systems analyst," he said. It was a profession with which he was familiar enough to be able to fake his way through a conversation, but also one he figured she would find far too dull to make a topic of conversation in the first place.

"Ah," she said, nodding. "I have to admit, financial matters are not my thing. I mean, I'm okay at them and I appreciate their importance, but frankly they make my eyes glaze over. No offense."

"None taken. A lot of people share that attitude. I understand perfectly. I feel the same way about the Arts. I get that they're important. But me? I prefer more tangible things." He slightly emphasized the penultimate word, letting her find innuendo there if she chose to.

She did. She raised her eyebrows and smiled knowingly. "Do you, now?"

Yif returned with the wine. He poured each of them a glass, then waited while they tasted it.

It was excellent, with a smooth rosy flavor that had a faint appley undertone. Reynard luxuriated in its tingly warmth as it suffused first his mouth, then his throat, then his belly. He had had a lot of wines over the years, but the Vävelaran stuff always surpassed all others.

"Are the establishment's esteemed guests now prepared for their ordering delight?" Yif asked, his hand raised half-way to the T-pad jutting from his jacket's breast pocket.

"I am," Reynard said. He looked at Solace. "You?"

"Uh....yeah, as long as you go first."

He ordered the Cobolaro Delight. After some dithering, Solace chose the curiously named Squid/Spinach-Noodle Whirlpool. Yif punched their order into his T-pad, which transmitted it directly to the kitchen, then headed away to tend to other diners.

"I don't understand myself sometimes," Reynard said, shaking his head. "I travel all this way from Shandar, and I'm still ordering seafood."

"You probably just need that touch of home to make yourself feel comfortable. Nioedo *is* a totally different place than Shandar. It'll take a while to adjust, I'm sure."

"True."

"Were you born there?"

"No, my family moved there when I was ten. I'm originally from Brambot."

"Oh, I like Brambot. That's a nice place. But still, no-where's quite like Shandar. I remember when I visited it a few years ago, I almost didn't want to leave. It's so beautiful! All those huge historic warehouses along the docks. And, um, what's that one place called? The big park with the old laser cannon?"

He nodded. "Tar Park."

"Right. And that street with the buildings with the gold façades."

He opened his mouth to say "Doubloon Street," then realized Doubloon Street had burned down in the Great Fire of 5776.

Very clever. She almost had him.

He was about to tell her he had no idea what she was talking about when an even better idea struck him, one that would flip her ploy right back in her face.

"Do you mean Doubloon Street?" he said with a frown.

"Yeah, that's it," she said, leaning forward. Her tone and expression remained calm and conversational, but her eyes shone with the excitement of a predator about to make a hard-won kill.

He shook his head in mock confusion. "That's been gone for...well, a long time. Hardly anyone's ever even heard of it. The only reason I know about it is because my mom was a history teacher, and she developed this kind of obsession with obscure Shandaran history. She had all these musty scrapbooks full of clippings."

"Oh." Solace had gone very still, eyes fixed on him, unblinking. "Um..."

"So, what, are you saying you actually saw it when you visited? You must be older than you look." He chuckled like someone who's said something witty.

She continued staring at him for a moment, then emitted a breezy laugh and made a backhanded swatting motion with her hand as if to shoo away crazy ideas.

"You're silly," she said. "No, I have to admit, I only saw it in a book. I figured it was just a locale I hadn't gotten to during my visit."

"Ah." Nice save.

Yif returned with a tray. Reynard and Solace shared a surprised glance. It seemed too soon for the meal to be ready.

It was. Instead of their dinners, the tray bore a platter of bite-sized appetizers.

Yif saw their confusion. As he set the platter in the center of the table, he explained, "These are amuse-bouches, artful creations of flavorful bliss, concocted to excite your tastebuds with quivering anticipation for the impending feast. They are an essential portion of the dining experience here at Bistro 27." He bowed and departed.

Reynard and Solace leaned forward and examined the items on the platter. There was a sphere of crabmeat drizzled with an amber-colored sauce; a cube of some dense white substance wrapped with ribbons of seaweed; a square of rich orange cheese with slender silver anchovies crosshatched atop it; a wedge of baked tofu dotted with small black seeds and topped with slivers of pimiento; a tight bundle of crisp red and green leaves arranged to resemble a rosebud; a tiny bowl made of sticky rice filled with a dollop of pink paté garnished with shreds of green onion; and ringing the platter, twelve crackers on each of which was a layer of creamy white spread decorated with a twelve-pointed star made of glistening red roe.

Solace looked up at him over the platter.

"Is there anything on here you particularly want to try?"

"Just one of those caviar cracker thingies."

"Mm. Yeah. Those look tasty."

They each took one of the crackers, which turned out to be just as blissfully flavorful as Yif had promised. The tastes and textures complemented each other perfectly—rough wheaty cracker, rich creamy spread, fishy roe crackling and popping against tongue and teeth.

After sips of wine to cleanse their palates, Solace chose the piece of cheese layered with anchovies, while Reynard picked up the leafy rosebud and sniffed it. It gave off a strong vegetative odor he didn't recognize. He thought he detected a hint of fish as well, but figured it was the residual aroma of the rosebud's neighbors on the platter.

When he bit into it, a complex mix of flavors filled his mouth. He didn't recognize the types of leaves, but the green ones were sharp and tangy, while the red ones were smooth and cooling. And nestled deep between them were shreds of sea stalker, a fish whose buttery flavor added the perfect touch to the amuse-bouche.

"Damn, that's good," he said.

"Mine too," Solace said around a mouthful of fish and cheese. She swallowed, sank back in her seat with a satisfied sigh, then took another sip of wine.

"Do you have a preference?" he asked, gesturing at the remaining appetizers.

She sat forward and studied them a moment, then picked up the white cube wrapped in seaweed.

"If you don't mind..." she said.

"I do not."

She popped it into her mouth. Her eyes immediately widened in surprise.

"Spicy!" she said. "It's some kind of radish, I think." She bit into it. Her eyes went even wider while her hand half rose to her mouth. "Mm! There's some kind of sauce in the center of it. It really breaks up the spiciness."

"But is it good?"

"It's fantastic." She glanced at the remaining items on the platter. "I'll bet there's a lot of eater's remorse here."

"How so?"

"Well, aside from the crackers, there's only one of each thing. I mean, there really should be enough of each for every person at the table, don't you think?"

He smirked. "I think it's a very clever ploy by the restaurant to give people incentive to come back."

He picked up the paté-filled bowl, raised it to his open

mouth, then stopped, realizing she was staring at him with eyes as narrow as razor cuts.

"What?" he said.

"You *are* Reynard." Her tone was vehemently certain on the surface, but underneath it he thought he detected lingering threads of uncertainty.

He gave her a long, steady look without a trace of emotion. Then he lowered his head, set down his amuse-bouche, and placed his hands palms down on the edge of the table as if he were about to push himself away from it.

He sighed and shook his head. When he looked back up at her, it was with an expression of mingled annoyance and disappointment.

"Look," he said, "you obviously think I'm someone I'm not and—"

Her veneer of certitude collapsed. She shook her head and held up her hands, palms outward. "No, no—"

Hiding his glee at her panic, he said, "I should go."

"I'm sorry." She was cringing in mortification now. "I am *so* sorry. It's just, you look and sound so much like this guy I knew…"

"Yeah, well, this is just too weird for me. I mean, I don't know if you're interested in me for me, or if it's because I remind you of—of your ex-boyfriend, or whatever he is."

She started to say something about how he wasn't her ex-boyfriend, but then realized the pointlessness of it.

"I'm sorry," she said again, this time with a serious, level gaze. "Let me just say in my defense that if you knew how similar you were to this guy, you'd understand. That said, I want you to know that I am having a very good time and I would very much like it to continue." She cocked her head and flashed a beseeching smile. "Can we just keep on with dinner, please? I assure you, it won't happen again."

He eyed her in silence for six seconds (he counted them), enjoying the sight of her struggling to maintain that smile. Then he heaved a deep sigh as if he were about to act against his better judgment.

"All right," he said. "But—"

"No more. Really."

They regarded each other in silence. He nodded with a small smile. She nodded with a much larger smile. He allowed his own smile to broaden in response.

So," she said, taking a cracker off the platter, "I never did ask what brought you to the Wellness Center this afternoon. Um, I mean, if that's not too personal or anything…"

He had been prepared for that question and was amazed it had taken her this long to ask.

"Oh, it was nothing too serious. Little gash on my hand. A knife slipped while I was cutting a cucumber. It was easy to fix. I was in and out of the Center in no time." He picked up his paté-filled rice bowl and popped it into his mouth. The paté was athelok, an animal somewhat similar to a bison. An unusual choice, but a very tasty one.

"Which biomage did you see?" she asked him.

He chewed his amuse-bouche with a thoughtful frown. "I don't recall his name, actually. Older guy? Short dark hair?" Those were safe bets. No doubt numerous biomages at the Center fit that description.

"Was it Doki, maybe?"

"That sounds familiar…"

"He's good. He rated close to Level 4, you know."

"No kidding! That certainly explains how he was able to heal me up so fast."

"Yeah, he's one of the decent ones."

"What, some of them aren't?"

She groaned. "Oh, don't get me started. I mean, they do

their work well, but biomages can be some of the most arrogant people on the planet. I think it's endemic to the profession."

"I had no idea."

"Sad but true."

"So, what led you to choose this particular career?" He was genuinely curious to learn the answer to that. After all, during their ill-fated T-Net exchange, she told him she had saved a fortune and worked only when and where she wished. Had she lost all her money? He couldn't think of any other reason she would choose to slave away at a thankless, low-paying job where each new day brought a fresh batch of losers leaking blood and pus all over everything. Of course, she would never admit to "Halfor" that she once had a fortune, but he hoped to glean some insight into the truth from whatever BS she offered up.

To his surprise, she gave him a small frown as if she found the question weird.

"It's good work," she said. "It helps people."

Oh, right. The whole do-gooder thing. How could he have forgotten? Still, he was astounded she would take it to such an extreme. She was an immortal, for fuck's sake. Why would she spend her days wallowing in filth and gore when she could help unfortunate schlubs just as much via, say, charitable donations?

"To be honest," she went on, "I don't know if I'll stick with it much longer. I've been there six years now, and I get bored if I do the same thing for too long. I'm fickle." She sighed with mock despondence. "We fickle women."

"Eh, it's nothing a domineering husband can't fix."

"Quiet, you," she said, laughing and raising her napkin as if to hurl it at him.

Yif appeared with their dinners hefted on a tray. In front

of Solace he set the Squid/Spinach-Noodle Whirlpool. This consisted of long spinach noodles twined together into a rope that had been coiled around the inner side of a deep, tapered bowl to form the titular whirlpool. Chunks of squid and slices of red, green, and yellow peppers had been arranged along the spiral's convolutions to form curving rays that radiated up from a pyramid of jalapeno cheese-stuffed olives that sat at the bottom of the whirlpool.

And for Reynard: the Cobolaro Delight, a cobolaro being a taxonomically unique ocean-bottom life-form resembling a seven-inch-high coral-colored barrel. Beneath their leathery hides, their bodies were soft and tender and segmented like an orange. The meat of the cobolaro had the color and consistency of scallops and a flavor many compared to sea urchin. There were various ways to serve cobolaro. In this case, the chef had opened out the segments like the petals of a flower and slathered them with melted halfling barrow cheese topped with nasturtium leaves. In the heart of the flower was a peeled and hollowed-out clambon—a tropical fruit whose closest relative was the pineapple—with half a dozen asparagus stalks protruding from the central hollow like cut flowers in a vase.

"I'd heard that genuine Nioedoan cuisine was as much about the visuals as the taste," Reynard said after Yif had departed. "But I'd always figured that was just hyperbole."

"Trust me, most of it isn't like this. It's only classy places like this that still go to these lengths." She picked up her silverware, then hesitated, staring at the food. "It's almost a shame to eat these. They're like works of art."

"Yeah, well, speak for yourself," Reynard said. "I'm hungry enough that my stomach's overruling my aesthetic sense."

He speared a cobolaro segment with his fork, tore it free

of the rest of the "flower," and raised it high above the plate to break the strings of cheese still attaching it to its fellows. When he slid the segment into his mouth and the mix of flavors hit his taste buds, he shut his eyes and his mouth curled into a delighted smile.

"Oh, this is amazing," he heard Solace say, her words muffled by squid and noodles.

He opened his eyes and looked at her. She too was smiling in delight, and her jaw wriggled a little as she rolled the food around inside her mouth, working it with her tongue to find the most succulent alignment of food and palate.

Shutting his eyes again, he began to chew, but slowly and gently, wishing to prolong the enjoyment as much as possible. The segment broke apart between his molars, the meat and cheese and greens crushed together, flavors deliciously mingling. Once the segment had been thoroughly pulped, he swallowed it down, then sighed in satisfaction and opened his eyes once more.

"Wow," Solace said. "Why have I never eaten here before?"

"The first time," he said, "but definitely not the last."

"More!" she said with a laugh, and plunged her fork into another knot of noodles.

They ate and ate, every bite as fantastic as the first. Eventually their plates were empty save for a few shiny smears of oil.

Yif reappeared and began to pile the empty plates on a tray.

"Are the gentle-entities still possessed of sufficient appetite and stamina to enjoy the ecstasy of one of our many superlative desserts?"

"Hm." Solace pondered this with a small frown, then

looked at Reynard. "Are you getting anything?"

"Gotta try something. If the main course is that tasty, I'm dying to know what the desserts are like."

"Oh, what the heck? I'm sure I can find a little more room in my belly."

Yif handed them dessert menus. The choices were many, and all sounded scrumptious. Reynard wound up ordering the quackberry pie, Solace the gnomish butterscotch-shrimp ice cream.

"Well," Reynard said as Yif departed, "this has been quite a night. I can't remember the last time I enjoyed a date this much."

"Me either," she said with a happy grin. "I had a great time."

"Great enough to warrant a sequel?"

The grin actually got bigger, though he got the impression she was trying hard to rein it in a bit. "Sure. That'd be fun. Unless, of course, you royally screw up in the next twenty minutes."

He bent his lips into an exaggerated pout. "Does that mean I can't fingerpaint on the tablecloth with my quackberry pie?"

"I think that would be a deal-breaker, yes."

"I shall try to refrain then."

She giggled.

"When's a good time for us to meet again?" he asked.

"Actually, I have tomorrow off. Would tomorrow work for you?"

"Tomorrow's perfect. I'm off, too."

"We could make a day of it."

"Sure. But, uh, seeing as how I'm still new to this area, do you have any ideas about what we could do? Frankly, at the risk of sounding touristy, I'd be kind of keen to see some of the notable local sites."

"That would be great," she said. "There are all kinds of interesting places to go. There's Makina Park, where everything's artificial: the birds, the trees, the dirt, everything. They've even got fake worms in the fake dirt. It's crazy. Then there's Dreamland Arcade, which is, like, fifteen floors of the world's coolest shops. That's always *my* favorite place. There's Anjulie's, the theater on Machine Street, though I have no idea what's showing there right now. And there's plenty of cool historical sites. There's the Hexagon, where the Central Computer was originally located. It's mostly underground, and it's enormous. There's one room that's half a mile long and contains nothing but rows and rows of databanks. And then just east of the city there's the remains of the Astropolis Platform, which is where the robots launched their spaceship city right before the War of Unification. The city's turned the place into a big museum with info on all the prominent robots who left and stuff like that. I was there once, and it was fascinating. I've always wanted to go back."

"That sounds interesting. Let's go there."

"Trust me, you'll love it."

Yif reappeared with dessert and the check. Reynard goggled at his gigantic slice of pie. The bulging crust couldn't contain the plump purple quackberries, which spilled out across the plate in glistening heaps.

"Well, you certainly get your money's worth," Solace said, regarding her own dessert with trepidation. The three scoops of ice cream in her bowl were the size of grapefruit. "I don't think I can eat all this."

"Me either. But I sure aim to try."

He stuffed a forkful of pie into his mouth and savored the way the tender berries burst between his teeth, their sugary juices splashing across his tongue.

"Oh, this is fantastic," he said.

"Trade bites?" Solace said, eyebrows raised hopefully.

"I don't know. I'm not sure I like the sound of butter-scotch-shrimp ice cream."

"It's delicious."

"You could be saying that because your misery wants my company."

"Oh, come on. Trust me."

"All right…"

They scooted their plates into the center of the table. With his spoon, he shaved off a curl of ice cream, while she forked up a couple of quackberries and a chunk of crust.

Reynard had expected the ice cream to be tolerable at best, but he should have known better than to doubt gnomes' culinary skills. Gnomes were renowned for mixing unlikely combinations of flavors and somehow making them work, and the butterscotch-shrimp ice cream was no exception. As he licked his spoon clean, Reynard made a mental note to look up the ice cream on the T-Net and see if it was available for sale anywhere.

Much to his and Solace's amazement, they managed to eat every last morsel of their desserts, though the last few bites were separated by increasingly long gaps and prefaced by deep breaths.

When they were done, Reynard paid the tab, and they headed out. As they passed through the lobby, the maître d' inclined its topmost appendage toward them and said, "Thank you for choosing to dine at Bistro 27. We hope to see you again soon."

"Oh, I'm pretty sure you will," Solace said with a laugh.

Outside, night had fallen, though it was hard to tell: The megalopolis blazed with lights of every shape, size, and hue.

The countless towers' lighted windows formed glowing grids of squares and rectangles; holographic signs and billboards enacted their preprogrammed animations; the headlights of cars and antigravity trains and flying robots streaked about. The city burned so brightly the night sky above it was dull gray, with not a single star visible. Even the full moon was only a faint, milky spot in the sky above Jimjin Tower's tallest spire.

"Can I walk you to your car?" Reynard asked.

"Um, actually I walked here. I live only a few blocks away."

"Oh. Well, in that case, can I walk you home?"

She opened her mouth, paused for a long moment, eyes probing his, then smiled and said, "Sure. Thanks. That'd be nice."

"All right then," he said, a little surprised he hadn't had to talk her into it.

She led him north to the corner of Seldon and Strontium Lane, then east down Strontium. Seldon's classy shops and eateries were replaced by apartment buildings that started out just as classy but grew less and less so the farther east they went. After only four blocks, they were in a neighborhood where peeling paint hung from window frames and most of the cars parked in the lots were more than twenty years old. Once again Reynard found himself wondering if she had lost her fortune.

"We're here," she said, stopping in front of a six-storey building whose holosign read "Friendly View Terrace." The sign flickered every few seconds, suggesting a dying drive.

"So, the Astropolis Platform tomorrow," he said. "Followed, perhaps, by another lovely dinner?"

She nodded. "Sounds good. And maybe after dinner we can even hit a couple of clubs. There's a place on Transformer Parkway I've always wanted to visit. I hear they've got their dance floor rigged up with antigrav plates, so you can actually dance on air."

"Ooh. That sounds like fun. We have to do that."

"It's a date, then."

"It's a date."

They smiled at each other in silence for a moment.

"Well," he said softly, leaning toward her a little. "I guess this is good night."

"I guess it is." She didn't draw back as he leaned farther forward, his shadow enveloping her.

He watched her face draw closer and closer till it filled his vision. Her eyes, looking both eager and scared, fixed on his then on his approaching lips then back on his eyes.

He felt her warm breath on his chin and smelled that unique and irreproducible scent of hers that always reminded him of exotic spices, and then their lips touched, lightly at first, tentatively, as if each of them were afraid of harming the other, but then pressing harder, more boldly, flesh pushing and flattening against flesh, their lips both advancing and yielding at the same time.

He tasted clams and butterscotch, the residue of dinner concentrated in her lips' tender crevices, a final tiny feast for him, much like the one he knew he must be providing her. And behind that were other flavors: the faint tang of salt from her skin, the coppery taste of her saliva, the hot, earthy traces of chewed food wafting up from her mouth's cavy depths.

She pulled away, took a breath, licked her lips. Inside his shadow, the whites of her eyes were gray as she looked at him.

"I have to go," she said.

"Yeah."

"Pick me up here tomorrow at, say, three o'clock?"

"Sounds perfect."

She nodded and regarded him a little uncertainly, as if she wished to say more but wasn't sure if she should. Then a smile broke through her uncertainty.

"Thanks again," she said. "I had a *great* time."

"Same here. I can't wait till tomorrow."

Her smile ballooned into a toothy grin that made her look like a teenager. "Me either."

"Bye."

"Bye."

He strode away. Though he didn't look back, he knew she was standing there watching him till he was out of sight.

The next day at three, he sat on the antigrav train The Silvercat Express as it streaked out of Nioedo at 120 miles an hour.

He wondered how long she would wait for him, and how mad or sad she would be when she realized he had stood her up. He wondered how much she would hurt. He wondered if she would cry.

As he watched the city's metal towers give way to suburbs and then to field and forest, he told himself she deserved it. Given how she had treated him during their last few encounters, she had earned every tear she might shed over this.

The question he carefully avoided asking himself was: If that were true, why didn't he feel more pleased?

9

Ravenshaft
8681 A.C.

Reynard slunk from the bushes, scurried across the sidewalk and the stretch of open grass, and crouched down next to the marble plinth atop which stood the bronze statue of Adam Frankenstein that dominated this section of Ravenshaft's Cryptic Acres Park. There he paused a moment, watching and listening.

Crickets chirred in the darkness beyond the yellow circles of light cast by the black cast-iron lamps that lined the park's paths. The lamps were solarite-powered, a touch of the old-fashioned that fit the locale well. The spiders and webs decorating them were old-fashioned, too, being completely non-interactive. They didn't move or scream or display informative diagrams, no matter how many times you scanned them with your Realms+ Card. Which didn't prevent the occasional idiotic tourist from trying, though.

Reynard saluted Ravenshaft's refusal to change its venerable ways. That alone was what made it Belladonna's last tolerable city. The rest of the realm had become far too tame and commercialized, campily playing up its weirdness and spookiness to attract new residents in an effort to mitigate the population drain caused by the ongoing space migration. But then, most realms had been reduced to the same thing, desperately flaunting their every plus like aging whores trying to compete with the younger, fresher girls down the block. And like those aging whores, the realms were doomed to lose. Why would anyone bother with a mere realm when whole planets had been terraformed to meet the needs and desires of every species, race, and lifestyle?

Ravenshaft, though, remained one of a kind. Unlike Lachrymont or Vile Vale or any other big city in Belladonna, Ravenshaft was still genuinely scary. The danger wasn't just theatrics to wow prospective denizens. It still had murky byways and labyrinths of alleys any halfway sane person would stay out of. Ravenshaft's disappearance rate was five times higher than anywhere else in the United Realms. No one knew why, or where those missing persons might be ending up, though many claimed this was where a lot of the nastier vampires gangs had decamped to, the ones who refused to play nice with the UR government and give up victimizing innocents. Reynard had also heard that Ravenshaft still had serial killers.

If so, they weren't in Cryptic Acres Park at the moment. Nor were the nasty vampires. Nor, thankfully, was anyone other than Reynard. The park's paths were silent and still. Even in sinister Ravenshaft most folks were fast asleep at three a.m. on a weeknight.

Most, but not all. Local Watch patrols, he knew, checked the park periodically throughout the night, so he had to act fast.

From a small cloth shopping sack he pulled a smoke bomb, a foot-long purple dildo, and a roll of thick tape sticky enough to adhere to cold marble. He tore off a strip of tape with his teeth and taped the dildo into the recess under the plinth's chilly stone rim. He had just bitten off another strip to do the same with the smoke bomb when his communicator shrilled.

"Thit," he hissed around the tape as he scrambled to yank the small silver device from his pocket. He cursed himself for forgetting to mute it.

He almost turned it off without answering it, but then reflected that it might be his lawyer with an update on the Charon property Reynard was bidding on.

He hit TALK and said, "Yeth?"

"Um...hello?" said a puzzled and very familiar female voice.

"Tholath?" he said, all his panic and plans momentarily erased by astonishment.

A pause on the other end, then: "Reynard? Is that you?"

He pulled the tape from his mouth. One sticky edge caught on his upper lip and tore away a sliver of skin, producing a quick, sharp pain like a bee-sting.

"Yeah," he said. He touched the tip of his tongue to the wound and tasted blood. "It's me."

"I couldn't tell."

"Sorry, I was eating." Over the uproar of thoughts and feelings and questions her call had unleashed, his instincts shouted at him to hurry up and finish the task at hand because the longer he squatted here with it half done the greater his chances of getting caught. He clamped the communicator to his ear with his raised left shoulder, and carefully taped the smoke bomb next to the dildo. "So, to what do I owe this unexpected pleasure?"

"I..." She paused, took a breath. "I need your help."

"You need my help," he said slowly and precisely, as if he were having trouble comprehending a statement so ludicrous. "It's funny, I seem to recall that the last time we got in touch, you abruptly cut ties with me without even—"

"Reynard, I don't have time for this," she said. The desperation in her voice stopped all his words. "We can talk about it later, if you want."

He stood up, knees cracking. "What do you need me to do?"

"Do you have a car?"

"Sure."

She heaved a relieved breath. "I need a ride."

"Don't *you* have a car?"

"Yes, but…I can't use it."

"Why?"

An exasperated grunt. "Reynard, please, I'll tell you whatever you want to know later. We need to get moving."

He sighed. "Okay. Fine. Where are you now?"

Ten minutes later he pulled his black ZipGo MeteoRight up to the southwest corner of Zonster Avenue and South Scapula, a corner occupied by the Thirteenth Church of Ilva, a looming basalt structure with a crenellated roof rimmed with gargoyles, all of whom appeared to be dormant (though you could never be quite sure with that bizarrely sedentary species).

There was no sign of Solace anywhere. There was no sign of anyone (aside from the gargoyles). The corner, and every street around, was dark and still.

He was beginning to wonder if he had misunderstood her, or if something bad had happened, when a figure detached itself from the shadows in the church's recessed and unlit front doorway and strode across the pavement toward the car.

It was her. She wore a black coat so long it enwrapped her from neck to ankles. Her hair was long, straight, and loose, a look that pleased him. It was how she had been wearing it the first time they met, and it remained his favorite.

He pushed the dashboard button that opened the passenger door. She climbed in, the old familiar scent of her filling the car, the rustles as she settled into her seat sounding loud in the enclosed space on this quiet night.

"Thank you so much for coming," she said.

In the shifting light of the multsy unit's holographic dashboard display, she didn't look too good. Her face was strained and haggard and seemed more lined than he remembered. Her eyes were bloodshot, and there were dark bags under them. Her hair needed brushing, too: Stray strands formed a frizzy halo, a witchy look appropriate to many residents of Ravenshaft, but not to her.

He also noted that the left-hand pocket of her coat bulged with something thick and squarish. It was about the right size for a neatly folded pair of women's elbow-length gloves. Then again, it was the right size for all kinds of things.

"So what now?" he asked.

"Do you know where Pumpkin Lane is?"

"The name rings a bell, but..."

She nodded as if she had expected this. "Just follow my directions." She pointed at the windshield. "Head straight down Zonster for now."

He drove. Ranks of dark buildings slid past. Here and there a lone lit window revealed the presence of an insomniac or a third-shift worker. The only sounds were the faint hum of the car's ZipTek engine and the murmur of voices and music from the multsy unit, whose volume Reynard had turned down to an indecipherable level, rendering the unit's ever-shifting holographic images completely inscrutable. Right now, for instance, it showed a top hat.

"Care to tell me what's going on?" he said.

When ten seconds passed without an answer, or rather

with Solace's silence being her answer, he looked over at her. Her eyes were fixed on the street ahead, her brow creased with concentration.

"I think our turn's coming up," she said quietly. Though she didn't look straight at him, he could tell by the way her eyes kept flicking slightly toward him that she was watching him in her peripheral vision.

"Solace." He filled his voice with disappointment. It was the tone you would use with a child who has done bad despite knowing better.

She slumped a little with a faint weary exhalation, her shoulders sinking. Blue light washed across her face as the multsy unit displayed an underwater scene of sharks swimming past a sunken ship. Her eyes never left the road.

"I just—I can't talk about it."

"Can't or won't?"

After a pause she finally looked at him. "Reynard, please. It's personal." Her eyes met his for a moment, then slid away to resume their watch on the street signs.

Before he could decide how, or if, to respond, she said, "Turn left up here, by the doll store." She gestured at the Coffin Road intersection, the northwest corner of which was occupied by Ghoulette's Ghastly Dolls. A sign in the window read: "Dolls of all kinds—rag, bone, china, mechanical, voodoo, and elsewhat!"

He turned down Coffin, a mostly residential street. The MeteoRight juddered on the brick pavement as they passed between the rows of houses, most of which sported the mansard roofs and spiked cast-iron fences that seemed to be Belladonna's national architectural motifs.

The dashboard holographic display flashed an image of a field of cornflowers. Simultaneously Reynard caught a faint whiff of the flower's scent, a sensation beamed straight to his brain courtesy of the unit's telepathic interface, which he had turned down along with the sound. Good thing, too; given how strong the muted version was, he would be gagging on it at normal strength.

Solace frowned at the multsy unit. "Could you turn that off, please? It's distracting."

"Sure." He pushed a button below the display. The cornflowers and their smell and the muffled strains of music all vanished.

"Sorry, but I just don't like multsy," Solace said. "It's intrusive, and it leaves nothing to the imagination. I don't want everything defined for me. I prefer a little mystery and personal creativity."

"Yeah. I'm not a big fan myself." Actually he didn't care one way or another, and he doubted she did very much either. He suspected that her grousing was a way of diverting her mind from her anxieties. And of diverting the conversation from her reasons for this journey.

He decided to let her have her way. For now.

As they had progressed down Coffin, the neighborhood had steadily deteriorated. The houses were in increasing states of disrepair, the lawns dead and brown, the gutters clotted with trash, half the street lamps smashed and dark. On the porch of one dilapidated house with shattered windows and a sagging roof, three figures sat in chairs, unmoving. It was too dark to tell if they were awake, or asleep, or even alive. In the distance a dog heaved out a chain of barks so savage it sounded as if it hoped to maim or kill by the noise alone.

"Turn at the next left," Solace said. "Frayn Street."

Reynard did so with a small frown. Why did Frayn Street sound familiar? As he maneuvered the car down the narrow lane, past houses with Condemned signs on the crooked doors, past illegible graffiti scrawled on walls, past junked cars sharing driveway space with grimy children's toys, Reynard dug through his memory to identify where he had heard the name before.

The mystery was answered by the appearance of a house on the north side of the street whose door was crisscrossed with the bright glowing orange stop-strips the Watch used to identify and (in theory) block civilian access to crime scenes.

Of course. This house had been in the news last week. The family who lived there—a husband and wife, five kids aged four months to twelve years, the wife's sister, and a pet pubble—had been slaughtered in the dead of night without the neighbors seeing or hearing anything. Or at least without any of them admitting to it.

Last he heard, the Watch had no leads, no evidence, not even a possible motive. It was just a family—normal, poor, and unremarkable. Now they weren't anything.

"Solace, if there's trouble maybe I can help," he said, surprised at the sound of his own voice. He hadn't known he was going to speak until the words were streaming from his mouth.

"You are."

"You know what I mean."

She sighed. He glanced at her. Though she had turned away from him to look out the window, he could see her face reflected in the glass. Her eyes were distant, preoccupied.

"Thanks, but there's nothing you can do beyond what you're already doing," she said, her gaze never wavering from the dark world outside.

The weary fatalism in her voice startled him. It was a tone he had never heard from her before.

"Turn right," she said.

He did, noting the new street was Pumpkin Lane, presumably their destination. It looked much the same as Frayn.

He kept expecting her to tell him to stop or pull into a driveway, but she didn't, and the car traveled down Pumpkin Lane for five minutes, then ten, the houses and occasional businesses growing sparser, with fields and copses and in one case an old weedy cemetery separating them. Before long he realized they had entered the city's far north side. Not the best place to be at night. Or during the day, for that matter. This was where Ravenshaft's high disappearance rate and high homicide rate were highest.

Soon the road began to wind amid low, rocky hills dense with pines that loomed tall and black in the night. In the valley between two such hills they glimpsed an ancient industrial building, its once-white walls now grimy gray. A loading dock door stood open, and in the depths of the structure a campfire flickered.

They weren't even technically in the city anymore, Reynard realized; they had entered the wild and desolate country beyond, a region called Black Pines.

"It's just up ahead," Solace said.

Out of the corner of his eye he saw her touch the bulge in her coat pocket as if to confirm it was still there. She quickly withdrew her hand and laid it atop the other one in her lap. Then she glanced at him. He stared straight ahead and pretended not to have seen a thing.

They jounced across a rickety tin bridge. Five hundred feet beyond it on the right, a large structure bulked amid the trees.

"There," Solace said. "Go in there."

He pulled the MeteoRight into a gravel lot that fronted a long, low wooden building whose sides were denuded of all but a few stubbornly clinging strips of blue-gray paint. The building had no windows, and where the front door should have been was a rectangle opening on blackness. A porch extended the length of the façade, and on it sat a line of weathered rocking chairs. No one was in sight.

Reynard parked the car in the middle of the lot, head-lights trained on the façade. He left the engine running.

"This it, then?" he said.

Solace didn't answer. Her eyes were fixed on the doorless doorway.

"Do you want me to—"

He had been about to say "kill the headlights" but she cut him off, turning to him and saying: "Whatever happens, don't get out of the car."

"What? But—"

"Promise me."

He hesitated, the very nature of the request inclining him not to grant it.

"Please, Reynard," she said. "Everything'll be fine as long as you stay in the car."

He stared at her, unsure how to respond. It was clear she believed what she was saying. The problem was, the request presupposed she had anticipated all eventualities, which not even the smartest or wisest or wiliest could ever truly do.

Despite his doubts, he said, "All right." That was what she wanted to hear. She wouldn't be satisfied till he said it. But just because he said it didn't mean he had to stick to it.

"Thank you," she said. She glanced out the windshield and went stiff. "Oh!"

He followed her gaze. While they had been talking, the front porch had filled with nearly two dozen individuals, mostly grim, hulking, black-garbed men. Bodyguards, from the look of it. There were four others present as well, pre-sumably the bodies to be guarded.

The first was a tall, thin man with long white hair tied

back with a red ribbon. He wore a cream-colored suit and white leather gloves and boots. His erect posture, haughty countenance, and position at the forefront of the group, with the toes of his boots nearly touching the edge of the tilted and dry-rotted wooden stairs that descended to the gravel lot, suggested he was the group's leader.

The second was a man barely five feet tall yet so fat he was nearly a sphere. He wore a multicolored waistcoat over a dark blue silk shirt, a pair of black pants, black leather boots, and a black beret. His eyes were narrow and suspicious as he peered at the car over a pair of tinted pince-nez glasses.

The third was a bald, skeletal man in a double-breasted white lab coat tightly buttoned all the way from the high collar to the hem midway down his shins. He sat on the arm of one of the rocking chairs, watching the car from under his lowered brows with a tired and faintly disgusted expression.

The last was a slim young woman whose bronze skin and jet-black hair marked her as a member of the Nations, and whose multicolored headband and fringed green-and-orange jacket sported designs particular to the long-extinct tribe called the Nanshee. The hand extending from the jacket's left sleeve was prosthetic, but unlike most prosthetic appendages these days, it was not covered with a Skinthetic shell to make it look real; instead the woman had chosen to expose the metal and wires for all to see.

Reynard's blood ran cold. The Nanshee designs. The mechanical hand. This could only be Nimbus, the former Nanshee tracker who was ranked among the most notorious vampires in history and was one of the select few known to have survived a battle with Hull, the legendary vampire hunter. As it was, the battle had claimed her hand and left her trapped all alone in an underground vault for several centuries, an experience from which she emerged half mad and packed with hate. She was one of the vampires who had opted to continue their ancient, brutal ways in secret and risk imprisonment or death rather than capitulate to the UR.

As soon as Reynard had identified Nimbus—and concomitantly realized that the eerily smooth, pale complexions of the figures on the porch was due not to the glare of the headlights as he had hitherto assumed but to their being vampires—he belatedly identified the white-haired man as Jelain Belloc, the discovery of whose so-called Torture Circus a few decades ago in Briésk had sickened the whole UR and set back the Vampire Rights movement a hundred years.

"Solace—" Reynard began, turning to her, hoping to urge her not to go, or at least to let him go with her.

But she was already opening the door and stepping out. As she turned to close the door behind her, she bent down a little and looked in at him.

"Just stay here," she said softly, then shut the door before he could reply.

He watched her walk into and along the beams of the car's headlights, her back so brightly lit it seemed as if he could see every thread of her coat and every strand of her black hair. Her huge shadow lurched about on the building's façade, those on the porch eclipsed within it. The shadow grew smaller as she neared the porch, as if she were losing puissance the closer she got to those who awaited her.

She stopped at the foot of the steps. One side of Belloc's mouth rose in a smug smile. Nimbus watched Solace with deceptive blankness. The fat vampire clasped his hands behind his back and puffed out his chest self-importantly. The bald vampire eyed Solace as if she were a distinctly uninteresting bug. The bodyguards stood as stiff as the posts that supported the porch's roof.

Reynard could see only Solace's back, but given the small, quick movements of her head and shoulders and the way the vampires were watching her, it was clear she was speaking.

Hoping to hear what she was saying, he rolled down the driver's side window. He could now make out the soft, feminine strains of her voice, but the hum of the car's engine, low though it was, muffled the words. He reached for the car's off switch, then stopped and lowered his arm. Bad idea. Turning off the engine now, with the undertaking well underway, would be open to misinterpretations that could get Solace hurt. Besides, if things went wrong, he wanted to have the engine running for a quick getaway.

Belloc drew back in surprise at something Solace said. He regarded her in silence for a moment. Then his eyes narrowed, and he turned to speak to the fat vampire.

Though Solace's words were lost to Reynard, everyone else's were clear as water, for one of the countless skills he had mastered over the millennia was lip reading. And what Belloc now said was: "Is this true?"

Everyone looked at the fat vampire. His only response was to scowl at Solace, then turn to look at the bald vampire and say, "Well? You'd know better than I."

All heads now turned to the bald vampire. He regarded Solace from beneath his brows for a moment, then shifted his gaze to the MeteoRight. Although it seemed unlikely he could see inside the car over the glare of the headlights, it certainly looked to Reynard as if the vampire's cold eyes were fixed right on him. After a couple of seconds the bald vampire's upper body gave a quick, spasmodic jerk, a movement that Reynard at first interpreted as a cough or a hiccup, then realized was the byproduct of a terse, humorless laugh. Shaking his head, the vampire turned back to the others and said, "Only for a month."

The fat vampire looked puzzled. Nimbus scrutinized the bald vampire, then fixed an appraisive gaze on Solace. Belloc's expression reverted to its former aloofness, and he said, "What about the other four?"

Solace responded. The fat vampire thrust a plump finger at her and snapped, "That's not true!" Both Solace and Belloc ignored him.

Solace then said something that reduced everyone to complete silence and immobility, except two of the black-clad bodyguards, who glanced at each other.

Eyes narrow with suspicion, Nimbus said, "Did you know about this?" to Belloc. Belloc said nothing, merely stared at Solace as if waiting for something.

Solace spoke for ten seconds straight, then dug into her left coat pocket and withdrew a small squarish object wrapped in a white cloth.

Everyone on the porch once again went very still, their eyes fixed on the white-shrouded object in her outstretched hand.

Belloc said, "Yes." The bald vampire stiffened and goggled at him.

Solace said something. Belloc said, "Indeed we will." Nimbus, the fat vampire, and the bodyguards were watching either Solace or Belloc. No one but Reynard was paying attention to the bald vampire.

Big mistake.

Over the years Reynard had gotten quite adept at scenting trouble. His livelihood depended on knowing when a mark had divined a scam, or who was an undercover Watch officer, or how close to cracking someone was. And right now, given the way the bald vampire sat there, his muscles tight as cables and his glaring eyes fixed on Belloc,

Reynard's instincts were telling him that this was one of those individuals who might appear fairly sane on the surface, but underneath it all are completely fucking batshit crazy and only one wrong moment away from going supernova on everyone and everything around them.

And that wrong moment was now.

Reynard's heart, already fast, started racing as the bald vampire sprang to his feet in one crisp movement. The vampire's eyes were slits, and his lips were pursed like the world's tightest sphincter.

Smiling calmly down at Solace, Belloc extended one pale, slender hand. Solace stepped up onto the bottom step, holding out the white-wrapped object.

The bald vampire breezed past Nimbus and the fat vampire, neither of whom understood what was happening; they only stared at him in mild puzzlement as he strode toward the delivery in progress. None of the bodyguards were doing anything either, even though a couple of them were watching the bald vampire's advance.

That's the trouble with people who are secretly batshit crazy: You think they're normal right up until the very moment they supernova in your face, and by then it's too late to do anything about it.

Reynard grabbed the handle to open the car door despite his near certainty there was no way he could stop the man in time. Even if he shouted something, no one would grasp what he was trying to tell them until it was too late. The bodyguards would instinctively see *him* as the potential threat while the bald vampire would ignore Reynard and continue stalking toward Solace and Belloc to do whatever it was he was planning to do. Something batshit crazy, no doubt.

As Reynard pulled the handle and the door snapped

open, he glanced at the porch and saw the bald vampire slip a hand under the flap of his long white coat midway up his chest. The vampire's slitted eyes glistened darkly in the headlights. His lips were compressed almost into nonexistence.

Reynard pushed open the car door, seeing as he did so that he had been right: The damn bodyguards shifted their attention to him, even the two who had noticed the bald vampire's inexplicable advance. But what the hell else could Reynard do? He had to try to stop whatever was going to happen, and he didn't have a whole lot of options as to how.

As he swung his feet out onto the gravel, the bald vampire's arm slid mid-forearm deep under the coat, paused, then began moving out, having found what it sought. Solace ascended to the second step, the white-wrapped object rising toward Belloc's open hand.

Solace froze. She had spotted the bald vampire approaching. He saw that she had seen him, and his upper lip peeled back in a mocking sneer, revealing two white fangs that shone white in the headlights.

Reynard twisted out through the door. In response, several of the bodyguards sprang to life, some baring fangs, others thrusting their hands deep inside their jackets much as the bald vampire had done, all of them ready to pounce on Reynard. Meanwhile, still unnoticed by the guards, the bald vampire's hand was about to emerge from under his coat along with whatever it held.

Solace said something to the bald vampire. The bald vampire stopped, blinked, frowned at her.

Reynard froze half out of the car, watching, waiting. A few of the bodyguards had realized something unusual was happening right there on the porch, though since they weren't yet sure what, they were dividing their attention between Solace, the bald vampire, and Belloc in hopes of discerning the truth.

Belloc turned and saw his associate standing only a few steps away, hand frozen under his coat. Belloc looked back at Solace, puzzled.

Solace spoke again. The bald vampire's mouth moved in a complicated way, as if he wanted to grimace and spit at the same time.

Belloc turned to the bald vampire and said, "I think she's right." The bald vampire only glowered at Solace in response.

Solace said something. Belloc gave her a faint smile. The bald vampire's shoulders slumped.

The hand slid all the way back to mid-forearm depth under the coat, then slid out again, empty. All the while the bald vampire's eyes never left Solace's face.

Belloc glanced at his compatriot—or perhaps now his former compatriot—and said, "An excellent idea."

The bald vampire stood rigid for a moment, eyes still fixed on Solace, then took a deep breath and shouted "Cattle!" loud enough for Reynard to hear it clearly over the engine's hum.

The bald vampire stormed back to his rocking chair and flung himself into it so hard the top of the backrest slammed against the wall. Face crumpled in a petulant frown, arms folded across his chest, he rocked rapidly. He looked like a child who hasn't been allowed to have dessert.

Belloc watched him for a moment, then turned back to Solace and said, "Thank you."

He plucked the cloth-wrapped object from Solace's still-outstretched hand. He began to unwrap it, then glanced up at Reynard, who still stood behind the MeteoRight's open door.

"Does he know?" Belloc asked.

Solace's reply made him cock an eyebrow at Reynard again, then lift one edge of the cloth and peek at the object beneath in a way that ensured Reynard couldn't see anything.

Feeling embarrassed for some reason, Reynard slipped back into the car and shut the door. When he looked again at the scene on the porch, Belloc was tucking the cloth-wrapped object into his pocket. Belloc then turned to Nimbus and the fat vampire and said, "That's that."

Nimbus gave Solace a wry smile and said, "Next time, just keep walking."

Solace said something that made Nimbus laugh softly.

Belloc turned back to Solace and said, "I sincerely hope we don't meet again." Without awaiting a reply, he whirled about and strode inside the dark building. While the others on the porch filed in after him, Solace returned to the car.

She got in and shut the door. Reynard didn't move, just sat there watching the others vanish one by one through the doorway. Except the bald vampire, who continued to rock, a hateful scowl fixed on the porch floor in front of him.

"We can go," Solace said quietly, her voice muffled. Reynard knew without looking that she was turned away from him to gaze out the passenger window. "It's over."

Reynard still didn't move. The last of the bodyguards disappeared inside. The bald vampire kept rocking and scowling.

There was a long pause. The only sound was the hum of the motor.

"Thank you," Solace said finally, the clarity of her voice indicating she had finally turned to look at him.

Reynard continued watching the porch. The bald vampire abruptly froze at the farthest point of the chair's backward rock, his legs stiff and braced, the chair resting on the rearmost two inches of its curved supports. He gave Reynard's car a long, spiteful sneer, then launched himself to his feet and stomped into the building. The chair, set in motion by his brusque rise, rocked unoccupied, its arcs fast and violent at first but quickly diminishing to slow, gentle rolls.

Reynard turned the car around, and they headed back the way they had come.

"You gonna tell me what that was all about?" he asked as they crossed the tin bridge.

After a pause she said, "I'm sorry, but I'd prefer not to talk about it." She sounded tired, wrung out, a little irritable.

"So, what, you drag me all the way out here, and I never even get to find out why?"

"I'll tell you some day."

He grunted. He didn't believe her, and he could tell from her tone that *she* didn't believe what she was saying either.

His disbelief must have been as obvious as hers, because she sighed and said, "Look, Reynard, I was in trouble, okay? I needed help, and you helped me. Do you really need to know why?"

After a long pause, he said, "I guess not." It was a lie.

He sensed her eyeing him closely as he maneuvered the car around the piney bends of Pumpkin Lane and the dark towers of downtown Ravenshaft drew ever closer. He kept his gaze fixed on the road ahead and his face as blank as possible, granting her no glimpse of his thoughts and feelings.

"Please, Reynard," she said after a time, her voice soft and imploring. "Please understand. Everybody has things they prefer to keep secret. It's not that I don't trust you or... or anything. It's just, some things need to be kept secret even from...people close to you. Often *especially* those people."

He didn't respond right away, wasn't sure if he wanted to respond at all. Out of the corner of his eye he could see her watching him, motionless.

"Yeah, I understand," he said finally.

"Thank you," she said in a voice so small and soft the words were nearly whispers.

The rest of the drive back passed in silence. He kept expecting her to ask how he was, or what he had been up to, or if it had been him who stood her up in Nioedo fifteen hundred years ago; but all she did was stare out the windshield at the minute wedge of the world illuminated by the headlights.

He nearly broke the silence himself at one point, when he found himself wondering why she had asked *him* to help her. Surely she knew countless people who would be willing to drive her somewhere or even loan her their car.

But before he could ask, the answer became clear to him. She had wanted someone she knew well, but who was not a regular part of her life and would therefore not be around very often to ask nosey questions.

His knuckles cracked faintly as his hands tightened on the steering wheel.

When they arrived at the intersection of Zonster and South Scapula, he made a tight U-turn and pulled up alongside the southwest corner in the exact position he had picked her up. The swath of the eastern horizon visible down Zonster's length had lightened to dark blue, first hint of the coming dawn.

She got out, then leaned in through the open door.

"Thank you again," she said.

"No problem." He offered her a bland smile.

She hovered there, watching him, waiting. Her smile wavered. No doubt she was expecting him to ask her if she wanted to stay in touch. He wasn't going to bother. It wasn't worth the trouble. At this point all he wanted was to go back to his hotel room and sleep and forget this whole incident.

"Okay, well…" She sounded confused. The smile stretched and quivered a little as she struggled to keep it in place.

There was a long pause.

"I owe you one, Reynard," she said, leaning farther forward so he would be sure to see the sincerity on her face. "Someday I'll repay you."

He repeated his bland smile. "Don't worry about it. I'm just glad I could help."

She opened her mouth. Nothing came out. She shut it. She flashed a strained smile.

"Take care," she said.

"Yeah, you too."

After another brief pause, as if she expected him to say something more, she stepped back and shut the door.

He made another, more rapid U-turn, tires squealing, and sped off toward his hotel. He didn't look back.

10

Giv-Golos Repository
9987 A.C.

Reynard sat on a white metal chair at a white metal table in a white room devoid of any other people or furniture. Bulging from the center of the ceiling like a necrotic pustule was the blackglass hemisphere of the Eye, a 180° lens that recorded all that went on in the room.

He leaned back in his chair, tilting it till it nearly toppled over. He lifted his feet from the floor and let the chair slam back down. He rested his chin on the tabletop. He sat back up. He examined his fingernails. He drummed tunes on his kneecaps with his open hands.

He had resumed leaning back in his chair when the door in the far wall slid open. The officer on duty, a chunky middle-aged man whose nametag read "Rixl," stood just outside, gesturing for someone beyond Reynard's line of sight to enter the room.

Reynard straightened up with a friendly smile that hid how scared shitless he really felt.

The fear wasn't due merely to his incarceration here in Giv-Golos Repository ("repository" being this era's euphemism of choice for "prison"). He had been in supposedly escape-proof prisons before, and he had found a way out of every one. True, Giv-Golos was an artificial planetoid constructed by geniuses with unlimited funding and millennia of prison history to draw on, and true, it was surrounded by a parsec of space that was empty of anything except monitoring systems and security drones, and true, it had technology so cutting-edge nobody outside the United Planets Welfare Administration had ever heard of it, and blah and blah and blah. The plain truth was, if a place existed, it was escapable. All you had to do was figure out how.

No, the really scary thing was the recent widespread acceptance of personality adjustment as a means of dealing with those inmates seen as unresponsive to normal methods of rehabilitation. Personality adjustment—another splendid modern euphemism for what might be more honestly labeled "mind rape"—was when a psychomage, one of those rare individuals blessed with powers over others' minds, altered your thought patterns to give you a more "socially constructive attitude." All the facts and memories in your brain remained the same. What changed was your outlook.

Reynard knew someone it had been done to. Bones Teh had been a mad, cackling, take-no-shit, take-no-prisoners DNAura counterfeiter who saw the world as a bastardly place in which you had to be a bigger bastard than everyone else to survive. Then he got arrested and spent a week in the UPWA's Titan Repository. The man who came out was someone else entirely.

The one time Reynard saw Bones after the change, he almost didn't recognize him. Bones's posture was upright, his eyes bright, and his face free of most of the lines that had once seamed it, facts that led Reynard to realize just how tense and worried Bones had always been underneath his crazy bluster. Reynard watched and listened in mingled horror and fascination as the disturbingly serene and constantly smiling Bones urged him to change his ways. Being a bastard, Bones argued, was self-defeating since it only increased the amount of unpleasantness in the universe, a universe Reynard himself had to live in.

"I mean, why make your own home more awful?" Bones had asked. "It's much wiser and more rewarding to think and act positively, to help people instead of taking advantage of them."

Of course, part of the point of this sunny-side-up lecture had been to keep Reynard occupied while the UPWA closed in. Only a combination of quick thinking and dumb luck had permitted his escape.

Fortunately personality adjustment was rare. Stringent regulations limited its use to only the most irredeemable criminals, whom the UPWA employed specially trained psychological evaluators to identify. Supposedly the evaluators had it down to a fine art, able to spot candidates for adjustment with only a few dozen properly asked questions.

And today, Reynard's fifth day here at Giv-Golos, was the day of his evaluation. If the evaluators were as adept as their reputation suggested, he was fairly sure he would be labeled irredeemable. His very existence was antithetical to the insipidly amiable mores of this modern-day space-faring society, and there was no way he would ever change without being forced.

His only chance was to con the evaluator into thinking he was something far different than he was, perhaps a poor, desperate soul who had gone a little overboard in an attempt to raise fast funds. It was doable. Evaluators were fallible just like anyone else.

Even so, the dread of failure squirmed in Reynard's every cell. The stakes were so high. The stakes were everything that made him who he was.

Muscles rigid, heart pounding so hard he felt the thrum of each beat in his ears, he faced the open door, ready for his evaluation, for this critical battle of wits.

Solace strode into the room. Reynard's face went slack with surprise, and all his careful plans vanished from his brain.

She stopped just inside the entrance, her back to Officer Rixl, her eyes on Reynard. Her scrutiny was remote, clinical. If she recognized him, she gave no sign. She wore a gold-embroidered white sherwani, a narrow white salwar, white shoes, and small rectangular glasses with gold bioplastic rims. Her long hair was held back with a plain white triangular clip. In her left hand was a paperback-sized white Databoard with the UPWA's twelve-pointed star logo embossed in gold on the back.

"You sure you don't want some accompaniment, Ms. Desidáre?" Officer Rixl said.

"Thanks, but I'll be fine. This one has no record of violence."

"I don't know, I've heard he's pretty tricky."

Solace, aka Ms. Desidáre, half turned toward Officer Rixl and grinned.

"I doubt he knows a single trick I haven't seen before."

Officer Rixl chuckled, then gave a crisp nod and shut the door.

Solace once again turned her cool gaze on Reynard.

"Mister…" With a twitch of a frown, she raised the Databoard and studied its screen. She pressed a button. "Mister Fuchs." She granted him a stiff, formal smile. "A pleasure to make your acquaintance."

"Likewise."

She sat down across from him, flicked out a stand at the bottom of the Databoard, and set the Databoard upright in the center of the table, its screen facing her. She pushed a few buttons on the screen. Glowing patterns of color flashed in her glasses, reflections from the screen's changing images. Reynard tried hard to discern any meaningful content in the reflections, but the images were too small and distorted for decipherment.

She looked up at him. "Do you understand why you're here?"

"Yeah, this is one of those speed-dating things, right?"

She blinked at him a couple of times, then returned to her Databoard. After pushing a few buttons, she scowled, then picked it up off the table and punched the buttons harder.

"This stupid thing's buggy. I knew I shouldn't have upgraded until they'd worked out all the kinks."

Reynard held out a hand. "Let me have a look. I might be able to fix it. I've got a degree in MiniZip Systems."

"Thank you for the offer," she said, not even deigning to look at him, "but that won't be necessary."

She tapped the screen a few more times, then smiled with relief.

"Ah. There we go."

She looked at him over the top of the Databoard.

"I have been tasked with performing a full psychological evaluation of you to determine if you are an appropriate candidate for a personality adjustment."

Reynard smiled. "You seem far too lovely a person to be engaged in such a morally dubious practice."

Ignoring this, she returned her attention to the Databoard. "I will ask you a series of questions. Simultaneously I will show you a series of images and I would like you to tell me your immediate impression of each image in a single word."

"What, at the same time I'm answering your questions?"

"Yes."

"What's the purpose of that?"

"Studies have shown that dealing with multiple tasks such as these reduces the possibility of deception, always a large risk with individuals with your background."

He felt his guts slithering about. So now she knew. She knew who he was, the sorts of things he did. He wasn't sure how *much* she knew. Certainly not everything. If the UPWA knew everything, they wouldn't bother with an evaluation; they would just go ahead and adjust him without a second thought. But they knew enough.

And now she did too.

She set the Databoard back on the table and looked at him over its top, her expression still blank and professional. It crossed his mind that maybe this wasn't really her. Maybe it was a descendant, a clone, an android—something with her form but not her memories.

But no. It was her. It had to be. The smell was hers, and that was something that couldn't be duplicated, not even by a clone.

"The images will appear on this." She swiveled the Databoard around on its stand so he could see the display. Several rows of fingertip-sized pastel-pink sense-field buttons hovered a millimeter above the surface of the Databoard's screen, which showed a bright blue sky through which puffy white clouds adorned with smiling faces were slowly drifting. The buttons were marked with various symbols denoting their function.

It was a top-of-the-line Acme Databoard, one of the newest models with fractal memory storage and infra-quantum shift-state encryption. Old hat to Reynard, of course. He had known how to hack those things to do everything except cook his dinner practically from the moment they were off the assembly line. If he could get his hands on it for just twenty seconds, he should be able to blunt-serve a message to someone who could bust him out of here. He had a few favors to call in. Then again, that damn Eye was watching everything…

"You are here," Solace said, "for tampering with a jump gate, endangering countless lives through the unlawful operation of a pair of Class-B starships, inciting a system-wide panic while concurrently wasting valuable UPWA time and resources by staging a fake chitii invasion using black-market morph gel, entering restricted Tholjaheim space, possession and usage of unregistered nano-gas, and breaking into the Forbidden Ziggurat with intent to rob it. Further investigation revealed evidence of drone-tampering, theft, fraud, and countless other crimes, including…" She paused, as if to muster the nerve to say the rest of it. "Including, post-apprehension, recoding your UPWA liaison officer's desktop holocube to broadcast visuals from the Man-2-Man Erotica Network."

Reynard chuckled at the memory. "It's just a matter of resetting it to the right frequency."

She swiveled the Databoard toward her, pressed a button with her thumb, then turned it back toward Reynard. The screen now showed a photo of a nude man striding out of a bedroom toward the viewer. In the bedroom behind him, a young blonde woman, also nude, sat on the bed with a pillow clutched to her chest. Her lowered gaze was dark, haunted.

"In a single word, please describe the feelings this photo evokes in you."

"Uh…"

"Now!"

"Um, aroused."

"Thank you," she said. "Now, why did you do what you

did?"

"I never admitted to—"

"Please don't insult my intelligence. We have irrefutable proof of your culpability on every count. What I want to know now is why."

"Why?" He shrugged. "I needed the money."

"You needed the money," she said.

"Well, yeah, why else does anyone commit a robbery?"

She heaved a sigh, as if she had been expecting better. "First of all, there are countless ways of illegally obtaining equivalent if not greater sums of money without insanely elaborate plans involving starship crashes and hoaxed invasions of malignant life-forms. Second, and more importantly, we have records of at least some of your MyCred accounts, which show combined balances of over seventeen million credits. Thus, you did not commit any of these crimes for the money. So, I ask again: Why?"

Okay. So the act-of-financial-desperation ploy wasn't going to work. Time for Plan B. If necessary, he had Plans C through X prepped as well.

"All right," he said with mock reluctance. "I confess. It was the challenge."

She frowned in puzzlement and shook her head. "The challenge? What do you mean?"

"To see if I could do it. The Forbidden Ziggurat is legendary as the most heavily guarded and inaccessible trove of ancient treasures in this entire galaxy. Over the years, countless thieves, conmen, and madmen have tried their hardest to get inside that place. So, yeah; the challenge. I almost succeeded, too. Which is more than everyone else who's ever tried can say."

She stared at him for a minute, then grunted and swiveled the Databoard around to face her. She began tapping away at the sense-field buttons.

"You're still lying," she said.

"Excuse me?"

"Even if what you say is true, you needed only to stage a simple collision between a pair of starships to create the debris shower required to mask your entry into Tholjaheim space. Why make one of the vessels infested with chitii?"

He shrugged again. "To keep everyone too panicked and preoccupied to notice me."

She shook her head as she continued punching buttons. "No. That doesn't make sense. The collision took place outside of Tholjaheim space, and the Tholjaheim don't care a whit about what happens beyond their borders. If anything, they'd track down every last bit of debris if they thought it was in any way a threat. In other words, the whole chitii infestation was extraneous to your needs, even antithetical. So, once again: Why?"

He watched her tap away at the Databoard for a minute, his eyes slits. Fine. She asked for it.

"I did it for the amusement," he said.

Her hand froze in mid-tap, index finger pointed at the screen as if in accusation. She looked up at him over the top of the Databoard.

"Amusement?" She sounded incredulous.

"Yep."

She blinked, then returned to the Databoard. She tapped, frowned, then tapped some more, the taps growing harder and faster until each jab made the Databoard rumble a few millimeters backward across the tabletop.

"Buggy little thing," she grumbled. As she continued tapping, she said, "So, is it feeling smarter than others that amuses you? Or is it the power?"

"Uh…"

"Ah, here we go." She swiveled the Databoard toward him. On its screen were the words, "Pretend there is a picture here. By the way, you are an asshole."

For the second time in less than ten minutes he could only gawp in surprise.

"Your reaction," she said. "In one word."

His surprise winked out. He fixed her with a frown. "Annoyance."

She gave a single terse nod, then swiveled the screen back toward her.

"You didn't answer my question," she said as she resumed pushing buttons. "What is it about doing these things that amuses you?"

"I don't know. Why does anybody enjoy anything? I just do. I guess I find the chaos entertaining."

"Causing it, you mean. Surely you don't like it when your own life is in chaos."

"Sure I do." He shifted in his seat, uncomfortable. He hated analyzing his motives. He simply did things he enjoyed and avoided those he didn't. Why did people want to make it more complicated than that?

Alas, that was exactly what she wanted him to do. Indeed, his very freedom, both physical and psychological, might depend on it.

"Unpredictability is...exciting," he said, allowing the words to pour forth, but not allowing himself to think about them too much or ask himself whether they were really true or only sounded true. "The unknown path. The unexpected twist. The endlessly complex configurations a vigintillion things can make. All of that is much better than routine, stasis, predictability. Life is chaos. Chaos is life. The alternative is death."

"The alternative to chaos isn't death. It's order." She

turned the screen toward him again. This time it read, "I am going to try to get you out of here. It won't be easy."

"In one word," she said.

He resisted the urge to sigh in relief and simply said, "Happy."

She gave a nearly imperceptible nod, as if he had given the expected answer, then swung the Databoard back toward her.

He admired her craftiness. The Eye overhead saw and recorded a fish-eye view of the room, but Solace was keeping the Databoard perpendicular to it so that the Eye could see only its upper edge. And she had accomplished this in a way that would arouse no suspicion. Smart girl. He entertained a brief fantasy of her joining him at his work, being his partner in crime....a notion her next words thoroughly quashed.

"I fail to see how you can enjoy chaos," she said. "Most people abhor it. Rightly, I should think."

"Chaos is just...it's the way of things. It's the way the world is."

"You sound like a Nünite." The way she said this latter word, Reynard could practically see the icicles depending from it.

"No. I don't hold with them at all. They make it a religion. A duty. An *order.*"

She swung the Databoard around. Now it read: "If you play along, I think I can guarantee you won't get adjusted. But I'm not sure yet of anything beyond that."

"Comforted," he said.

With a nod, she swiveled the screen back around, then resumed jabbing it with her finger, occasionally frowning and grumbling about tetchy mechanisms to maintain the charade.

"So," she said. "What's your take on it, then? On chaos, I mean?"

"I don't know that I have a *take* on it, exactly. I mean, I haven't made some kind of religion or philosophy out of it or anything. I just accept that it's the way things are. I don't think it's good or bad, right or wrong, divine or demonic. I just go along with it because it's there and it seems stupid to me to deny its existence. Everything is chaos. Clouds shift. Species mutate. Lives begin and end, and sometimes those lives end exactly where they started and sometimes a billion miles away. Nations are founded, struggle, thrive, fall, get forgotten, get rediscovered. Universes turn and end and begin again and spawn new ones. It's all just time happening." He paused, recalling his excursion into the Black Cathedral. Hadn't that crazy old woman said something similar? No, wait. That had been something about sound and time, hadn't it? Or was it all connected somehow?

"That strikes me as a fairly disempowering worldview," Solace said and turned the screen to face him again. It read: "You need to sound at least a little contrite. Give me something to work with here. I have to convince them you're not irredeemable."

"Contrite," he said, with a small smile like a pupil who knows he's said exactly what his teacher wished to hear.

There was a brief moment where her eyelids tightened and her eyeballs fluttered in place, and he realized she was trying not to roll her eyes.

She turned the screen back toward her. "Interesting response," she said. A pause, then: "So time is chaos?"

He shrugged, disgusted with the conversation. It was ridiculous. They were trying to parse things that defied analysis.

"It's all just words," he said, flicking up his hand as if

tossing something into the air. "And words are lies. Words aren't reality. Reality is a messy thing that our words can never fully describe. It's a sloppy, unpredictable, recalcitrant bitch of a thing that defies all theories and vocabularies. It's bigger than us and stronger than us and pisses on all our silly attempts to understand it. It will outlive all our words and concepts and doings. It will outlive *us*. And anything we can say about it is complete and utter bullshit that says more about us than it does about reality. All we can do is try to understand our puniness and lack of understanding, and accept reality's incomprehensible vicissitudes, its chaos."

Solace was staring at him with an expression both thoughtful and impressed, which was gratifying. He wondered how long it would take her to spot the inherent contradiction of his statement that all words are lies.

At the start of his monologue, she had been pushing buttons on the Databoard, but she stopped once he got rolling. Now she tapped at them frantically. He got the impression she was changing what she had written.

"Interesting little speech," she said. "But explain to me how that relates to your chitii hoax, not to mention all the other things you're guilty of."

She turned the Databoard toward him again. It read: "I think if we make this ideologically based, a demonstration of philosophy, rather than harmful criminal intent, we should be able to shorten your stay here and keep you from adjustment."

"Glee."

The sides of her mouth twitched upward with an imperfectly suppressed smile.

"Well," he said, following her lead, "I guess I want to do more than just accept the unpredictability of things. I want to expose others to it and help them learn to accept it, too."

She lifted her head just enough for Reynard to see her face while limiting the Eye's view to the top of her head and the tip of her nose. "Yes," she mouthed, and gave him a wink. Then she went back to tapping on the Databoard's buttons.

"If you try to simply tell people these things," he went on, "they don't really get it. Sure, they *say* they get it, and maybe on an intellectual level they do, but people need to understand it on a deep, primal level, below the threshold of rational thought. They need to understand it in the gut."

She nodded and turned the screen around.

"Nice!" it read. "Keep going! And if you can be more contrite, I think we might even have a chance at only some community service for you."

"Disbelief," he said.

She cocked her head and shot him a querying look, as if his response baffled her.

But she couldn't be any more baffled than he was; he didn't understand how she could promise so much. After all he had done, why would they let him go with only a token punishment? Or was he underestimating this era's obsession with embracing diversity?

"I'm truly sorry if I hurt anyone," he said, taking up her suggestion as she resumed tapping away at the Databoard. "I really am. If I had to do it all over again, I'd do it very differently, I assure you."

She glanced up at him over the rims of her glasses and flashed a small smile.

Perhaps it was because of his ebullience that adjustment now seemed unlikely, or perhaps it was simply because he had been locked up and layless for nearly a week, but whatever the reason, he felt an unexpected jolt of lust at the sight of her like that, her eyes fixed on his over those cute little glasses, her warm brown face standing out starkly against all the sterile whiteness around her, her pink lips bowed in a smile. He remembered their kiss in Nioedo and was suddenly seized with the desire to lean across the table right here and now and smash his lips to hers, to hell with the Eye and the UPWA.

His expression must have conveyed a hint of his thoughts, for her eyes widened a little and her smile drained away. Then she quickly whisked her gaze back down to her Databoard. She seemed unsure what to do with the board for a moment; her index finger wavered above the buttons while her eyes darted all over the screen, settling nowhere.

"Um, yes. Um…" She cleared her throat. "You're sorry, are you?"

"Absolutely. I never meant to cause any real harm. I just think it's good to unsettle people a little every now and then. People get too comfortable in their routines. It makes them soft, complacent. I think occasional challenges and discomforts are important for growth. It's only by meeting and overcoming challenges that we can become stronger." He nodded, head bobbing hard with the zeal of a proselyte. He didn't know if he believed a single word of it, but it sure *sounded* good.

"Interesting viewpoint," she said. "But did it not occur to you that your staged collision could have caused widespread and possibly severe damage? The debris could have gone anywhere, especially since it was so close to a jump gate. Plus, the panic incited by such stunts is very real and damaging. And not just psychologically; the fright many people experienced when they learned about the apparent chitii infestation could have led to heart attacks, strokes, accidents."

"Honestly, that never even occurred to me."

"You need to work on your empathy."

He groaned inwardly. Empathy had become a corner-stone of society, a byword heard from every tongue and transmitter. Empathy, understanding, accommodation—all these mewling pleas for togetherness were absurd. Everyone believed that adhering to such ideals made them wiser, better. But all it did was create a society of sheep, coddled and trusting and stupid. Which was fine with him, of course. It meant his shears were always buzzing.

But then he looked at Solace as she sat there awaiting his response—at her calm and assured bearing, at the small secure smile on her lips, at her white outfit that perfectly matched the white room—and he suddenly realized this was precisely the kind of world she preferred, the kind of world she came from and had yearned to return to ever since the Cataclysm. This was her element, her paradise.

And in the wake of this realization, he was amazed to feel his opinion of that world change a minute amount. He still disdained it, but now his disdain was leavened by a grudging acknowledgement that it might harbor some value beyond his own easy enrichment.

Then again, he reflected, perhaps his shift in attitude wasn't so amazing: A world like this had created Solace, and Solace had just helped save his ass from adjustment. Thus, there was value to a world like this. Simple logical self-interest. That was all.

"I'll do that," he said. "I'm sure my empathy can use improvement."

"Good," she said, her smile broadening. As she returned to her Databoard she said almost off-handedly: "Empathy is important. We're all in this together."

We're all in this together. He had heard that tired phrase a million times and had always dismissed it as Pollyanna twaddle. Now, though, out of nowhere, he intuited the truth at its core. It wasn't just the simpering love-thy-neighbor bullshit he and nearly everyone else imagined it to be, the latest iteration of good old Mogo Lobilozo's "all one flesh, all one blood." No, there was something more to it than that, something more akin to his own beliefs, shockingly enough.

He and Solace were a perfect representation of it. He was a Trickster, a con man, a liar, a thief, the child of a crude and cruel medieval world where people wiped their asses with leaves and problems were solved with knives and swords. She was a Good Samaritan, a helper, a nurse, a teacher, the product of a high-tech utopia full of peace and quiet and unobtrusive machines. Two people could not be more dissimilar. Yet here they were, linked despite all logic and expectations.

And that was the truth behind it: that he and Solace and everyone else were all just bits of debris adrift on the river of time, the vagaries of the current bringing some of these bits together in unpredictable configurations then wrenching them apart, perhaps to meet again one day, perhaps to remain eternally sundered; but all the while sliding forward toward no certain or meaningful end, the motion—the chaotic joinings and divisions and rearrangements—being all there was.

He knew he had taken on a distant, spacey look, but he felt no great urge to change it, not even when she peered at him, her smile fading, the folds of a tiny frown forming between her eyebrows.

"Are you all right?" she asked.

"Fine," he said quietly, his eyes never leaving hers.

Her frown deepened. He realized she had no idea what was going on in his head. But had she ever? And had he ever really had any idea what was going on in hers? They were aliens, strangers, even though they had known each other for ten thousand years. They had shared comedies and tragedies; they had lied to each other and divulged awkward truths to each other; they had amused each other and angered each other and helped each other and failed each other. And yet they didn't really know each other, because they couldn't, because while we're all one flesh and one blood, while we're all in this together, adrift on the same river, we're each of us unique, a solitary and remarkable soul sheathed in a numb casing of meat and blood, forever severed from true communion with another.

All one, all alone. Forever.

An itch on his right eyebrow broke the spell. As he grimaced and scratched it, she tore her eyes from his and frowned distractedly at her Databoard.

"I'm thinking of joining the Nünites," he said, returning to the thread of the world.

"That fits," she said with a slow nod, clearly still a little perplexed by his weird zone-out a moment earlier. "Would you like me to set up a meeting with a Nünite minister?"

"I…" Of course he didn't. In his opinion, Nünites were blithering idiots. Who ever heard of trying to codify chaos? It was stupid. But he had to play along to save his skin, the most valuable possession he owned. "Yeah, that'd be great."

She pushed buttons on her Databoard. "I'll set something up, then." She flashed him a bright, upbeat smile. "I'm happy to say, I think we can help you become a healthier member of society without having to turn to an unfortunate last-resort method like personality adjustment. It sounds as if all you require is the proper outlet for the expression of your personal value-system. Just to be sure, though, let's do a few final tests."

She turned the Databoard around. It read "Awesome, Reynard! I predict you'll be out of here in a couple of months if you keep playing along—and I know you can do that."

Was that last comment some kind of jab? He looked in her eyes, but saw only twinkling good humor therein.

"Gladness," he said.

She gave a hearty nod, then swiveled the Databoard back toward her and began punching buttons again.

"I'll work out a program for you," she said. "Regular meetings with the Nünite minister, some community service, and so on. You're not irredeemable. You're just in need of guidance."

She flashed him another upbeat smile, one of those smiles it's impossible for even the crankiest curmudgeon to avoid returning, and then turned the Databoard toward him one last time.

It read: "You're still an asshole."

He stared at it for a second, his expression carefully blank, then looked up at her and with a small, pleasant smile said, "Bitchy."

Events unfolded exactly as she said. The very next day a Nünite priest visited him in his cell. Reynard played the part of the eager new convert to the hilt. Within a week, he was transferred to a lower security wing. A month later he was released from the Repository, but on probation, with orders to perform regular community service, attend Nünite meetings every third day, and visit a counselor once a week. The counselor was a smiling, overly trusting fool whom Reynard could run intellectual rings around in his sleep. Reynard didn't see Solace at all after the evaluation.

A year later, after the entirety of his sentence had been

served, when he was, then, a free man, he hacked into the Repository's Galacticom node in hopes of learning how he could get in touch with Solace. (He had tried more orthodox channels already, but had been told by the Repository's public interface liaison [i.e. help-desk worker] that information on specific employees could not be distributed to the general public.) The personnel databanks informed him that Solace Desidáre (where, he wondered, had that strange surname come from?) had tendered her resignation eight months earlier, abruptly terminating five years of impeccable service. Her file contained nothing after that except a note added three weeks later by an obviously frustrated administrative employee, reading, "All sprocking mail to Ms. Desidáre's sprocking node returned as sprocking undeliverable! And no sprocking physical address on sprocking record!"

Reynard laughed when he read this, but behind his laughter lurked disappointment. He had been hoping to get in touch with her instead of enduring yet another encore performance of her disappearing act.

He started to navigate out of the Repository's node, then stopped.

What was he thinking?

While he was here, he might as well do a little creative reconstruction of their node to help its users understand chaos on a deep and primal level...

11

Haven
11012 A.C.

Reynard strode down the long white corridor toward Elevator A223 on Level 38 of the Monolith-Class Astrocruiser *Haven*. The inner pocket of his polychromatic vest was heavy with the bug-popper porn crystals he planned to give to Hem Sithawoo, head of small-vehicle maintenance in Level 499's three-mile-wide hangar. In return for the crystals, Hem promised to sign over to Reynard an Atom-Class Cruiser currently slated for recycling. The cruiser was one of the old non-sentient models, but Reynard planned to modify it to resemble a modern sentient one. The voice issuing from the ship's onboard speakers, however, would be his own, remotely broadcast from a secure location where he could also monitor the ship's occupants via various sensors hidden onboard. This was only one fragment of an insanely elaborate plan to engineer the utter ruination of Arzt ba ta Kuweimorai, the Intergalactic Senate's Assistant Secretary of Trade.

He stopped at the smooth white elevator door and pressed the Up button. With a brief cheery chime, the door slid open after only five seconds, a bit of unexpected luck that made him smile. With over four thousand levels on a ship of this size, the wait for the elevators could be excruciating, despite the hyper-fast MetaShell technology that powered them.

As he stepped into the empty compartment, he heard a weak, wavering voice say, "Hold on, please."

He turned. A tiny old lady in an iridescent pink robe was hobbling down the corridor toward him. When she saw that he had seen her, she smiled and nodded as if he had already sworn to hold the elevator. Of course. Because everyone was in this together, and that meant doing good deeds for your fellow travelers through life.

Reynard returned her smile, then pressed the button for Level 499. He caught a quick glimpse of the woman's smile collapsing into a gape of shock an instant before the door slid shut between them.

He chuckled as the elevator streaked upward, the only sign of its ascent being the changing of the large luminous numbers on the wall. The levels raced by so fast only every fourth number appeared. He loved this new technology. He would be at the hangar in about ten seconds unless...

The numbers stopped at 52.

"Shit," he hissed.

With another chime, the door opened, and Solace started to step aboard, casting him one of those automatic smiles you give strangers you're forced to briefly associate with. When she saw it was Reynard, however, she froze right in the middle of the doorway, her eyes the size of planets. Reynard was likewise frozen, his mouth agape, no doubt looking exactly like the old woman down on Level 38 when he closed the elevator door on her.

Reynard regained his composure first. "You'd better get inside," he said. "You don't want to get snipped in two by the door."

Which was a joke, of course. Everything in this defanged age had multiple safeguards that prevented anything even remotely unpleasant from happening. He guessed that of everyone on this ship, only he and Solace and maybe a couple of history geeks knew of the days when elevators could actually be dangerous.

Solace acted as if those days were still here. With a clipped yelp, she propelled herself into the car, twisting her head around as she did so to make sure the doors weren't about to shear off her backside.

Then she remembered the safeness of things, and gave a small, embarrassed laugh.

"Old habits," she said. She checked the elevator's destination, then pressed the button for Level 996.

"So how've you been?" he asked as the doors closed and the elevator began its ascent anew.

"Fine." She glanced at him. "You?"

"Good."

"Good." She gave a terse nod, then turned to watch the shifting numbers on the wall.

He studied her profile, hoping to gauge her feelings, but her expression was blank, unreadable. Not the greatest sign. Maybe now that she had learned the truth about him she wanted nothing more to do with him. Maybe her helping him escape from Giv-Golos had been, to her, a squaring of accounts and a final act of fellowship in commemoration of all that had gone before. Maybe it had been her way of saying goodbye.

Still, giving up wasn't his style. Where there's life, there's hope.

"So, are you residing on-ship," he asked, "or just en route somewhere?"

She opened her mouth to reply, then hesitated as if debating with herself whether or not to tell him the truth.

"Technically I'm living here," she said finally, giving him a cool, even look. "But when we reach Pompulop 9 tomorrow, I'll be taking off on a long work-related trip."

"Ah." Of course. A long trip. How convenient. "What kind of work are you doing these days?"

"I'm with the Outreach Society. You know, the group that works to bring new worlds and species into the Pax Galactica?"

"Ah."

"Are *you* living here?"

"No. Just en route…elsewhere."

"Mm."

With another chipper little chime, the doors opened. Level 499.

He stepped into the doorway and turned to face her, feeling compelled to place one hand on the edge of the retracted door even though his rational mind knew it wouldn't budge until its multiple sensor fields detected no obstructions. She wasn't the only one whose old habits refused to die, it seemed.

"Maybe we could meet before you leave," he said. "Have dinner or something."

"Uh…" She glanced at the display on which 499 was now blinking while 996 still glowed steadily beside it. "Sure."

Was she saying that only to get rid of him? Her still-inscrutable expression made it impossible to tell.

"Solace, look—"

She raised her hands, palms out, and for the first time she gave him what appeared to be a genuine smile.

"Save it for dinner, okay?" she said.

He smiled in return. "Okay. I guess we have a lot to talk about, don't we?"

"I guess." She licked her lips, took a breath as if she were about to do something dangerous, then said, "I'll meet you in the Black Hole Lounge at six o'clock. You know where that is?"

"I know. Level 1728. Just down from the Pleasure Pyramid, right?"

"Right."

His smile broadened. "It's good to see you again, by the way."

She stared at him in silence a moment, a brittle shine in her eyes that made him wonder if she were about to start crying. But then she made her face return the smile.

"It's good to see you too," she said.

"See you at six."

"Okay."

Eyes fixed on her all the while, he backed out of the elevator and into a white hallway identical to the one on Level 38. They smiled at each other as the door closed between them. He remained there for several seconds, smile slowly fading, then turned and headed on his way.

When he stepped into the Black Hole Lounge's dimly lit interior at five to six, he grunted in mingled surprise and relief to find Solace already seated at the long black bar, sipping one of those cloying shnozzberry martinis that were all the rage these days. All things considered, he had been more than half sure she wouldn't show up.

Far more surprising than her mere presence was what she was wearing. Her torso was sheathed in a skimpy black dress nearly nonexistent in the leg and so low in the chest it was a miracle her nipples weren't visible. She also wore transparent high-heeled pumps, another faddish choice that showed off her slender, beautifully pedicured feet, the nails of which, like her fingernails, she had painted with nanite-filled polish programmed to display swirls of color that shifted languidly like smoke. Her long black hair had been waved since their encounter in the elevator, and the shining serpentine tresses framed a face embellished by a hint of black eyeshadow, deep red lipstick, and a pair of pendant earrings that looked like real diamonds.

He sat down beside her, the bar-stool's fake leather upholstery producing a faint creak that made him a little nostalgic. He hadn't seen real leather since the Universal Biodignity Act of 9051.

"You look fantastic," he said.

She smiled at him with those dark red lips, eyes fixed directly on his, then lowered her gaze with affected demureness.

"Thanks," she said in a coy, girlish voice.

He blinked at her, nonplused to hear her adopt such a tone.

The bartender, a female wochobüshkan with dusty blue skin that faded to white at the tips of her two waist-length head-tentacles, appeared, handed them menus, and asked Reynard if he would like anything to drink.

He flashed Solace a smile then said to the bartender, "I'll have a Queen Pithylia."

Solace frowned slightly. The bartender blinked at him, her black, whiteless eyes uncertain, the ends of her tentacles curling up into stiff hooks, a sign of nervousness.

"Um, I'm not sure what that is," the bartender said.

He started to explain how to prepare it, but she interrupted him: "Sorry, but open flames aren't allowed on *Haven.*" Noting his disgruntlement, she said, "It's, like, a security measure." Noting the unchanged disgruntlement, she added, "Fires are dangerous."

His mood plummeting fast, Reynard cocked an eyebrow. "Have you ever even seen a real fire?"

The bartender opened her mouth, shut it. "Um..."

"Reynard." This from Solace. He looked over at her. She shook her head.

He sagged a little as a silent sigh escaped him.

"Gimme a vodka," he said. "Neat."

Back on familiar ground, the bartender gave him a sharp nod and bustled away, overcompensating for her inability to meet his primary desire by meeting the secondary one with almost military efficiency.

"A Queen Pithylia?" Solace asked. "Did you really think she'd be able to serve something like that?"

He shrugged. "I guess I hadn't thought that far ahead."

She reached out and patted his hand on the bar top.

"Don't worry, we'll get you good and drunk one way or another." Leaving her hand on his a moment longer than necessary, she gave him another coquettish smile, then settled back and picked up her menu. "We'd better order soon," she said, perusing the items on the menu's holo-screen. "I am absolutely *ravenous.*" She packed the last word with unmistakable innuendo.

He stared at her in baffled silence. Why was she being so uncharacteristically flirtatious? Given their less-than-ideal encounters the last few millennia, not to mention their meeting in the elevator earlier today, he had been expecting coolness, even animosity. What kind of game was she playing?

Unsure how to proceed, he picked up his own menu and scrolled through the entrees.

The bartender returned with Reynard's vodka.

"You two ready to order?" she asked.

"Yeah, I am," he said. To Solace: "You?"

"Oh, I'm definitely ready," she said with a quick glance at Reynard to underscore the double entendre.

"Glad to hear it," he said with a smile, hiding his growing

mystification.

Choosing to be oblivious to this exchange, the like of which she had no doubt witnessed in here a thousand times before, the bartender said, "So what'll it be, then?"

"The Oysters Deluxe for me," Reynard said. It didn't include real oysters, of course. It didn't include any living things. Not even plants. Only villains and barbarians ate anything other than synthedibles anymore. Even the drinks he and Solace were sipping had been made from inorganic chemicals. Thankfully, synthetically produced foods were designed to replicate the flavors and textures of the finest examples of real, old-fashioned biological food. In Reynard's opinion, the invariable perfection got rather monotonous.

"And the lady?" the bartender said.

Solace shot Reynard a sultry sidelong smile. "I'll have what he's having."

"Good choice. I'll have that out for you in a picobeat." She hurried away.

Reynard regarded Solace as she sipped her martini, unsure whether to be pleased or perturbed by her behavior. Had it been any other woman delivering these innuendoes, sending these fuck-me glances, he wouldn't have thought twice about satisfying her desires. Hell, he would have had her back in his room already. Or in her own room. Or maybe in the nearest closet.

But this wasn't any other woman. This was Solace. And she wasn't acting anything like Solace...

Or was she? As he had reflected during their encounter in Giv-Golos, no two people could ever truly know each other. Her coquetry tonight could simply be a facet of her personality he had never seen before. He knew next to nothing about her sexual behaviors, her preferred bedmates. Maybe she was one of those women who act prim and proper on the outside, but secretly lust for dangerous men. Maybe discovering the truth about him had made him more alluring to her.

Noticing his scrutiny, she cocked her head.

"Anything wrong?" she asked.

"No. It's just…well, I'm a little surprised you don't want to talk about, you know, what happened before. About—"

She leaned forward and again laid a hand on his. The touch shut him up in an instant.

"Let's not talk about the past," she said. "Now's the only time there is, right?" She curled her fingers, the tips of her nanite-covered nails lightly grazing his skin.

He stiffened and sucked in a breath. In his pants, his penis stirred and began to strain against the fabric enclosing it.

She gave him another seductive smile, then picked up her martini. As she dropped her gaze to guide the slim red straw into her mouth, he allowed his eyes one swift sweep over her body: her shining black hair cascading over her bare brown shoulders, the smooth swells of her breasts, her slender legs stretching away into the shadows beneath her snug black dress. He felt almost dizzy with lust at the thought he might see that body unclothed before the night was done, feel it warm and writhing beneath him, taste it, touch it, possess it. He still didn't entirely grasp why this was happening, didn't have a clue what emotional undercurrents or ulterior motives were driving her, but what difference did it make? If she wanted him to fuck her, then that's exactly what he would do.

She looked up from her drink, only her eyes moving, swiveling in their sockets to fix upon his. Her dark red lips formed a smile around the straw inserted between them. The pink liquid in the glass slowly drained away as it rose through the straw and disappeared inside her.

The bartender returned, bearing a pair of steaming plates which she set on the bar before them. That was another good thing about synthedibles: All they needed was a quick heating up.

"Enjoy," the bartender said as she departed. Reynard thought he detected a trace of amusement in her tone, and wondered how much of the exchange she had witnessed.

He took hold of the oyster fork that was stuck into one of the fabricated oysters like a sea-god's trident piercing the body of a vanquished foe. Twisting the fork, he tugged the fake meat free of its dark striated shell. It came away with a slick tearing sound, leaving behind a few rubbery shreds that clung to the pale interior of the shell, which was synthetic just like the meat. He never ceased to be amazed at how much effort the makers of synthedibles devoted to replicating every last taste, texture, color, and smell of real organic food. For a society that claimed to abhor the killing and consumption of living things, the overwhelming demand for such slavish reproduction seemed hypocritical, to say the least.

"Mmm," Solace said, her mouth full. "This is delicious."

"Yeah."

"You know," she said, holding up one of the faux oysters on the end of her fork, "some people say these are an aphrodisiac."

"Maybe I should've ordered something else, then." He shot her a smile. "I mean, with you sitting here, an aphrodisiac is kind of superfluous."

She grinned and forked the oyster into her mouth.

And so went dinner: As the pile of empty shells on the sides of their plates swelled, as their glasses emptied then filled then emptied again, they flirted and traded trivialities, neither of them sharing anything of importance about themselves. She told colorful stories about her days working as an assistant at the Yohelé Orgasm Institute in the mid-10300s. He bragged of adventures he had had, leaving out all serious illegalities and whatever else he thought might disquiet her.

By the time dessert arrived—two slabs of rich, creamy synthedible mint-chocolate chip ice cream cake—Reynard's face felt flushed, and he had to squint a little to make out the logos on the bottles behind the bar. He was drunker than he had been in…well, centuries. Since that party on Smasmu IV, if he wasn't mistaken.

The truth was, he avoided drinking whenever possible. Given his activities, where the slightest lapse of focus could bring hordes of Harmony Facilitation Officers down on his head, anything that muddied thought and perception was asking for disaster. And since any place, person, or event had the potential to be bent to his ends, he saw himself as always on the job. For occasions when he had to drink socially, he had taught himself how to nurse a single drink all evening while making it seem as if he had gulped down half the bar.

He couldn't understand why he had drunk so much tonight. It was as if his body had been acting of its own volition, continually grabbing his glass and raising it to his lips while his mind had been preoccupied with Solace's pleasing yet decidedly uncharacteristic behavior.

Since Solace didn't strike him as a heavy drinker and weighed a good forty or fifty pounds less than him, he figured she had to be at least as drunk as he was. But however closely he watched her, he couldn't tell for sure. Sometimes she seemed quite tipsy, making jokes and comments that under normal circumstances she surely would have thrust aside as inappropriate or insipid the moment her brain conceived them. At other times, however, her eyes shone with such craft and her speech flowed so elegantly he felt clumsy and outmatched. He hated being drunk.

The bartender returned to clear away the dessert plates and find out if they wanted anything more. Reynard asked for a glass of water and the check. After the bartender had brought them, then bustled happily away with a twenty-cred crystal, which covered all food and drinks plus a hefty tip, Solace cocked an eyebrow at Reynard.

"Water, huh?" she said.

"Absolutely. After all, I'd hate to get so drunk I don't remember this wonderful night."

"Hmm. Maybe I should stop too." She eyed her half-finished peach martini—her fifth martini of the night, and her second peach one, she having grown tired of shnozzberry half an hour back—then shrugged. "On the other hand, I hate to waste it." She downed the rest in one big swallow.

With a satisfied sigh she pushed the glass away, then swiveled around to face Reynard, her elbow on the bartop, her chin on her palm, her index finger toying with her pendant earring as she regarded him with a coy smile.

"So," she said, "if we're not gonna be drinking any more, we'll have to find some other way to occupy our evening."

"I don't think it's technically evening anymore. I believe we're officially in night territory at this point."

"Evening, night, morning, whatever. Time is relative, right? And it flies. It flies relatively."

"Sure," he said, her strange comments making him wonder again how drunk she was.

"So what can we do with our flying time?" she asked, her low, insinuating tone making it abundantly clear what she wanted to do.

Smiling, he leaned forward until his face was only a few inches from hers. The stink of peaches and alcohol washed across him. He laid a hand on her smooth brown knee.

"Well," he said. "I might be able to think of a few things to keep us busy."

"Hmm." She sucked her upper lip between her teeth and pressed a finger onto the back of the hand on her knee. "And where should we do these things?"

"Oh, not here," he said, looking around in mock alarm. "I'd hate to make these fine people jealous of all the fun we'll be having. After all, I don't want to make anyone feel bad."

"Want to make 'em feel good, eh?" The finger twisted first one way then the other.

Reynard inhaled sharply, nostrils flaring. He flipped his hand over and grabbed hers.

"Let's go," he said, rising, hauling her up off her seat.

She stood there looking at him a little uncertainly for a moment, but then tilted her chin up, eyes sparking with willed boldness, and gave his hand a squeeze.

"Yes, let's," she said.

He led her out of the bar to the elevator, pleased to find he was steadier on his feet than he had feared he would be. Moving around made the feelings of drunkenness abate a bit.

While they waited for the elevator, her hand still clasped in his, he leaned in close, his bicep pressing against her warm, soft breast, his cheek grazing hers, and nuzzled her earlobe. She drew in a breath, the sound clear and sharp so close to his ear. She had just started to turn her head toward his when the elevator emitted its single chime and the door slid open.

An elderly couple shuffled out. For a second Reynard

thought the woman was the one he had let the elevator door close on earlier; but no, it was just another collection of droops and wrinkles and outdated clothes.

The woman spared them only a brief, disinterested glance as she and her companion walked past, but the old man's eyes, bright and quick in his seamed gray face, darted back and forth between Reynard and Solace before fixing on Reynard. The old man gave him a grin and a single vigorous nod, as if in encouragement.

Reynard pulled Solace onto the elevator, trying to maintain his passion but failing. The old couple had dampened his mood. Part of it was the memory of the old woman from earlier and how he had let the doors close on her. For some reason it bothered him now. He found her shocked look no longer amusing but sad and pathetic. And the old man's silly go-get-em nod hadn't helped either, somehow reducing this whole endeavor to farce or banality.

Solace didn't seem to notice the shift in his mood, or perhaps she did but intended to swing things back in her favor, for as soon as he had pressed the button for Level 2744, his level, and the elevator door had closed, she threw herself against him, forcing him back against the wall, and began licking and nipping his neck. Her body, barely covered in its skimpy black dress, pressed against his from chest to thigh. His passion rekindled, his penis swelled pulse by pulse.

He seized a fistful of her black hair and tugged her head back, off his neck, baring her face to his. Her eyes were as clouded with lust as he knew his own must be. Her lips were parted, revealing a glimpse of white teeth.

He leaned in and kissed her. As their lips joined he felt her exhale a tiny sigh into his mouth as if relinquishing a piece of herself into him, and she made a small noise that might have been a whimper or a moan. Her hand squeezed his. His squeezed hers. He wrapped an arm around her back, and clutching her tightly, twirled around so their positions were reversed; now it was he who was pinning her to the elevator wall, their bodies welded together, his groin nestled in the crook of her parted legs.

The elevator stopped with a chime. The door opened.

For a moment they continued kissing, pressing, clutching. Then he broke away and, still grasping her hand—he hadn't let it go since they left the bar, he realized—he dragged her out of the elevator and down the white corridor to his room.

He had his key-crystal out well before they got there. He swiped the crystal over the scanner next to the door, and the door whooshed open. Stuffing the crystal back into his pocket, he stepped across the threshold and yanked her in after him. Unprepared for the hard, sudden tug, she stumbled forward and slammed into him, sending him stumbling in turn. For a second they did a clumsy dance there in the dim foyer, where the light streaming in from the bright white hallway faded through infinite gradations of gray toward the black of the room's unlit interior. Their shoulders knocked. Their hips bumped. Their legs tangled and tottered. Their hands remained clasped through it all.

They miraculously stayed upright and took advantage of the collision to resume kissing with wild abandon. Without even looking, he flung out his free hand and slapped the touch-switch that activated the room's lights a moment before the door whisked closed and cut off the light from the hallway.

Still kissing, bodies still pressed together, they stumbled into the main room, weaving and turning and careering as if their opposing passions could find no balance, condemning them to remain in constant chaotic motion.

He caught quick glimpses of the room as they staggered about: the tall crystalline entertainment column that served as both container and player of countless films and songs and images and mood-shows; the square black table and two silver chairs sitting before the curtained display screen, which was currently switched off but could be programmed either to show the universe passing by outside the ship or to radiate varying levels of imitation sunlight; and there in the midst of it all, the neatly made bed, its perfect orderliness awaiting disarrangement.

He hoped to maneuver her toward the bed, but instead their turbulent course somehow ended with his back banging into the wall beside the entertainment column. She wrenched her hand free of his grasp, and it joined its mate in roving over his body, clutching, stroking, clawing. In no time his shirt was untucked and pulled up high enough to expose his belly and the line of dark hair plunging from his navel to the waistband of his pants. Her crotch ground against his, teasing his stiff penis with wonderful friction.

He broke the kiss and drew back a little to take a breath. As she peered at him impatiently, desperate for more, he saw that her eyes were glistening, an effect he at first attributed to her intense desire. But then a tear slid from the corner of her right eye and streaked down her cheek.

"Solace," he said. "What—"

Before he could say more, she hurtled forward, pinning him to the wall. Her lips smashed into his, pinching his lower lip against his teeth. He caught a quick taste of blood.

"Solace," he said, his words muffled by her mouth.

She seemed not to hear him. Her onslaught didn't slacken a bit. Her mouth and hands and body continued moving, touching, caressing. Though he tried to give himself over to the arousal her actions elicited, the image of that tear coursing down her face kept recurring.

He yanked his head back. She tried to follow his lips with hers, but he turned his head away, denying her access.

"What's wrong?" she said. "I thought you liked it."

"I did. I do. But…"

She cupped the bulge in the front of his pants.

"Well, you'll like the rest even better," she said, flashing an impish grin full of teeth, exultant in the power she knew she possessed over him. But that exultation imperfectly masked something else, something fragile and sad. Looking closer, he spotted the shiny lines of shed tears running down both of her cheeks.

"Sol—"

She launched herself against him again, slamming him against the wall so hard that the entertainment column wobbled on its stand. Her hand, still on his penis, stroked it up and down.

He allowed himself to enjoy the feeling for a moment, then gripped her by the forearms and pushed her away.

"What are you doing?" she said, words clipped with annoyance. "Why do you keep stopping?"

She tried to move forward again, but he held her at arm's length.

"What?" she snapped. "This is what you want, isn't it? This is what you've always wanted! Well, take it!" The words were both an order and a plea.

He shook his head. "Why are you acting like this? What's wrong?"

"What a stupid question!"

"I don't think so."

She twisted in his grip, trying to get away now, but he held her tight.

"Stupid!" she said.

"Stop it!"

"Fuck you!" She wrenched herself from his grasp and stumbled backward, glaring at him like a feral animal. "What the hell's wrong with you? I'm finally giving you a chance to fuck me like you always wanted, and you can't even fucking do it!" Her voice was a shriek. "Why are you just standing there? Take me! Fuck me! Just...just..."

She burst into tears. She made no effort to cover her face or turn away, just stood there sobbing helplessly, eyes clenched shut, cheeks streaming with tears, arms limp at her sides.

Seeing her like this roused something inside him he had never felt before. He wanted her to stop crying, but not for the reasons he had wanted girls to stop crying in the past—because their weeping annoyed him, or because he thought if he comforted them they would put out for him; no, for the first time he wanted her to stop crying because seeing her cry pained him. Seeing her face contort in misery was like seeing something that shouldn't exist—a square circle, a black whiteness—and he felt compelled to do whatever he could to ease that misery.

Without a word he stepped forward and gently wrapped his arms around her, half expecting her to either pull away in defiance or go limp, ceding all power to him. Instead she showed no response at all at first, leading him to wonder if she was so far gone in her agony she wasn't even aware of him. But then he felt her arms closing around his back.

Though her sobs soon tapered off, she remained in his embrace, her cheek on his shoulder, her eyes closed, a damp oval on his shirt from her tears.

"I'm sorry," she said finally, her voice shaky and low.

"What's wrong?"

There was no response for so long he became convinced she wasn't going to answer at all, but then she sighed and said, "Sometimes I hate this world. I don't understand it anymore."

"You what?" he said, mystified. He had been expecting some tale of romantic woe, of her being jilted and deciding to vent her aggressions on him.

"I don't…" She sniffed, the sound becoming something of a wet snort as she sucked back snot. "I don't understand all this technology anymore. I sit there trying to work this silly KristalLine crap, and I feel so fucking stupid. I mean, I'm over eleven thousand years old. I'm from a world that was pretty technologically advanced in its own way, but I can't make these damn crystals do what they're supposed to. And then there're those gendermorphing procedures. Men becoming women. Women becoming men. How can you be sure of anyone anymore? Any man you meet could have been a woman the week before. I mean, I don't want to sound intolerant or—or judgmental or anything, but I—I just don't understand how people could do that." She heaved a husky sigh. "And their fashions—all these ugly fashions. The goddamn twirly things they attach to their crotches and the metal fins and the tacky fucking glow-piping. And—and…" A pause, then: "And I lost my Gem Node. All my contacts were on it."

"You didn't back it up anywhere?" He tried hard not to make it sound accusatory or belittling.

She didn't say anything, but he felt her shake her head.

After a moment she said in a small quiet voice, "Can we lie down?"

His heart jumped, and his cock gave a tentative twitch. Did she still want to have sex?

"Just to lie down," she added quickly, as if reading his

thoughts. "But…" Her voice was hesitant, almost embarrassed. "Could you still hold me? Please?"

"Whatever you want," he said, feeling far less disappointed than he would have expected.

He led her to the bed and they lay down atop the covers, still embracing. She didn't look at him, just kept her head lowered, eyes closed. His arm soon went numb under the weight of her shoulder, but he said nothing, choosing to let it go dead and heavy rather than disturb her.

Her breathing slowed and deepened so much he thought she had dozed off. But then she mumbled, "Thank you," her voice drowsy-thick. A minute later, her breathing grew even slower and deeper and more regular, and he knew she was asleep.

He remained exactly as he was, numb arm and all, not tired enough to sleep, but relaxed, comfortable, at peace, floating in a strange sort of contentment with the scent of her filling his nostrils as if it were the only smell in the universe. He gazed at her sleep-slack face for a few minutes, examining every curve, every line, every tiny hair, then with a small smile, he rested his cheek against the top of her head, and they lay there together in silence, on the bed, in the room, on the vast ship as it traversed the endless void.

An hour later she muttered something that sounded like "Nectar for that," and rolled over, off his arm.

He watched the back of her head for a minute to make sure she was still asleep, and when he heard her deep regular breathing, he got up as slowly and quietly as he could and went in search of a bite to eat.

She awoke six hours later, sat up, looked around. Reynard sat at the round white table in front of the display panel, which he had turned on low, allowing just enough soft white light to filter in around the edges of the drawn curtain for him to play Twelve's Delight, a variety of solitaire that utilized a deck of 144 cards.

"Hi," he said as she blinked at him.

With a small frown, she looked down to check her clothes, then back up at him, her expression a little perplexed. "Um, hi."

"Are you hungry?" he asked. "I could get you something. The kyeta juice is especially good." He nodded at a nearby glass that sported congealing traces of a green liquid on its interior and around its rim.

"No, thanks," she said.

She climbed out of bed and came over to the table. After silently watching the game's ever-changing columns, rows, and crosses for a minute, she sat down opposite him.

"You ever play this?" he asked as he drew a new card—the Purple Bird—and looked for a place to put it.

"No. Cards games aren't really my thing."

He set the Purple Bird on the Black Crown, then added both of them to the Fortune pile. Next he moved the Orange Door next to the Green Stone. This freed up the Silver Sword, which went atop the Blue Sphere, and those two, too, went into the pile.

With no more available moves in the layout, he drew another card from the stock. Yellow Heart. Perfect. He set it atop the Red Hand at the bottom of the only open column.

As he placed these two cards in the Fortune pile, Solace cleared her throat and said, "Can I ask you something?"

He tensed, knowing that when someone asks if they can ask something, the thing they want to ask probably isn't good. He looked up to find that she was eyeing him with a sad, somewhat rueful expression.

"Sure," he said, drawing another card. Gray Eye. Shit.

"Was that you in Nioedo? Back in the 7400s?"

That was exactly what he had been afraid she would ask. He hesitated, caught between the warring impulses of lying and telling the truth. Then he realized that the fact of the war itself, and the telltale hesitation it produced, was already the declaration of the winner.

"I thought so," she said, and gave a faint sigh that was little more than a minute shift of her chest and shoulders.

Unable to keep his eyes on her, he dropped his gaze to the game and drew another card: Brown Star. Interesting.

"If you meant to hurt me, you succeeded." She emitted a small humorless laugh. "You succeeded very well. You caught me at a…a vulnerable time. The man I'd been with for nearly a decade had died a few months earlier."

"Oh. I…I'm sorry."

She nodded, looking down at her hands, which sat folded on the tabletop. Her nails were plain and pink. She must have deactivated the nanites at some point.

"I hadn't dated at all since then," she said, "hadn't even felt like it. Frankly I'd been a complete mess. I was finally getting over it, ready to move on, when you popped up, except of course I didn't know for sure it was you. Either way…" Her voice trailed off. After a pause, she heaved another, deeper sigh. "I understand why you did it. I do. And I can't really blame you. The thing with the T-mails—I'm sure that hurt you quite a bit, and I'm sorry about that. I really am. I knew it would hurt you, but…" She shook her head. "I had to. Some of the things you said…"

"Like what? I never could figure out why you disappeared on me like that."

She shrugged as if it were unimportant now, as if too much time had passed for the answer to be meaningful. Which was true.

"It was just…some things you said struck a nerve. It made me realize we didn't know each other half as well as we thought we did."

"Does anybody?"

She stared at him for a long moment, giving the question more thought than he expected or even wanted. He was suddenly afraid she would say yes.

Instead of answering, she sighed once more and lowered her eyes to the cards arrayed on the table.

"I'm sorry I did that," she said.

"You could have tried talking to me if you had a problem with something." His gaze roved over her face as she continued examining the cards. He now found himself wishing she would have answered the question after all.

"I know. I'm sorry."

"Yeah. I'm sorry too. About, you know, Nioedo. It was…cruel."

She nodded, never raising her eyes from the table.

He watched her watching the unchanging layout a moment longer, then drew another card. Prismatic Book. Excellent. He placed it atop the White Tower, then added them to the Fortune pile. This unblocked the Yellow Crown, which he moved onto the Brown Star. Those two also went into the pile. There were only about two dozen cards left now. He was amazed he had gotten this far. This was the one game he had never won without cheating.

"Yeah, well, we've both hurt each other now," he said. "Does that make us grown-ups finally?"

She looked up sharply, blinking, surprised that he had made a joke, albeit a rather feeble one. Then she laughed.

"I think perhaps it does," she said.

He moved the White Crown onto the Red Eye and added both of them to the pile. He turned over the last card in the stock. Prismatic Star. So *that's* where it was. Figures it would be the last one. Still, he had been doing great without it. He set it next to the Green Sphere, then added both the latter card and the Red Bird beneath it to the Fortune pile.

As he looked for a new spot to place the Prismatic Star, he said, "I must say, it's kind of a surprise that we wound up having this intimate little heart-to-heart."

"How so?"

"Well, I mean, after Giv-Golos I half figured you wouldn't want to have anything to do with me ever again."

She cocked her head and gave him a puzzled smile. "Why? Because of that 'bitchy' remark you made?"

"Uh, well, no. Because, you know…you found out. About me. What I do."

She gawked at him a moment. Then she smiled as if he had said something endearingly ridiculous.

"What?" Reynard asked, squirming self-consciously.

"Reynard, I've known about that since Drell."

Now it was his turn to gawk.

"You what?"

"Seriously, did you really think I wouldn't hear about the guy who tried to con the government? It was all anyone could talk about for weeks. And given that the description of the culprit sounded quite a bit like you, and given also how you failed to show up for our scheduled meeting the very day the culprit was believed to have fled town…well, I mean, I'm not completely stupid."

After gaping at her a moment more, he let out a little laugh. "Son of a bitch." He shook his head. "That's…" He froze, his smile dying away. "That's why you're always dis-appearing on me, isn't it?"

She opened her mouth then paused, not sure what to say or how to talk about something she had always assumed to be understood but tacit.

"I'm sorry. It's just…" She moved her shoulders in a vague shrug as she fished about for the right words. "I don't know what to do with you, Reynard."

He lowered his gaze and stared at the cards in silence for a long moment. When he looked back up, he had his coolest, cockiest smile affixed to his face, the smile of a man not a single thing in the universe could touch.

"Yeah," he said. "I guess I wouldn't know what to do with me either."

She smiled back at him. He pretended he didn't see something sad in her eyes.

As he returned to his game, scanning the remaining cards in search of the best move, he said, "We'll be reaching Pompulop 9 in a couple of hours."

"Yeah," she said with a sigh. "I should probably think about being on my way. I still have to pack."

"Yeah."

He shifted the Green Bird two spaces left, an action that unlocked a whole sequence of moves he felt sure would win him the game.

But it didn't. The shifting of cards to the Fortune pile stopped dead with only four cards left on the table. Reynard sank back in his chair with a groan.

"Problem?" Solace asked, amused.

"Stupid game," he said. "It's unwinnable."

"Couldn't you, like, go back a few moves and do them over again differently or something? I know it's technically cheating, but I won't tell anyone."

"No, it's not anything I did. Hell, I pretty much played a perfect game. It's just the way the cards fell when they were dealt. See, I can't remove either of these two topmost cards without one of the two underneath them. If the cards in either stack were switched around, I'd be fine, but…" He shook his head.

"Sorry," she said, still looking amused. "Maybe the next game'll be better."

"Yeah…"

She rose. "I'd better go."

He rose too, and walked her to the door. They stopped in the doorway, facing each other.

"Hey," he said, "maybe we could actually stay in touch this time around."

She winced. "I hate to tell you this…"

He sighed, grinning. "How did I know this was coming?"

"It's just, my mission for the Outreach Society is taking me to GC229, which is way beyond the jurisdiction of the Intergalactic Senate. I'll be out of reach of all standard com contact for at least two years."

"Yeah, I figured it'd be something like that. I'd give you a com number you could reach me at, but…" He shrugged. "Well, I never keep the same com number that long. Occupational hazard."

"Yeah."

"Well, good luck with your mission."

"Thanks. And thanks for…everything."

She rose up on tip-toes and kissed him softly on the side of the mouth.

"Till next time," she said.

"Yeah," he said.

They shared one last smile, and then she turned and left.

Reynard stood there staring at the closed door for a minute, then walked slowly back to the round white table. After surveying the remains of the game, he started gathering up the cards to put them away.

12

Across the Universe
12013 A.C.

Reynard was flying his private one-man cruiser *Remember the Whatever-It-Was-Called* through the Nerual System, on his way from Melikatara Red to the Wheel, when a call came through on the ship's PsyCom interface panel. Seeing from the video screen's InfoTab that it was from a lawyer, he nearly refused it, assuming it was an ad, or worse, a repercussion from some past misdeed. But before he could, the lawyer, a saddarite named Ebb Tw'twitto m'Mashgor whose dark green skin glistened with a fine coating of slime and whose long black horns were buffed and polished and adorned with a series of ornamental metal bands, said hurriedly, as if he suspected (or had been informed) that Reynard would be unlikely to give a lawyer much of a chance to speak, "I have been instructed to contact you by a Ms. Solace 10-NT."

Reynard wasn't sure which surprised him more: the fact that a lawyer was contacting him on Solace's behalf or the fact that the lawyer was using her real surname.

"What's this about?" Reynard asked, heart suddenly pounding too hard, too fast. Somehow he already knew.

"I, ah, I am regretful to inform you that Ms. 10-NT is no longer among the living. She has had a meeting with an unfortunate accident."

He said nothing, could think of nothing to say, just slumped back in his force-mesh chair and stared unseeingly at the stars moving past on the main display screen.

"What…" He had been about to ask "What happened?" but wasn't sure he wanted to know the answer. He remembered her unhappiness last time they met, and he feared she had committed suicide. If she had, he didn't want to know.

The lawyer knew what he wanted, though, and had no similar qualms about discussing it.

"Ms. 10-NT was, ehm, the unfortunate victim of an unusual accident involving an outgassing of methane on a pleasure moon. She was hiking with friends and, as said, there was an outgassing, a stray spark, an explosion, and she was, ehm, unfortunately bisected by debris."

The story was so bizarre and ridiculous Reynard had trouble processing it.

"Bisected?" he asked. Who the hell used a word like "bisected" in this context? Yes, he knew the saddarite brain functioned in ways that made the species excellent in matters of great complexity, such as law, logic, and psychohistory, while making them terrible in matters of common discourse, but this was particularly egregious.

The lawyer cleared his throat. "It was said to be, ehm, it was said, instantaneous. No pain. Probably no real awareness of what was happening."

Reynard was silent. He was still having trouble getting past the absurdity of the whole thing. She, an immortal over twelve thousand years old, a survivor of the Cataclysm, the War of Unification, the Last Great War, the Toy Box Massacre, a career at Giv-Golos, and so many other things, she getting cut down in some senseless accident. How could something like that happen? He wanted to punch the universe.

The lawyer spoke on, as lawyers always do, saving Reynard the need to talk.

"The, uhm, the will (such as it is) does not name you, but you are, eh, listed among the listees in a document listing those to be notified in the event of her death." A pause. "A document I noted, seeing the date upon it, that was prepared sixteen hundred years ago." A longer pause, as if he expected Reynard to say something. When Reynard didn't, m'Mashgor said in a low voice that suggested confidentiality, "She was a human, though, was she not?"

Reynard had been expecting him to ask if she were an Elder, but now realized that that was a silly thing to expect. The lawyer had probably never heard of Elders. Elders had been a big deal back on Eridia, but here in the larger universe, with hundreds of thousands of known sentient species, Eridia and all its history barely even qualified as trivia.

"She was very healthy," Reynard said dryly.

"Ahm!" The sound was halfway between an exclamation of understanding and a laugh, as if the lawyer weren't sure enough of his grasp of human physiognomy to know if Reynard's comment had been a joke or not. "Yes. Ehm, the funeral is to be held on the *Final Voyage* Funerary Satellite in the Lü System in the Kirfa Galaxy on Stardate 9003.12."

Reynard did the math. That was April 15, 12013, Eridian Standard Time. Two days from now. And here he was halfway across the cluster from the Kirfa Galaxy. From her. What was left of her.

Bisected.

Something the lawyer said earlier finally sank in.

"She didn't leave me anything?" he asked, not caring if he sounded greedy or mercenary. It wasn't that he wanted anything; he was 13,000 years old. There wasn't anything she could give him he hadn't already had or didn't know how to get. At least no physical thing. No, what prompted the question was hurt. He was hurt that she hadn't left him even some little token to show that she was thinking of him.

"Ehm, no?" It came out as a question, as if the lawyer were asking, "Should she have?"

Reynard said nothing, just stared off into space again, not feeling anything now. Or perhaps feeling too much, too many conflicting things for any one of them to predominate, with the result that they canceled each other out in a sort of emotional white noise.

"No message either?" he asked after a long pause.

"No, no message. Just the, ehm, the invitation."

She surely hadn't expected to die at all, he told himself. Whatever will she had drawn up had probably been a half-hearted, lackadaisical effort prompted by a whim that passed almost as soon as it had appeared.

Or perhaps he was just telling himself comforting lies. He realized he would never know for sure.

"Will, ehm, will you come?" the lawyer asked.

"Of course I will!" he snapped, and severed the connection.

When Reynard arrived at the *Final Voyage*'s inanely named Departure Hall he thought for a moment he had come to the wrong funeral. For some reason, he had always pictured Solace as a private, introverted person with only a select few friends at any given time. But beyond the double doorway, the bright, high-ceilinged hall was packed with several hundred sentient entities: humans, robots, gnomes, saddrites, caulimbos, nyow-ha, ssleth, dwarves, elves, and more, including several species he didn't recognize. Voices of various pitches and timbers conversed in dozens of languages. Skin and hair and scales and casings of all hues shone under the overhead lights. Mechanisms whirred. Wings rustled. Tentacles and tails curled and undulated.

A hush fell over the immediate crowd as Reynard walked in. Practically everyone present wore funeral garb that was in tune with the era's lazy unisex styles—most wore loose-fitting black gowns and pull-on cloth shoes. Reynard, on the other hand, was decked out in a black three-piece suit and tie. His black dress shoes gleamed as if they had been carved from obsidian. His slacks' front creases were sharp enough to slit a throat.

He didn't know if Solace would have liked the style, but he was pretty sure that she alone of all the people in this room would have remembered days when clothes like these were worn, days so ancient he hadn't been able to track down a genuine suit in any size or condition, and had had to have one fashioned for him based on images from a crumbling magazine housed in the archives of the Early Human History Museum on Skron 3. He had had to drain one of his Inner Rim MyCred accounts to get everything done in time for the funeral, but money was for spending, and he could think of no better way to have spent it.

As he strode through the gawping crowd, dress shoes clacking conspicuously in the midst of all these cloth-shod padders, he glanced around in search of the casket and soon spotted the sleek black metal cylinder sitting at the far end of the room beyond dozens of arrow-straight rows of black folding chairs. The casket rested on a magnetic track that led to an airlock. At the ceremony's climax, the casket would be fired from this airlock on a trajectory that would take it into the heart of Lü, this system's star.

Since the sight of a genuine corpse rather than, say, a PsyCom entertainment simulation would be too traumatic for this age's delicate sheep with their neurotic fear of anything that wasn't artificial, funerals were always closed casket affairs, with a final view of the dearly departed provided by an EMbed memorial, a short free-floating audiovisual recording that played on a perpetual loop above the casket. Usually these recordings depicted the deceased laughing, or reciting a short, upbeat speech, or uttering some characteristic phrase.

Solace hadn't wanted any of that. No EMbed images, no silly catch-phrases, and no hiding. An ancient-style open-casket funeral would have been far too boorish and provocative a gesture for someone of her considerate sensibilities, so as a halfway measure she had demanded in her will that her casket be equipped with a small square window to display her face to the mourners. Even this was deemed so extreme that the management of the *Final Voyage* had felt compelled to send a warning message to the funeral's attendees.

Indeed, many mourners avoided approaching the casket during this informal pre-ceremony viewing, and most of those who braved a look at the face behind the glass came away pale and distressed. One old man stared through the window a long time, then turned away, his stringy neck quivering as he swallowed hard, his eyes lost and bewildered.

"She still looks like a normal person," he spluttered. "Except...she doesn't move."

Reynard hung back until the casket was clear of mourners, then slowly walked over to it. His heart felt tight and dense and achy as if it were compressing itself smaller and smaller, like a spent star collapsing into a black hole.

From the moment he had learned of her death until now, he had been constantly busy, what with the mad rush to procure his outfit and then make it here in time for the ceremony. These tasks had consumed all his thought and energy, leaving none for Solace herself.

But now all of that was done. All the items on the list had been crossed off, all the light-years devoured. Now there was just him and the casket.

He stood beside it and gazed down at the face behind the glass window. The old man had been right: She looked perfectly normal, her countenance smooth and calm, her closed eyes restful, her long black hair neatly arranged, not a strand out of place. It was an old, old cliché, he knew, to say that the freshly dead looked like they were sleeping, but that was indeed how she looked. So much so, in fact, that for one brief moment he tried to tell himself that this was all an elaborate trick she was playing on him, that she had decided to trick the trickster to teach him some silly lesson about how wrong it was to mess with people's lives, and at any moment she would open her eyes and crack a smile, revealing those perfect teeth, and—

She didn't move. The old man had been right about that, too. Her face never changed. Her eyes did not—would never again—open. She was gone. This thing laid out before him was not her. It was just an assemblage of slowly decomposing meat and bone. Soon it wouldn't even be that. It would be a billion scattered atoms whirling about inside a solar furnace.

In his mind he suddenly heard her voice saying something she had said thousands of years before in reference to her daughter:

"The world—*my* world—was a better place with her in it."

There was a soft, deliberate shuffle of feet behind him, a timid sheep signaling impatience without risk of rudeness or confrontation. Reynard glanced back and saw a small crowd awaiting their turn to pay their respects.

Barely hiding his irritation, he took one more look at her still, calm face and walked away.

He hung around next to the refreshment table for a while, his thoughts straying from Solace to the living bodies in the room around him. In a weird way it felt like a betrayal of her to even consider thinking about anything else this soon. But that was exactly what he did, as if his brain needed to occupy itself with something beyond the fact of her nonexistence lest it go mad.

A scan of the crowd confirmed he didn't know a single person here. Listening in on several conversations, he discovered that a large percentage of the mourners were either artists of one sort or another, or employees of various political and governmental organizations, many of them affiliated somehow with the Intergalactic Senate. He also learned that in recent years Solace had owned and managed Re:Sound, a popular nightclub on Krizz T-19, which seemed to be either a moon or a space station; he couldn't tell which.

He was in the midst of an excruciatingly boring conversation with a pompous and half-inebriated dwarf named Doven do Kombeltot, who worked as a political analyst on Mezureth 5, when there was a sudden shift in the room's pattern of noise, with some voices falling silent while others began whispering urgently. Reynard and Doven looked around. The funeral coordinator, an aging male elf, had stepped up to a podium near the head of the casket.

"Thank you for coming," the elf said with a small smile that managed to radiate both sorrow and serenity. "Please, be seated."

Everyone made their way to the rows of folding chairs. Reynard made sure to sit well away from Doven.

"We are here to deliver our final farewells to Solace 10-NT," the elf said, and then launched into the usual string of soothing platitudes people expected on occasions like this.

After reciting a mawkish poem, the gist of which was that death was merely a gateway to other things beyond the ken of the living, the elf opened the floor to those who wished to say a few words about the deceased.

Many did. Over two dozen people gave speeches of varying length about Solace, her good heart, her optimism, her love of people, her keen aesthetic sense.

"Everyone loved her," one man said, a ruggedly handsome fellow whose blue eyes and high cheek bones glimmered with tears. Reynard couldn't help wondering if he had been Solace's boyfriend. "She was a beautiful, wonderful, generous person, one of the best I've ever known."

"Her taste in music was impeccable," said an older woman with a pair of cybernetic eyes implanted in her forehead above her biological ones. "She always knew the best songs. She had a real knack for ferreting out the great new performers no one else had heard of yet." The woman turned and looked at the casket, her face crumpling up, the smile she was trying for twisting out of her control. "Where am I going to find new music now, Solace?" She broke down and had to be escorted back to her seat by the funeral co-ordinator.

"What I remember best about her," said a large, matronly woman, "was her writing. She was the most magnificent writer—poetry, prose, the occasional omnitainment. She always claimed her work wasn't very good, but to those of us she allowed to read some of it, it was clear she was being overly modest."

"She was so full of life," said a yellow-haired gnome girl.

"She had more energy than anyone else I ever knew. When we all went out hiking or skiing or whatever, she'd always be at the front of the group, laughing and living it up. She was always *doing.*"

"She was a romantic at heart."

"She could be a real cynic at times."

"She had the most contagious laugh."

"Sparkling wit."

"Amazing fashion sense."

"Endless generosity."

"No tolerance for fools."

"She was—"

"She had—"

"She loved—"

"I'll miss her."

After the reminiscences and a tedious and generically hopeful sermon by a Reformed Dodecite Church minister, everyone filed past the body one last time, a process that took nearly half an hour. Reynard found himself stuck in line between a vegetal entity that resembled a seven-foot-tall artichoke and smelled faintly like rancid cheese, and the yellow-haired gnome girl, who introduced herself as Tinda Gobozizzio and blathered on about her work as an aide in the Intergalactic Senate and the awfulness of the recent spiries swarm and how truly truly *ultra* Solace had been, until Reynard's unresponsiveness forced her to redirect her chattiness to the fellow behind her.

As each mourner said their last goodbye and moved on, as the line advanced body by body, as the black casket drew closer and closer, Reynard felt numb and empty. His body was a thing that moved automatically. His feet walked, his heart pumped, his blood pulsed, his eyes blinked and swiveled. But inside that biological machinery, he felt dead. He kept telling himself he should be brimming with despair or outrage or one of the other emotions a mourning man should feel. But he didn't. There seemed to be nothing left inside.

The line moved. He moved. Time passed.

When he got to the casket and looked down at her for the last time, realizing it *was* the last time, he felt something like panic rise up inside him. He suddenly didn't want to leave her side, couldn't bear the thought of her body burning to ash in the heart of a star. He wanted to tear open the casket, snatch up her body, carry it away somewhere to preserve it forever.

But he knew he couldn't do that, so he took one final look at her face, willing himself to preserve the image, freeze it in his mind, make it a memory that would never fade or grow distorted, knowing even as he willed it that it was impossible.

Last look: The closed eyes, the straight nose, the lips behind which lay those perfect teeth, the light-brown skin, the black hair.

He turned and walked away, feeling as if he had failed her somehow.

After the line had finished worming past the casket and everyone returned to their seats, insipidly upbeat music began to blare from hidden speakers. It was only after several bars had played that Reynard identified the tune as a hideously mangled version of Hathendomonia's *deisan* solo from the Unity Symphony.

He felt his throat tighten and tears sting his eyes. Not wanting to cry in front of all these people, he forced his feelings back by focusing on the shittiness of the rendition.

For some reason all modern performances of it sounded flat and feeble, no matter how accurately the notes and rhythms were played. Perhaps it was due to alterations in the manufacture of the instruments, or subtle evolutionary mutations in the mouths or fingers of the species that played them. But whatever its cause, the change had definitely not been for the better.

It suddenly dawned on him that Solace might have chosen this music specifically as a last, secret farewell to him. He got up, made his way over to where the funeral coordinator stood at a small control panel that worked the lights and the speakers and the airlock, and asked the elf who had picked the music. With a small, pleased smile, he told Reynard it was what they always played.

"Everybody loves this one," he said. "So beautiful."

Reynard returned to his seat without another word, the swift rise and fall of his hopes having left him feeling deader than ever.

She hadn't expected to die, he told himself. Hell, neither did *he*. If he were to die suddenly in a stupid accident, no one would have any idea what to do with his body or who to contact; he hadn't drawn up any instructions whatsoever.

Yet she had, haphazard as they were. And she still hadn't left him anything except an invitation to say goodbye.

As the barely recognizable *deisan* solo soared to its hopeful end, the airlock's transparent inner hatch opened and the casket moved silently down its track and into the airlock. The hatch closed. After a pause just long enough for Reynard to wonder if something had gone wrong, the outer hatch opened. Without a tremor or sound, the casket shot from the airlock and disappeared into space. The outer hatch rolled closed.

The music ceased. The funeral coordinator returned to

the podium and with a small bow said, "On behalf of Solace 10-NT, I thank you for coming to see her off on her final voyage in this sphere of existence."

As the other mourners made their way to the door, Reynard stood staring at the closed hatch. In his mind's eye he saw the casket shooting through space on its way to its rendezvous with Lü, its destined end as ash. He imagined the stars' reflections passing across that small, square window, across her restful face, tiny white dots sliding by like bits of debris on a river.

A hand touched his arm. It was the funeral coordinator.

"We've got another funeral in ten minutes," the elf said. "I'm sorry, but you'll have to move along."

He left for Eridia the next day. Even with jump-gates it was a three-week journey to the old homeworld, which he hadn't visited in over nine hundred years. He had been having too much fun in the wide and wild universe to give a crap about that dull, depopulated green-and-blue nursery.

He landed his cruiser at a spaceport on the east coast, about seventy miles north of Drell, which had dwindled from a thriving metropolis to a largish fishing village surrounded by mossy ruins. There weren't enough people on the planet for there to be metropolises anymore.

From the port (technically known as the Mashkiter Wampoliter Memorial Spaceport, though who or what the fuck Mashkiter Wampoliter was, Reynard had no idea), he traveled by warp train, a ridiculously old-fashioned mode of transport in this day and age, to a town called Fa'lill'e, about which his PsyCom chip offered no information beyond its location and population. It was dark by the time he arrived, so he got a room at Mimizz'ii'naa's Inn, grabbed a bland dinner at the Inn's food synthesizer, and went straight to bed.

The following morning, after consulting the most recent topographical map of the area his PsyCom chip could find (a whopping 313 years old!), he bought a backpack and some food and set out on foot due north.

He got there at noon.

The sun baking his scalp, the armpits of his shirt damp with sweat from his trek, he stopped in the middle of a field and looked around while small yellow-and-black butterflies wobbled about above the high grass that encircled him.

All he saw in every direction was trees, grass, stones. And in the distance to the north, the Salt Stairs.

He stared at those mountains long and hard, comparing them with the mountains in the ancient fragments of memory that remained in his brain.

The two matched as much as they ever would. He was in the right place. He was where New Portland had once stood.

But there was now no trace of it.

Of course not, he told himself. It had been overrun and abandoned twelve thousand years earlier. What had he expected? A monument to a city no one remembered? A few bits of brick? Maybe a rusting chunk of one of the robot invaders?

Still, it seemed wrong that it was gone. The place was important to him. It was where he had met her. Its erasure from the world felt like an affront.

He wondered if Solace had ever come back here, if she had even thought about doing so. He wondered what importance this place had held for her.

During the journey here, he had tried not to think about her, focusing only on the needs of the moment, much as he had on his way to the funeral. Now he allowed his thoughts to return to her, here in this place that meant nothing anymore to anyone except him.

He pictured her smile and remembered the first time he saw it in a tunnel that no longer existed under a city that no longer existed. And he realized he would never see that smile again. He could wait until the mountains before him had become dust, until the world was a cloud of ash expanding through the galaxy, until the very universe itself burned out, and still he would never see it again. It was gone. Forever.

Without warning, all the strength left his legs, and he dropped to his knees. At the same time, unbidden, unwanted, a horrible choked howl rose up from within him. He had never made a sound like this before, didn't want to now, but he had no control over it; it tore itself from him in an endless, unwavering stream and echoed away across the fields toward the far, doomed mountains.